I0818198

MIDNIGHT
CROWN

www.rebeccagarciabooks.com

Edited by Belle Manuel

Paperback ISBN: 9798846140752
Hardback ISBN: 9781912405961

CONTENT WARNING:

Please note this is a dark fantasy romance intended for readers 18+. Please go to my website to read the complete list of content warnings:
www.rebeccagarciabooks.com/contentwarnings

DEDICATION:

This book is dedicated to all of you
who've wondered what it's like to fuck a vampire

QUOTE:

"Someone I loved once gave me a box full of darkness.
It took me years to understand that this too, was a gift."
— *Mary Oliver*

Young God—Halsey
Raise the Dead—Rachel Rabin
Darkside—Neoni
Gods & Monsters—Lana Del Rey
Beggin for Thread—Banks
Breathe—Tommee Profitt
Hypnotic—Zella Day

Click here to listen to the entire playlist

PRONUNCIATION GUIDE

Achais–Ark-ice
Aniccipere–Ann-iss-sep-heir
Azia-Az-Eye-Ah
Baldoria–Bal-door-ee-ah
Draven: Dray-ven
Erianna–Air-ee-anna
Hamza–Ham-zah
Jaiunere–Shaun-air
Kalon–Kal-on
Laveniuess–Lav-en-nwass
Niall: Nye-ill
Ravena–Rav-ee-nah
Salenia–Sal-ee-nah
Sangaree–Sang-ah-ree
Sanmorte–San-moor-tey
Seraphina–Sair-ah-feen-ah
Sargon–Sar-gone
Trailic: Tray-lick

SANMORTE
LAKE OF
LAVENIUESS

ROYAL CASTLE
BLACK MOUNTAIN RETREAT
OF
MARES

ONE

Olivia

Blood trickled from the woman's neck, creating rivers between her wrinkles. The new vampire to court, Niall, closed his eyes as he lost himself in the mortal woman, fangs deep inside her. It had only been a day since his arrival. He'd spoken to me once, introducing himself as the adopted son of Kalon.

The color drained from her face as he pulled her against his body, laying her on the table. His tan glowed under the dim lights of the banquet room, coined as the feeding room by most here. Behind them, crimson red drapes hung over the windows and walls, pooling on the ground as if blood slicked the ancient stone. People hurried past them, moving between tents erected to create privacy. Niall clearly didn't care about that as he dug his nails into the woman's arms for all to see.

I wondered how long she'd been here, and if she'd come by choice. So many ventured to Sanmorte from other kingdoms, curious about what it would be like to be with a vampire. Most were misinformed. They fed off rumors about the beautiful sangaree—the name of the race for blood vampires, and wholly different from the aniccipere who fed on people's souls. Some believed they might be turned, no matter how much the royals of each territory tried to squash those whispers. As far as most mortals were aware, vampires couldn't be created, and only a couple thousand were left, which was entirely inaccurate.

I leaned against an empty table, taking the weight off my feet. Glowering at every vampire who wiped their bloodied lips, racing out of the feeding room in a blur, I sighed. They fed the rumors, even if they wouldn't admit it to the king. It was in their interest to keep a nice supply of food coming in. Bile bit up my throat as I imagined people jumping ship, illusioned by the fantasy of these monsters, only to be beaten, raped, and thrown in blood dens.

At least they were somewhat willing, unlike the mortals trafficked, stolen from their homes in the night. Most were from home, Baldoria. I could tell by their accents. That's why my mom and I lived so far from the coast; they seldom came far inland to snatch people.

Tilting my head, I watched helplessly from the other side of the room. My heart raced as the sound of moaning erupted from inside one tent. My imagination ran wild with what was happening inside. They could insist mortals gave consent for sex all they wanted, but no one could genuinely give permission when they were high on venom.

I recalled the ecstasy that pulsed through my veins after I was bitten, following the initial pain. Although I despised the monsters, I couldn't help but desire the feeling again. I shrugged away the fleeting thought and returned my focus to Niall. The woman released a brief gasp, eyes closed, with a slight smile on her tired lips.

I turned my head to find my father at his usual place at his throne, but he'd gone somewhere with my mom in the time I'd been watching Niall. I returned my gaze to him as he wiped his mouth on the back of his sleeve, amusement threading in his stare.

I ground my teeth, refusing to look away, ensuring he knew how vile I thought he was. He didn't have to kill her. He could have fed and stopped himself before she lost too much blood. I clenched my fist, and he smirked. Dark waves bounced around his shoulders as he walked away, probably to find his father.

Rushing toward the bench, I caught myself before toppling as a lord's wife almost knocked me in my stride. "Careful," I snapped.

She bowed her head, reluctance straining behind her hateful stare as she continued walking. They all hated me, except for my mom, who stood at her throne, her attention wandering over to me every so often. In just three short days, I would become Shadow Kissed and die at an altar, only to return as the Princess of Sanmorte and a vampire. A fact that seemed to rub most of the castle the wrong way.

Inhaling sharply, I lifted the skirts of my garnet-red dress and kneeled at the side of Niall's victim, praying there was a slither of life left in her body. "Please," I whispered. "Can you hear me?"

My heart palpitated. I didn't trust any bloodsucker in this room, especially as they eyed her body. I'd seen a couple of them abuse people long after they died, taking advantage of the corpses left behind.

Reaching for her curled fingers, I gasped at the icy touch. She was too far gone, but she deserved dignity. "I won't let them defile you," I promised, as if she could still hear me. Placing my arm under hers, I attempted to lift her, catching my breath as her weight crushed against me.

Fingers squeezed my shoulders. "Gods, Draven!" I jumped, dropping her back. Her head thudded against the chair.

He glanced at the woman's body. "Another one. There are mounds of bodies being burned every week." His eyes slid over the room. "They just can't control themselves."

"Where did you come from?" I asked breathily, my heart pounding against my chest.

"I came to find you." He lowered his voice. "You shouldn't be doing this."

I leaned in closer, smelling the scent of his spice-laced cologne, and whispered, "I can't leave her to them."

The muscles in his arms tensed. "But remember what happened the last time you tried to interfere?"

I stilled, remembering the noble who screamed at me when I forced him off a mortal. The king had stopped their rage, using my station to try and force their respect, but it wasn't something that could be demanded. "Yes."

His pleading stare burned into mine. "They'll kill you, daughter of the king or not. You can't stop them all. We're out of our depths here."

I chewed on the inside of my lip. "We should just give up then?" I scowled, then released a long exhale. "I'm sorry, it's not your fault. I just hate them."

"I know."

I found home in his sea-blue gaze, remembering a simpler time before all of this. "At least there are only a few soul vampires here. In the city, I saw a corpse after an aniccipere finished feeding on them, and it was the most horrendous thing I've ever seen." A shiver tingled goosebumps over my skin as I tried to block the image from forming in my mind.

I felt their icy stares before I saw them. The vampires watched me, daring lacing their frowns.

Draven brushed his thumb over the back of my hand. "Right now, we must focus on surviving." He glanced over to where my mom stood, her maroon lips pulled tight. "Let me take the hit for this one."

"Are you insane?" I reprimanded. "They won't think twice before killing you. I am a royal. You are disposable to *them*." I examined his navy, high-necked tunic with gold embellishments. His sword remained sheathed, but his fingers tightened around the hilt as he watched the vampires looking at me.

We both had a death sentence, but for now, we remained mortal. I gritted my teeth, my gaze flashing toward Kalon, who'd arrived to feed. My eyes flicked over to the large grandfather clock. It was a quarter past noon, lunchtime. He slid his eyes over to me before disappearing into a tent. It had been two days since my fate had been sealed, and Kalon had been unnervingly quiet for that time.

I hated him, and he despised me all the same. I could have told my father that his brother had tried to have me killed and knew of my true identity. But the truth was the only leverage I had. Honestly, I was concerned that I wouldn't be believed even if I tried to voice it.

Draven placed a hand on my shoulder, anger lacing his chiseled features. He was getting his muscle tone back after coming close to starvation for weeks, but the dark circles under his eyes were still prominent. "We will get out of here. Then we can tell the world what's really going on here."

"Not this again." I stepped out of his hold, lowering my voice to a whisper. "We can't escape. Maybe you can, but not me."

He balled a fist. "There *has* to be a way."

"There isn't." I tried to keep my expression stoic, but I'd always worn my emotions for all to see. Pain cracked through, creasing lines on my forehead. I hated to be so blunt with him, but I didn't want him hoping for something that could never be. There were people I needed to help, and I couldn't do that if I tried to save myself. Sebastian would be the first to be executed if I even attempted to leave. Then Erianna and Zach would follow shortly after. My mom would probably be okay, but they would never stop hunting us.

"You give up so easily."

"I've already chosen my path, Draven. Besides, we would probably die before we could get past the forest."

His tightened grip told me he would not let this go. "I'm tougher than you know."

"This isn't about how tough you are. Neither of us is a match against a castle of immortals, and I know they'd only bring me back. But you, they would have no need to keep you. Right now, you're only serving as a guard because me and Mom begged Sargon."

Flickering orange soaked the table from a lamp on the wall, illuminating the golden tones in Draven's hair. My father agreed to let him live, only if I promised to turn him into a vampire once I turned. He thought it would be ceremonial to have my first kill be my best friend, making him a permanent soldier in the castle. It was a gift, he said, but that wasn't how I saw it. I needed at least one person I loved to make it out of all this darkness.

I agreed to the terms if only to bide more time. As soon as the metaphorical leash around my neck was loosened, and I was trusted with free rein of the castle and its grounds, I would get Draven out of here, with safe passage back to Baldoria.

Grazing the side of my neck with my index finger, I turned my attention back to the room. The holiday of romance and love, Adormai, approached. The countdown also ticked down the minutes to my death. Silky roses of red and white entwined a metal arch over the thrones, and bouquets sat upon tall pillars.

Draven stepped in front of me. "I got this. I can move her." He leaned over, lifting her corpse from the bench, and laid her in his arms.

I stared for a moment longer at her face, wondering how it felt to die. Blue tinted her lips, and her skin grayed. I watched, hoping that wherever her soul was now, it was at peace. I swallowed thickly as I faced my mortality, a thing which would be taken away soon.

"They'll try to stop you," I warned, glancing at the greedy eyes of the vampires. "I shouldn't have tried to move her. It was stupid."

I felt their gazes bore into me as Draven laid her down, slumping her rigid body on the old stone floor for a few seconds as he held his breath, repositioning her against him. "It's fine. I want to move her body. I'll just say I'm clearing up."

The pianist in the corner of the room, and a string quartet, who were present at every feeding, started playing. A deep, thrumming melody filled the space, matching my stormy mood.

"You should go," Draven insisted. "Find your fiancé. I can handle this." The word left his mouth, leaving a tang of bitterness between us. *Fiancé*. After all, I had chosen Sebastian over him. Draven had offered to save me from marrying someone I didn't know, but I refused to do that to him. If I took Draven as my husband, I would commit him to a forever of immortality, forcing him to become the thing he'd fought his whole life against. I couldn't do that to my best friend.

I looked down at the woman. "You can't carry her on your own," I remarked, careful not to point out that he was still weak. His bronzed tan never returned, but he finally had color in his cheeks. "And you shouldn't. You'll get in trouble."

"Neither can you."

"I don't care..." I trailed off. Vampires around us sank into deep bows and curtseys, and my stomach hollowed. "Draven, put her down," I snapped, but it was too late.

Cold danced down my spine. I felt his presence towering over us before turning to look at him. "Your Majesty." His ancient-gold crown circled his forehead, freshly polished with enough rubies to feed a kingdom. His blazing red hair and emerald eyes matched mine.

"Daughter," he addressed me, awkwardness threading through the word. Neither of us had spent much time together since he discovered who I was. Something changed in his eyes, the anger burning behind them softening when he looked at me. "What is this?" He moved his attention to the woman and Draven.

"Niall's leftovers," I snapped, hatred clinging to each word. "We were moving her."

"You!" he barked at Draven, his liquor-tainted breath hitting us as he closed the distance between us. "Many would kill to be in your position, boy. Yet you show such blatant disrespect. Return to your post now."

I grabbed his arm. "Please don't! It was my idea—"

"Do not argue with me, Seraphina," he ordered, still focused on Draven. "The servants will take care of the bodies at the night's end. Go back to your post."

I held my quarrel behind clenched teeth. The vampires would first take advantage of her body before she was burned along with others. Every week I looked out my window, I saw the fires as they sent ash billowing into the sky, their name and identity forgotten to the winds. The smell was overpowering, so I always kept my window closed tight.

I glanced behind my father, observing a man as he licked his lips, hungry eyes on the woman's crumpled body at our feet. "Please." I softened my tone. "Can she be removed now?" I asked, hoping that the excitement of my return and agreeing to take my place as the princess wasn't wearing off. "Draven can take her outside and just burn her now."

"No," he ordered, his voice thick with a warning. "Leave her there. We have plenty to attend to before the night ends, and my guard needs to return to his post."

Draven didn't budge, instead, he glanced at me. "Olivia?"

"It's fine, Draven. You should go." I inhaled deeply as the corner of his eyes crinkled, and pity thinned his lips into a line.

Sargon's fingers flexed, his gaze burning into Draven's. "Your loyalty is to me, boy. Not Seraphina."

Draven glared back. "I'll always be loyal to *Olivia*."

I stepped in front of him before he could anger my father more. "He's loyal to us both," I promised. "We go back a long time, that's all. We're both grateful to you for showing him mercy."

Draven bit back his words, showing restraint. "So grateful."

Try to sound less sarcastic, I begged in my mind, hoping he could somehow hear my thoughts.

"Go," Sargon barked at Draven, then took my arm. Sargon moved the woman's head to the side with his foot, stepping on her fluffy, gray hair as he walked us away from her.

Everyone continued about their business, pretending not to look at us, but I caught their eyes.

"The entire court is watching you," Sargon said as the room's drunken chatter and melodic music continued. "You may one day be their queen, should I choose to retire. I forgive your naivete, as you are young, but you must give up your old way of life. You can't be their savior." He gestured vaguely to several mortals waiting beyond the tents, sitting at tables, waiting to be fed on. "It is a delicate ecosystem here. I allow my people their desires, and as for the mortals, they do not need saving. They are perfectly content."

I matched his pace, joining him up the three steps to his throne. "Is it naïve to want to give a dead woman some dignity?" I asked, trying to keep my tone light and curious. "She's probably been a slave here for most of her life."

He shrugged, sitting back in his tall throne carved up to a point. "I wouldn't know. We don't keep count of our servants' time here."

My fingers flexed, and I clasped my hands behind my back, not wanting him to see the rage pricking through me, singeing my veins. "Where's Mom?" I asked, changing the subject, noticing she'd disappeared since he'd walked into the room.

"Ravena is arranging your ceremony. I've allowed her to handle the preparations."

"How kind of you," I stated, struggling—and failing—to keep the bitterness from my voice. "If I may be excused, I need to find Sebastian."

"Seraphina," he said before I could leave. It felt wrong to be called by my birth name. "I implore you to stop all this nonsense. It is not in a vampire's nature to show restraint. You have my protection, but even a king cannot control every one of his subjects. If you meddle in the wrong one's business, they may kill you." He paused for a moment. "I can't lose you again." His nostrils flared; a breath baited against his lips.

Was that fear I could see beyond those ancient eyes?

"The gods have given us a gift," he continued. "We are rulers, by blood, chosen to bring peace to Sanmorte."

Glaring at the crowds dancing between the tables, sliding up and down each other, grinding and exploring their desires without shame, I couldn't help but hold back a scoff. While I didn't begrudge anyone for embracing their darker side as the god Laveniuess wanted, I disagreed with how far they would go. Everyone had good and bad inside them, but I judged them on their choices. Most of them enjoyed killing and humiliating mortals. They believed themselves to be the most powerful beings in our world. Therefore, they acted without apology, taking what felt good to them.

"This is peace?" I asked.

"We are safe here," he explained, leaning forward, staring at the same scene as me, "to be who we were made to be. Mortals hunt us, condemn us for our natures," he explained, as if I was already one of them. "They do not kill lions because they hunt and kill, yet we are not given the same kindness."

I couldn't help but flinch when he touched my shoulder. I spotted Kalon gliding through the hordes of vampires, his poise far more regal than ours. He'd finished feeding from his tent then and didn't even have a spot of blood on his pristine white robes.

"Vampires have cruelly ripped people from their homes and families for centuries," I said. "Lions hunt for food, but vampires do it for sport. You can restrain yourselves and feed without killing, yet choose not to." I thought back to Sebastian, telling me how his family was mercilessly slaughtered before him. "Why does that deserve kindness?"

His icy fingers gripped my wrist, twisting me around to face him. His lips deepened into a frown, a grim look crossing his expression. "Be careful, daughter," he warned, worry flashing in his features. "They will never accept you with this kind of talk. While you can say it to your mother or me, you cannot go around spewing out this treason."

"It's not treason."

"In three days, you will become one of us yourself. I only hope the transition will allow you some understanding of your people."

"What if it doesn't?"

"Then gods save your soul."

I blinked twice. "You think the gods would be angry at me?"

He slid backward, taking a goblet of blood from a servant, swirling it before taking a sip. "Why don't you tell me when you meet them in your death, as temporary as it is?"

I thumbed the side of my neck. "I'll meet them?"

He only nodded, shrugging the statement off as if he'd just made a passing comment on the weather. "I have matters to attend to. Stay out of trouble." He strode away before I could respond. I listened as he ordered a servant to find and bring Hamza to him.

Scanning the room, I searched for Sebastian, who hadn't bothered to show up to feed. I'd hoped to find him here, but he'd avoided me since our engagement was forced upon him. Moreover, he hadn't come to see me since he was brought up from the dungeons, escaping execution.

Instead, he'd learned how our fake betrothal had become all too real, and his wish to be mortal and escape this life was lost forever. I was sure he hated me for it, even though I'd saved him. He was the one who'd betrayed me. I asked him to turn me in the dungeons so we could escape, but he handed me over to Sargon instead, attempting to bargain for his freedom. A pang of hurt shot through my heart as the memory drifted back. I had stupidly believed he cared about me.

I reached the doors to the foyer, stopping upon seeing Astor. My undead ex-boyfriend draped his arm around Gwen, the woman he'd betrayed me for when he chose immortality over me. She flicked back at her blonde curls, her painted-red lips curling into a grin when she saw me looking.

I walked away, my cheeks heating against the cool breeze in the foyer. Heaviness sunk through my torso as I stared up at the spiraling staircases. I felt like an idiot. Sebastian had fooled me into thinking he cared, just like Astor had countless times.

As I climbed the ancient steps to my bedroom, I found distraction in the burning in my calves. The sounds of the monsters indulging their desires followed me to my room. Every part of me wanted to run and never return to his place. But there was no escaping.

TWO

Olivia

I closed my eyes as I ran my fingers down the long, black veil hanging on the back of my closet. It would serve as my wedding veil and the one I would wear during the Shadow Kissed ceremony. My heart hammered at the thought of the dagger being plunged into my body.

Music reverberated throughout the castle, vibrating up to my bedroom. Adormai was approaching, and parties were in full swing.

The clock next to my bed ticked past eight, letting out a loud chime. I turned my back to the veil and dropped onto my bed, lying back against the several pillows.

Sleep evaded me as the night wore on. I couldn't bring my thoughts to a peaceful baseline where I could rest. I'd never put a lot of thought into my death until I was at its doorstep with the promise to return to the land of the living. When I would go through the ceremony and wake, I would become a creature hungry for the blood of those I wanted to protect.

Sebastian had been confident that vampirism wouldn't destroy me. I worried he overestimated my good nature because something sinister was hidden under the surface. Whenever I thought about Astor, Hamza, or Kalon, a wave of unrelenting anger consumed me, desperate to make the world crumble.

The last of the sun's rays faded from the mountainous horizon, creating a reflection of my room in the windows as darkness consumed the sky. Everything soaked in a soft orange hue when I switched on the lamp.

I had been moved into the second grandest room in the entire castle, forcing Kalon out of it. I wouldn't have cared to accept such a lavish bedroom, but knowing it would anger my enemy made it too tempting to turn down. He'd been downgraded to the third nicest room. The room, papered with gold between beams of wood that ran up to vaulted ceilings, housed a large, four-poster bed big enough for several people if I wished.

The king had all new furniture brought in for me; a plush, gold footstool and matching futon. In front of the fireplace were two cream sofas with gold finishings and an area rug sprawling out over the polished wood floor.

I supposed it was my father's way of showing me he cared, although he never said as much. But, especially after our last conversation, I doubted I'd ever hear it now.

I walked over to the dresser, tilting my head at my reflection in the oval mirror. Azia had removed the brown hair dye we'd used to hide my red hair, to conceal my identity. While I appeared the same, there was something off. Perhaps it was my expression, now permanently anxious, with rage behind my green eyes, replacing the girl I was once.

A knock sounded at my door, jolting me. Had Sebastian finally come to speak with me? Unless it was my father, but he wouldn't knock. Instead, he'd just walk right in.

Anxiety prickled in my arms as I walked to the door, slowly pushing down the handle. As I opened it, my mind raced with what to say to him. I both hated and wanted Sebastian and resented him for making me feel both.

Astor's face came into view, and I took a long breath. "It's you," I said with the enthusiasm of a teaspoon. "What do you want?"

"I'm glad you finally agreed to speak with me." He ran his hand through his ash-brown curls.

My brows knitted together. "I didn't."

He strolled past me, gazing around my room wide-eyed. "Kalon must have made your guards let me come through. After I saw you leave the feeding room, I asked your guard for an audience. Again. I just got a message to come back now."

I made a mental note to fire whoever was guarding the entrance to my room. "You need to leave," I recalled his anger at seeing me in the banquet room.

"Why? Expecting your new man?" he asked, spite twitching the corner of his mouth.

"That's none of your business."

He arched an eyebrow, his gaze intrusive as he looked me up and down. "I thought you were smarter than this, Liv."

My jaw tensed. "Don't call me that."

"You were always so dramatic." He reached forward, grazing a finger against my cheek. "You were doing so well, working on that. Being here with Sebastian it's changing you. You used to be so gentle."

I curled my fingers into fists to stop myself from launching at him. "You have no right coming up here and—"

"You're better than this." Shoving his hands deep in his pockets, he shook his head. "You deserve more than Sebastian Vangard."

"Since when do you care what I deserve after everything you put me through?" I inhaled sharply. "I'm surprised my mom hasn't cut off your head yet," I snapped, changing the subject. "She knows everything. Or Draven. Has he seen you?"

His mouth twisted. "I'm aware," he said, his intensity matching my own. "She came at me yesterday. Luckily, Kalon intervened. I have his protection, and Draven would be smart not to come at me, too. He's only a mortal."

"Of course, you're working with Kalon," I seethed.

"He trusts Gwen, and she trusts me," he said with a shrug. "Look, I came to make things right."

Our relationship felt like a lifetime ago, although it had only been months. At the time, I hadn't known the real reason for his distance. I stared at the man I once loved, who faked his own suicide so he could become immortal and had cost every man and woman at the guild their life—including my mom. She was now a vampire because of him. "I will never forgive you for what you've done."

"Seriously? I kept your secret. I didn't hand you over, and I could have."

"Oh, fuck off," I shouted. "Just get out."

"You never used to be like this!" he shouted, raising his voice above my own. "You've changed."

My nostrils flared, and my chest tightened. "You changed more. I can't believe I ever loved you."

"I was always this person, Liv."

"Call me Liv again and see what happens," I dared. "You lost the right to that when you betrayed us."

"Then what do I call you? Olivia? Or maybe you'd prefer Seraphina?" he asked.

I tilted my head, regarding him carefully. He was right. I had changed, and as the cold circled the room through the cracks around the old, arched windows, I couldn't help but give in to the sinister smile creeping over my lips. "To you? I'm Your Royal Highness."

Slowly, he pulled his hands from his pockets, standing straight. "I suppose you think you're all-powerful now?" He took a step back, scoffing under his breath. "I came here to help you, but now I've seen what you've turned into, I wonder why I bothered."

I rubbed my temples, closing my eyes briefly. "You are so delusional, I can't..." I shoved a hand in the air. "Just leave."

"You're going to regret marrying him. Your father may be king, but that won't last forever. Even immortals eventually die."

Flexing my fingers, I stomped over to him, closing the distance between us. "That's treason!" My eyes burned with fury as I glared into his stare. "So go ahead, say that again. I dare you. I have no qualms telling my father what you said."

His breath hitched, and he stepped back. "I'm not afraid of you, Liv."

"You should be," I warned. "In three days, I'll be a vampire. Except, unlike you, I will have power, a crown, and armies that can hunt you to the end of the kingdoms."

Disappointment etched into his crumpled features as he slowly looked me up and down, his posture changing. "I miss the old you."

"I'm sure you do. She was easier to manipulate."

"I never manipulated you."

A rich laugh tinkled from my mouth. "Erianna once told me something that changed my life. She said you're often treated how you allow others to treat you."

"What does that even mean?"

"It means I was afraid of pushing boundaries against you, my mom, and anyone else who walked into my life. For so long, I believed I would lose all of your love if I did."

He rolled his eyes. "It wasn't like that."

"It was." Tears fell down my cheeks before I could stop myself. "Every time I caught you in lies when you would talk to girls behind my back or take days to text me back, you would threaten to leave.

I had to beg you to stay." I pointed my finger at his chest. "I had to console *you* when *I* was the one hurting. You made me think it was my fault. That somehow I was responsible for you doing those things because I was never enough for you!" My shouts turned to screams, and my nose became blocked as the tears fell thick and fast. "Now that I don't want you, you can't stand it, can you? You see that I'm wanted by Sebastian," I lied, but Astor had seen those moments, and they appeared genuine enough. "Now that I am finally standing up to you, and I'm not begging for drips of your love, you're here, at my door, trying to make things right."

He shook his head. "That's not true. I was good to you. I always cared for and loved you."

"You don't treat someone you love like that. All I ever wanted was your love, but you could never fully give it to me."

"Don't play the victim, Liv. You did stuff, too."

I rubbed my forehead, unable to stand there for another second with him. For years, all I knew was Astor. But as I recalled those memories, they became a poem about how my life once was. It was a beautiful story, but it was one I looked at through rose-tinted glasses, and I was tired of it. "Get out of my room and leave this castle. Go back to your girlfriend and the city, and stay there. I don't want you near me."

"Kalon needs me here."

"Kalon isn't in charge!"

He shook his head, mumbling as he walked to the door.

"What was that?"

He glanced over his shoulder before opening the door. "I said, neither are you."

"Fuck you, Astor," I shouted, my heart racing, unable to contain the anger searing inside.

He turned, veins visible under his skin as his muscles tensed and fingers curled into fists. "You know what? I'm glad I turned. I regret nothing."

"Don't," I warned, knowing where it was heading. "So many people died because of you."

"So? It was them or me, and I will always choose me. Is that what you want me to say?"

My mouth dried. "No."

"Then what? I protected you. Do you think that was easy? Nightshade knew about Ravena anyway. All I did was confirm it. Don't you think I've been punished for not telling them the truth about you? When everyone found out who you were, they almost killed me."

"I'm sorry they didn't."

He stepped forward, rage roiling in his features. "You can think of me as a traitor all you want and hate me forever, but the truth is I saved us both from death. You should be grateful."

I shook my head. "You only saved yourself."

His shoulders tensed. "That's not true, and you know it." The muscle in his jaw feathered. "And I would do it all over again and not bat an eye."

My chest tightened. "You don't mean that."

"I do, and I still care about you because I'm here, trying to help."

I scoffed, stepping back. "How are you possibly trying to help?"

"I know you don't want Sebastian. So whatever game he's playing with you, I'm offering you an out. You could marry me, instead. I know you still love me. You're crying for me, so don't pretend otherwise."

The audacity of this prick. "I'm crying because I'm angry. Because I'm reliving everything. I finally see things for how they really were."

"I don't want you to cry." He moved to hold my hand. "Look, I know you're upset, but things are different now. We're different. I would be good to you, Liv. *Baby*."

"Based on our history, I disagree, but it's nice to know your ego's still in check."

His eyes darkened, showing me a side to Astor I hadn't seen in all our years together. The man in front of me was as much a stranger as almost everyone else here. "This has nothing to do with my ego. Gwen, Velda, Kalon—" He ticked them off on his fingers, mania threading through his eyes. "—they would kill me if they knew what I was offering. But I would do it for you."

"So you can have more power," I stated.

"Is that so wrong? To want it all? I want you, too."

My stomach lurched. "Perhaps not, but you made one fatal mistake in all of this."

"What's that?"

"You said I didn't want Sebastian." My lips curled at the corners as I relished seeing the torment behind his eyes. "But you're wrong. He's a far better fuck than you ever were." Lies, all of it. I hadn't slept with him, although the moments between Sebastian and me lingered. My breath hitched as I recalled the feel of his lips against mine. I closed my eyes for a few seconds, and I could almost feel the way his fingers tangled in my hair when he'd kissed me.

"You're lying." Astor's expression deepened; the lines of his face were far more prominent than I'd ever seen them. He never moved his intrusive stare from mine as I watched betrayal drown him. Then, closing the distance between us, before I could ready myself for the blow I was sure would happen, his lips were on mine, enveloping me in a moment of lost love.

"No," I shouted into his mouth, pushing him away. "Never do that again," I bellowed, breathless, as I stumbled back.

His lips trembled, his gaze darting up and down.

"I will have you killed if you do," I threatened, darkness filling me up I didn't even know was there.

He clenched his jaw. "Fine, but never say I didn't offer you a different path." He turned, speeding out before leaving me with my mouth open and many more vicious words fresh on my tongue. I took in a deep breath, filling my lungs to capacity. I wouldn't shed another tear over that asshole. He didn't deserve a single one of them.

I slammed the door behind him and let out a small scream behind closed lips. How dare he kiss me like that? If I told Gwen what he did, I was confident she'd try to kill us both. But maybe it would be worth it? Touching my lips with my shaking fingers, I could still taste the kiss on me and with it the pain of feeling him one last time, the man I'd loved and devoted myself to for years.

He was the ultimate proof of how much of a monster someone could come by becoming immortal. Although, he'd betrayed the guild before he was a vampire. If it wasn't for the years of moments we'd shared, I would have had him executed already.

I'm sure my mom already tried, but my father was far more willing to accept my requests than hers. He'd made her into a vampire instead of keeping her as a sorceress, which would be far more useful to him. She said it was because he couldn't bear losing her again, but I knew better. Making her into one of them ensured she remained at his side forever, and divorce was illegal here. It made sense, but vampirism was also a punishment. She'd taken everything from him, or so he believed, and now he'd stripped her of the main thing she loved about herself—her magic.

It meant far more to her than it ever did to me.

Wiggling my fingers, I felt my powers move under my skin, ready to be used. I'd practiced a little but didn't give them too much thought. They'd be gone soon, anyway.

A sigh crept from my lips, and I sat on my bed. I gazed at the veil before turning off the light and falling back on my pillows. Slowly, I drifted into dark daydreams of Erianna, wingless and hiding. Of Anna being fed on as a mortal blood bag. I had no way of helping them right now. I tried, but the king had already allowed me Sebastian and Draven's lives and saw it as a weakness to forgive two more traitors for their sins.

Sleep came quickly, and in the middle of the night, sometime between the first drips of purple in the indigo sky and sunrise, I swore I could feel someone watching me from the shadows as I wrestled with my nightmares.

THREE

Sebastian

Victory.

Listening to Sargon's speech, bringing the entire throne room to a cheer, anyone would think it was inevitable. My eyes moved to Kalon, who stood at his brother's side in the throne room, nodding as if he believed every word.

Liar.

Along with a handful of nobles, he and I knew we had no chance if Asland launched their attack. Kalon was as sly as they came, a wolf posing as a sheep, but he was smart under all of that. Probably more intelligent than anyone else at court—and just as hateful.

Sanmorte was stuck in the dark ages while the rest of the world had moved forward. We'd lagged in technology and weaponry, refusing to acknowledge there was even a modern era. I knew it, even missed it. I had a cellphone, but it stayed in my nightstand drawer, gathering dust. There was little point in using it when only a few in this kingdom had one.

It was useful sometimes, however. Like when I'd gone to Baldoria to spy on Olivia, ensuring she was the lost princess, stealing her away before Kalon's secret order—Nightshade—could sink their teeth into her. I'd used it to keep in touch with Zach and Erianna, who'd not wanted to get back into the technological world since. It made sense. They'd spent most of their lives in this kingdom and were centuries old. While I had only been a vampire for three years.

Applause erupted around me as Sargon finished spewing his bullshit, and I clapped, forcing a clenched smile. As a senior royal, I stood up front on the first step leading to the thrones. Soon, I would be Prince of Sanmorte, consort to the princess, who I was glad was not here.

Olivia and I hadn't spoken once since I'd been brought up from the dungeons and told I would be her husband. My throat tightened as I thought about how I would be dead if she didn't choose me as her groom.

I ran my finger along my neck, imagining my head on the executioner's block. When a hand touched my shoulder, I almost heard an ax slicing through the air. I jolted, a rare reaction and one I wish I hadn't shown. Weakness was like poison in this court. Once it took root, it left a mark forever.

Gwen sped to my side, pursing her lips. The last time I'd seen her was only days ago, when she was sucking my dick in the dungeons when we both believed I was about to be executed. She came to say goodbye and wasn't aware that I knew she'd been behind the plot to frame me. Gwen believed it would be Olivia who would take the fall and not me. She should have known better than to believe Kalon. I'd learned that a long time ago.

Gwen waved as Sargon smiled in our direction. He lifted his goblet of blood, which splashed over the edges, spitting crimson onto the polished stone.

"Are you still mad?" she asked, her voice lower than a whisper.

Chatter rose, and the crowd dissipated as the king sat back on his throne, pulling a disgruntled Ravena onto his lap. Mortals were led in and sat at the tables, perfect specimens for today's lunch.

I glanced down at her. "No."

"Good." She chewed on her bottom lip. "Because I am."

I couldn't help but smirk, and I didn't bother trying to hide it. She'd wanted to hurt Olivia and had almost cost me my life. "I don't regret what I said in the dungeon," I said simply, then headed to the table to eat.

Her face reddened as she leaned in, blonde waves spilling around her face. "Astor can't know."

I spotted a mortal woman I hadn't seen before. Her piercing amber eyes sparkled, unlike the others.

"Sebastian!" Gwen scolded, and I rolled my eyes.

"Why would I care if he knows or not?" I'd only let her do it because I thought I was going to die. So hurting her was a bonus when I told her I was just using her for her mouth. It was a low blow, even I had to admit that.

"You wouldn't want me telling Olivia, would you?"

My shoulders tensed, anger roiling in my chest. Olivia and I weren't together. We were faking our engagement until recently anyway, and I had no commitment to her. I shouldn't care if she found out, and yet…

I shrugged away the feeling, clenching my jaw. "Tell her. I don't care."

"We both know that's a lie," she hissed in my ear.

I turned my attention back to the mortal woman. Someone else had gotten to her first. I watched him slurp against her throat, draining her blood. Clenching my jaw, I turned my focus back to

Gwen. "I'm not going to say shit. I don't care about either of you enough."

"You didn't always feel that way. We had a connection once."

I grabbed her wrist, pulling her close. "You destroyed any fragment of friendship or attraction we shared the moment you tried to hurt..." I paused. "Me."

"You mean Olivia." She tore her arm from my grip, scowling. "You act as if we were never a thing."

"What we had was only ever physical."

Hurt flashed through her blue eyes, and for a second, a twinge of regret ached in my chest until I was reminded of what she'd done. Gwen was the first to help me when her mom made me into a vampire. She wasn't the kindest person, but she was good to me for a time. She taught me what it was like to have fun as an immortal and ignore the guilt that came with what I was. We'd shared in threesomes at court, drank from the same people, getting caught up in the moment.

"Go." I softened my tone a slither, only for our memories. "Like I said, I won't say anything."

"You've changed." Gwen stood. "You care more now. It's unattractive."

I peered around her, spotting Astor and Velda walking in. Gwen pushed her hair over one shoulder, waving at them. She'd never committed herself to anyone before, and I couldn't help but wonder why Astor meant so much to her. He was a coward, a man who'd use his friends to shield his own death.

"Then why did you suck my dick?" I asked, tilting my head.

She shook her head, then strode away.

Tugging on the sleeves of my newly tailored suit, I gazed at the woman who'd intrigued me from the start. Finally, the man feasting on her neck paused. Enough was enough.

"She's mine now," I stated, clearing my throat as he wiped his mouth. I recognized the lord, Jerimiah.

"I'm still feeding."

Challenge shone through my eyes as I waited, unmoving. I didn't care about treading carefully around the nobles anymore. I would soon be a prince anyway, and my freedom would be gone. Taking what I wanted had never been so easy, especially when I had nothing to lose. "I said, she's mine now."

He looked from me over to where Sargon, Ravena, and Kalon stood and talked, then let the woman drop onto me. "Of course, Your Highness," he spat.

I caught her head in my hand, watching Jerimiah stand, then hurry away, a low growl reverberating behind closed lips.

The ecstasy of our venom was already deep in her veins. Those amber eyes rolled to the back of her head, her lips parting as a word breathed through. "More."

I wiped away the blood trickling down, then brought my lips to the other side of her neck where he hadn't bitten. My fangs pierced into her delicate skin, gushing blood through my teeth and coating my tongue. She shuddered against me, her fingers gripping my arms as I gulped her blood, clinging onto her as the frenzy took over.

I groaned as I took more, knowing I was close to the limit but not wanting to stop.

She slipped her fingers under her skirt as the venom in her system tipped her into euphoria. "More," she said again, and I gave in, sucking hard on her neck, pulling her tighter against me. Her movements slowed, and I stopped. No matter how good it felt, I couldn't kill her.

Instead, I lay her down on the bench, biting into my wrist and bringing it to her mouth. Slowly, she drank, and the color on her face returned. Usually, I wouldn't dare break the law here, at least not so openly. Feeding mortals our blood was off-limits, especially when so many of them wanted to become vampires, too—and that was precisely what they needed to become one.

But Sargon wanted to keep a constant stream of food, with the promise of immortality one day. Unfortunately, most of them died before that happened. Often, vampires would be overcome with desire and hunger to stop, draining them. This was why more and more mortals were taken from the neighboring kingdoms to keep us fed.

The woman I'd fed on, who didn't look any older than twenty-five, smiled and wiped my blood from her lips. Her eyes fluttered open, her fingers still dancing between her legs.

The promise of vampirism wasn't the only reason we had volunteers. They also enjoyed the rush of our venom, which, while excruciating at first, turned into ecstasy.

She ran her other hand over her breast, the outline visible under the thin fabric of her white dress, and rolled her nipple between her fingers. "Take me," she offered when she saw me watching.

While tempting, she wasn't in her right mind. Suddenly, Olivia flashed into my mind, slipping unwanted into my thoughts. She'd hate this, and I wished I didn't care. More than anything, I wished I could rip my heart from my chest and feel nothing.

"Sorry, love," I told the woman. "Here, come with me."

I led her out of the throne room and to one of the secluded bedrooms. She walked inside hazily, then fell onto the bed. I closed the door behind her, leaving her alone and away from the greedy eyes of Jeremiah, then headed for the staircase.

The smell of liquor and blood hung heavy in the air as I removed my jacket. My wings extended through the slits in my shirt, stretching out in the foyer, rolling relief into my back. I flapped them against the bitter air, kicking off from the ground.

A smile crept over my face as I took flight, gliding between the staircases, then landed on the second floor. Only when I spotted Olivia did I pause, the smile falling into a frown.

Good gods.

I caught my breath, the tips of my wings tingling as I watched her move wearing a trailic of all things. Her round ass was covered only with black lingerie and see-through sheer fabric. I glimpsed her full breasts under her lacy bra, her nipples hard as the cool air circled the staircase.

She walked down the long steps toward the west wing, the opposite direction from where Sargon would hold his war meeting shortly. I stepped back, moving into the shadows of the unlit corridor.

Her red waves swung down her back as she descended. I never thought she would wear a trailic. It was nothing but a ridiculous tradition they forced at court. Still, I licked my lips as desire built inside of me. Before I could pull myself away, my dick pulsed against my pants. The way she slid her fingers down the side of her neck to play with her necklace stole my next breath.

It was physical. Purely physical. That was all I wanted—to bed her. I told myself that repeatedly, tearing myself from the temptation to go to her. I strode in the opposite direction, forcing thoughts of Olivia from my mind, but desire begged me to turn back.

No. I had to find Zach and Erianna. I'd gotten them out of the dungeons before at least Zach's wings could be removed as punishment for their treason. Unfortunately, Erianna had already suffered her cruel, unjustified fate. Still, they'd remained in hiding ever since, posing as servants, living in the tunnels behind the walls.

When I was prince, that would change. There were some perks to being a royal, even if it was a life shackled by duties I never wanted. I'd chosen to become a Master of Travel back in the City of Nightmares for a reason. I had my freedoms and the luxuries that came with the title.

FOUR

Olivia

"I can't believe you did this!" I shouted at my mom who sat on the sofa in her bedroom. Fortunately, Sargon wasn't here. "It's sick." I ran my hands down the sides of the trailic, my power seething under my fingertips.

She sighed. "It's tradition."

"I hate tradition." I turned to look in the full-length ornate mirror on her wall. The dress hung over my body. If it wasn't for the black lingerie underneath, the whole court could see everything. It was the only item of clothing left in my closet when I woke up this morning.

She averted her gaze. "It's customary for the woman to wear these in the days leading up to a wedding."

"Yes, you said before."

"You refused to wear it."

"I know." I balled my fists. "That's why I can't believe you, of all people, forced my hand."

"You wouldn't listen to reason, so we *had* to remove all your clothes. I'm trying to protect you."

Self-consciously, I covered my chest with folded arms. The trailics were made from the thinnest of tulle, with beads and pearls dangling from the ends of the sleeves and bottom of the hem, imitating water droplets. "I won't wear it in public. It's bad enough I had to walk to your room with it on."

"Olivia, honey. The people see you refusing to conform to their traditions and customs. They already begrudge you as their princess. Don't push them further away. We are nothing without the loyalty of our subjects. I need you to be accepted by them. Because if you're not, and you keep rebelling, then..."

"They'll kill me?"

"Perhaps." She sat on the end of her bed. "I also must play a part I don't want. We have to do what we do to survive."

"What if I don't care about surviving?"

Her raven hair reflected the sunlight arrowing through the arched windows. "Don't be silly. If you didn't care about surviving, you wouldn't be here, trying. You wouldn't have agreed to turn. You will wear this trailic."

"So everyone can gawk at my body?" I shuddered at the thought.

"It's not like that. Women used to wear nothing before their weddings a century ago. It's so bruises and bites can't be hidden to eliminate any signs of abuse."

"Yeah, because vampires are sick."

"Yes." Her expression hardened. She seldom showed any compassion or softness on her strong features. Even when I was a child. All I ever heard was how it was important to always appear strong. Any signs of weakness were bad. So I didn't know why I thought she'd allow me some kindness now.

The idea that the outfit was for our own good was ridiculous, seeing as their blood can cure any injury, and therefore vampires could cover up any abuse. "I think this so-called tradition only exists so they can have another reason to satisfy their lust."

I wanted nothing more than to wrap a dressing gown around myself and hide away.

"Regardless of the reason, you must try to fit in here. This is a start. I won't hear another word."

"Mom!"

"It's this or nothing at all," she said with a pained expression, then turned her back to me.

A sob choked up my throat. "Please, don't do this. I don't trust any of the men here."

She stared at the window, arms folded. "I'm sorry. Regardless, I expect to see you at the party tonight. It's in your honor, after all."

"Mom." My eyebrows furrowed. "Look at me!"

She didn't move.

"I can't believe you." I sucked in a deep breath, my hands shaking.

"Don't push this anymore," she warned. "Sargon is at his limit. Draven stays alive by our grace. If you continue to rebel, Sargon will take it out on him. Do you want that?" She spun to face me, her dark stare razor sharp, piercing right through me. "Do you want his death on your hands?"

I swallowed thickly, my chest growing heavier by the second. The thought of him dead-dead, not even a vampire, buried six feet under or burned and sent to the heavens, was too much for my soul to bear. I didn't need to say anything.

She nodded. We both knew I would not risk Draven's life, and I hated her for it. I hated how she couldn't do more to protect him—or me. That she lied to me in the first place about all of this. I hated I felt that way because I loved her so much, and the warmth I needed from her wasn't there. It never was. So, I at least needed the powerful, take-no-shit mom who always protected me. But, unfortunately, that was lacking, too.

My magic coiled around my center, darkening my emotions as I headed out of the room, slamming the door behind me.

***

After remaining in my room for as long as possible, I walked down to the party. If it wasn't for the thought of Draven suffering the consequences of me not attending, I wouldn't go.

I hurried around a corner, taking the long way to the room where the corridors were emptier. Even though everyone would see the half-naked me at the party, I wanted to avoid people as much as possible.

Every room along the long corridors was decorated with red and white roses, midnight-black drapes, and crystals made to glisten like stars. Red floated around my ballet-style shoes as I disturbed the rose petals scattered over the ground. Lights flickered from candles placed inside glass lanterns hanging from the beams above.

Adormai celebrated passion, love, and desire, making it the most erotic and romantic holiday. In Baldoria, many celebrated by planning their weddings on the blessed day, or proposed. Here, the people mostly took it as an opportunity to partake in more orgies. Everywhere I turned, naked bodies were tangled together in moans of passion. I kept walking, not stopping long enough in any room until I reached a wedding.

I paused at the chapel, once used to worship the gods, wondering why they did away with it. We didn't have chapels or churches in Baldoria. We knew we could worship the gods from anywhere. Perhaps my father or his father before him had come to the same conclusion.

Darkness hung behind the stained-glass windows of the chapel. The candlelight on the tables fractured against the slices of color, forming beautiful scenes of the goddess Salenia bathing in a river.

In the window next to her, the god Jaiunere stood naked at a large tree, picking from its fruits and placing them into a basket while several mortals bowed at his feet.

When the heat from the sunlight hit me, I smiled. There was something beautiful about the room, with its ancient pews currently filled with a host of vampires and one aniccipere. I breathed in the musky scent, peering behind the witnesses to whoever's wedding was taking place. Neither of the participants had arrived yet. Old books of worship were stacked dustily against an old bookshelf at the rear of the room. At the front, an arch had been erected, entwined with roses in full bloom.

So many weddings would happen, but none were celebrated like Sebastian's and my nuptials. Seeing the bride emerge from the double doors on the other side of the chapel in a dress of black only reminded me of my fate.

Our wedding would be followed by the shadow kissed ceremony, where I would become a vampire. There were weddings every day leading up to the holiday. Which surprised me, considering how lawless and uncommitted they could be. Marriage, I'd learned, was important to them. According to the vampires, divorce wasn't a thing here as it went against everything the goddess Vaneria believed.

An aniccipere stared at me from the crowd, his beady eyes hungry with desire. I saw very few of them in the castle. I tilted my head, and the creature glowered back, his lipless mouth curling into an unnerving smile. His nostrils flared as he inhaled, licking his mouth as if he could somehow taste my soul. I shuddered, moving away from the doorway, and pressed my back against the stones of the wall. Jagged edges dug into my hips and lower back.

Out of all the vampires, the aniccipere were the worst. The half-demon, half-mortal creatures didn't drink the blood of their victims. Instead, they sucked out their souls, destroying the body in a painful, merciless feeding.

I turned to face the long corridor, feeling the uneven ground under my shoes. Then I saw him. Hamza's soulless eyes found mine. The emptiness and lack of light behind them sent a shiver down my spine. He licked his lips, grooming his dark beard with two fingers. He was conventionally handsome, especially when in his suits. It only made him more dangerous. People were drawn to him like moths to a flame. We had a word for people like him in Baldoria: psychopaths.

I felt nothing from his emotions when he approached me. The same as I'd felt when he'd brought me to the auction before Sebastian got me out. I pulled back my empath gifts, heightened by my magic.

"Beautiful Seraphina." He stopped before me, undressing me with his green eyes. "You are delicious in that dress." He traced a finger over my clavicle, and I shoved him away.

"I could have you killed," I threatened, attempting to stand tall despite him being a foot and a half taller than me.

His lip curved at one side. "You *do* have all the power now," he said, his voice charging with realization, and challenge flashed in his gaze. "As I'm sure you recall, I enjoy the fight."

"Then I'll be sure not to give you one." I pushed past him, but he grabbed me by the wrist, his icy fingers tearing me back. A spark of desire pierced through my barrier.

He needed to feel something. I could feel the want emanating from him in thick waves, enough to emotionally drown a person, and I was that something. I felt how he did when he saw me. Forbidden and powerful. He knew he couldn't have me, and the danger he'd be in if he tried. I was the one who'd gotten away, and since the auction, I was all he thought of. His feelings took a form of their own, and for a second, I was sure he would snap and force me to be his right here.

My heart palpitated, my mouth drying as I looked at him, ready to use my powers if he tried. I was not immortal yet, but there was a reason the vampires feared and coveted us. Our magic could disarm them. I only wished mine was stronger.

"I'm late for a meeting with my father," I said, annoyed at the tremble threading through my words. "He won't appreciate it if I'm late."

He shoved me back against the wall, scraping my shoulder against a painting. He pressed his hard dick against my hip as he shoved his mouth against my earlobe. "I could take you still. I doubt the king would kill me, even if I fuck his daughter."

"You're not that important."

He grinned against my skin, his eyelashes whispering over my temple. "You'd be surprised." He paused. "I want you, and I will have you."

I was tired of feeling helpless against them. Like these creatures could take whatever they wanted with no repercussions. "I'll have you killed for this."

A laugh tinkered from his mouth, spreading goosebumps over the back of my neck. "Unlikely, but just in case, maybe I should kill you after. This castle is full of people who would do anything for a taste of your blood," he hissed against my ear. "The list of suspects would be too long."

Darkness uncoiled from my center, filling me up as if it had been there all along, dormant and waiting. His free hand reached my throat, his touch so soft I could mistake it for that of a lover. I shouldn't have walked down here alone, but I'd heard Erianna was somewhere around here.

His grip tightened, his nails digging into my skin, blocking the air from reaching my lips. A low growl sounded as he pressed against me, his dick pulsing. His hot breath tickled against my temple, and my stomach churned, my chest tightening. Instinct begged to grapple with his fingers against my throat, but logic swayed me the other way. Brute strength would do nothing against a vampire, but I could hurt him. If I could get enough power.

Closing my eyes, finding solace in the blackness, panic pressed against the walls I'd built up as he unzipped his pants. Magic pricked my fingers, purring with my darkness. His grip loosened as he struggled to pull up the skirt of the dress, tearing it instead. I sucked in a deep breath, filling my lungs with oxygen, looking down at his dick through blurry eyes. He pushed forward, shredding the fabric of my clothes until they were tattered at my feet.

"Don't stop," I begged, hoping the distraction would stall him for a few seconds. Instead, my voice came out croaky, but genuine.

Surprise flashed over his expression, lines forming on his forehead. His hand trembled on my thigh, the corner of his eye twitching as he moved back an inch to look at me.

My power begged to be released. "You wanted this, so don't stop now," I said, my tone breaking in places. Then, glaring down at his cock, I grabbed it in my fist, and he jolted under my touch. "Now burn, you sick fuck."

Every ounce of magic in my body released into my bloodstream, traveling from my fingers and into his genitals, erupting a throaty scream from Hamza. He tried to push me off, but the magic kept my hand rooted, sending scorching heat into his dick.

The stench of burning flesh hit my nostrils, and I breathed it in, delighting in all the senses; the blazing heat of the touch, watching him sizzle and melt as shock waves moved through him with nowhere to go, hearing his screams bring people pouring into the corridor. I could almost taste his fear as his emotions muddied, slowing as his skin melted from his muscles, liquifying, bubbling down to his bones. Finally, the skin under my touch melted away, and I finally let go.

His body thumped back, hitting the stone, sending a loud crack echoing against the wall as his head split open and blood poured out. I didn't take my eyes from him until his final breath. I enjoyed seeing him suffer, relishing in his torture. He was gone—vermin wiped from this world, because I willed it so.

I'd been led to believe they were the powerful ones, to be feared, but I realized now it was me. Heat crept through my body, setting my nerves on fire when icy hands touched my shoulders, making me jump back. Then, shaking my head, I suddenly noticed everyone staring.

Shock rippled through me as muscle and skin regrew around his bones, his eyes regenerated, and his body returned to life. I let out a sharp breath, pain screeching through the adrenaline numbing me. Lifting my hands, I saw the large welts and blisters. I'd not only burned him, but my hands, too.

How the fuck was he coming back to life? I'd melted him to nothing. Watching him regrow again forced last night's dinner up my esophagus.

"Let's get out of here."

His voice broke me from my shock, dragging me back to him. Sebastian. My soon-to-be husband, and until now, the man who'd avoided me since our captivity.

"I melted him," I stated.

"Don't feel bad."

"I don't."

I wanted to stay and watch, but the concern etched onto Sebastian's face forced me away. We walked down the corridor, and he handed me his jacket. I pulled it around myself, glancing back at Hamza and the putrefying mess on the surrounding ground from his old body.

The crowd disbursed as we approached, none of them looking at Sebastian. No. All eyes were on me and radiating from them was fear. I could almost taste it as we left the corridor.

Once we were out of the main corridor, Sebastian's wings exploded outward in a swirl of black. Before I could protest, he swept me into his arms, his hand firmly against my thigh as he took off.

Finally, landing us at the door to my bedroom, he let me go. I toppled back, and he moved to the guard at my door, whispering something. He moved out of the way, and Sebastian pushed me inside, locking the door behind us.

He looked me up and down, his eyes manic. "What happened?"

"Hamza tried to rape me." I swallowed thickly.

He turned, his eyes darkening. "Motherfucker!" He slammed the door so hard it shattered the wood. Splinters stuck out from his knuckles when he glanced back at me, cursing under his breath. He paced forward, stopping in front of me. A world of words swam behind his dark-blue eyes, an ocean of the unspoken hanging between us, but nothing left his lips. Instead, his eyes darted down at my body, his jacket and black, lacy lingerie the only thing on me. Cold swirls hit me, erecting the hairs on my arms.

"Sebastian, it's o—"

"Don't say that." He stepped back. "If you hadn't had your powers—" His voice broke off at the end.

I didn't want to stare at his tortured expression. Instead, I averted my gaze to the window, shock still numbing me.

"Your hands," he said, reminding me of the welts covering them.

"Yeah." I stretched out my fingers, examining my palms. "It was worth it."

He touched me gently, and I flinched. His features softened, and he regained control over his emotions. I'd never seen him lose it like that. "Can I heal you?" he asked, his voice gentler than I was used to.

Swallowing thickly, I nodded. His fangs elongated, and slowly, he sunk them into his skin, his eyes evaluating my reaction the whole time.

Blood erupted from the puncture wounds on his wrist, and as much as I wanted to refuse the help, I couldn't ignore the stinging sensation swimming up my arms from the burn. Soon, the adrenaline would wear off and the pain from my injuries would take over. I knew how it worked, and I wasn't so stubborn that I would suffer unnecessarily.

Closing the distance between us, I pulled his wrist to my mouth, placing my lips around the cut. His blood trickled down my throat, feeding the power inside of me. As I gulped it down, trying my best not to gag against the tangy thickness. The magic moved with me more than ever before, and it was still untapped, with unending potential. It was a part of me. A part I wasn't prepared to give up. But I had no choice.

I ran my tongue over the marks, tasting what was left before the skin healed, then wiped my mouth on the back of my hand. My gaze climbed his body, meeting his. We hadn't been alone since we were in the dungeons, when he'd promised not to turn me in. I begged him to turn me there so we could escape. He'd lied to me, and I'd saved him, but as he stood, observing me, I saw how much he didn't want this.

"Thanks," I spluttered.

"I'm going to murder Hamza for this."

I grabbed his arm. "Don't." Reason splashed through me. "Sargon will kill you."

"I don't give a fuck. He can't get away with this."

My eyes clamped shut. "I'll tell my father what happened. He'll execute him. Please." I tugged his arm, and he let out a long exhale, brushing his thumb over my hand.

The skin peeled away, revealing a new layer as I watched my palms heal, marveling at the magic in their blood. They had an elixir of immortality in their blood, from the goddess Salenia. Sometimes I forget it could do some good—like heal. "Sebastian…"

"Hamza has too much power here," he said apologetically. "Sargon won't kill him. He might lock him away." He shook his head and slowly released me. "Wait here for me. Go into the bathroom and lock the door."

My heart pounded as I struggled to come to terms with what almost happened to me. Sebastian headed for the door, and I wanted to shout at him to stay. For what? Comfort? Affirmation? But I didn't. I watched him leave.

When I closed my eyes, I saw Hamza. I felt his breath on me still.

Suddenly, my powers were everything to me. My one defense against those who'd use and hurt me. I clung to them, biting my nails into my freshly healed palms, heading for the shower, wanting nothing more than to wash the scent of Hamza from me.

I turned the water all the way up, needing every piece of him off me, but no matter how hard I scrubbed, his scent clung to me. Or perhaps I imagined it?

Bile bit up my throat, burning my mouth. I folded, retching into the shower, my hair pooling around my face, water seeping into my eyes and mouth. My mom's screech pierced through the room as I heard the door open, banging back against the wall.

"Olivia!" Her fists pounded against the closed bathroom door. "Honey." Her breathless pleas thawed my icy heart. "Are you hurt?"

Sebastian must have told her. I wanted to shout back that he didn't hurt me. That he didn't get far enough, but I couldn't. Because it wasn't true. Every touch lingered on my skin. I turned up the heat of the water, watching pillars of steam swirl up as I stepped under the stream of water. "I'm okay," I finally managed, my voice catching as I swallowed against a sob climbing my throat. He hadn't hurt me. I'd hurt him. Yet, I'd never scrubbed myself so hard before as I reached for more soap.

She talked outside the door, leaving me to my privacy as my mind carouseled with scenes of what could have happened. There was no way I was becoming a vampire, not even at my father's wishes or to become the damned princess of Sanmorte.

"Your father's here," my mom said through the door, her tone gentle. "When you're ready."

I heard him say something behind her, but I couldn't make it out through the pouring water. She shouted something at him, then the room fell silent.

How was I going to tell him I refused to be the princess? Would Hamza die? No, they needed him. Politics had no room for justice.

If they didn't kill him for this, I would take matters into my own hands.

Dark magic tingled in my hands, as if it agreed with me. I dressed, wiped my eyes, and washed away the vomit before opening the door and facing my father.

FIVE

Sebastian

The dungeons were colder than normal as the winds outside gusted snowflakes into the cells.

I'd heard Sargon had Hamza arrested for treason, but they didn't know what to do with him. He couldn't kill him. Hamza had too many followers and played both sides for centuries. The aniccipere from the south who hated the monarchy believed he was on their side, and the nobles and elites in the city saw him as a loyal man to the king who helped them achieve their goals.

"What are you going to do?" Hamza taunted from behind bars. "It's her word against mine. Why was she walking around almost naked if she didn't want to get fucked? Tradition? She's the king's daughter. He would have pardoned her from wearing a trailic if she only asked."

I took a step closer, whispers of cold air circling around my neck, reminding me of the last time I'd been in these dungeons. The executioner's ax had been sharpened the night before I was supposed to die.

"The last time I was down here, I was so close to death I could feel her breath on my neck." I paced the stone walkway outside the iron bars separating us. "I've seen her before," I told him, barely glancing in his direction. "The Grim Reaper."

Silence befell the dungeons. The last prisoners had been taken out to the scaffolds that morning. Hamza peered around me, striding to the bars, coiling his long fingers around them. "You got the guards to leave."

The corner of my lips lifted. "Yes. I told them the king said I could come down here."

His nose scrunched, fingers curling around the bars. "Then they're not very smart. They didn't take me up on my offer of a thousand stagma to let me go."

"They wouldn't. They're members of Sargon's private guards," I said, recognizing them from their meetings with the king. Midnight Lotus was supposed to be a secret, but everyone knew about Sargon's loyal group. I pushed my hands into my pockets. "There isn't enough stagma in the world to save you. Not when you're in here for treason."

"My mistake," he admitted, a muscle in his jaw feathering. "But they won't kill me, you know. Not even the king is *that* stupid. My followers would come for him, and your bitch of a girl."

I reined my anger in, instead sharpening it, honing it. He'd always been difficult to figure out. Knowing a man's fear meant owning his soul, but until now, I couldn't put my finger on what Hamza's was. Yet, as he stood in a dungeon awaiting a trial he would inevitably win, I realized. "You have always been a selfpreservationist. You're unfeeling, always chasing darkness. You love no one."

He shrugged.

"Except for yourself," I added. "Do you feel her presence?"

The foul-smelling cells next to him echoed my words back to us. The only sounds were a leaking pipe in the distance and the scurry of rats clawing at the ancient stone.

"Whose?"

"Deaths," I answered.

His throat bobbed, and he brought a hand to the back of his neck. He averted his gaze, slowly turning his head to look behind him. As he moved, I ran my arm through the narrow bars, gripping his throat. I felt the vibration of his low scream on my fingers, reverberating in his windpipe. Grasping tighter, I forced his face into the wrought iron bars until we were only inches apart.

"There is no peace in death," I spat, our noses almost touching. "No happiness, only relentless torture beyond this veil. Do you fear it, Hamza?"

His eyes widened, a thread of fear swimming in his dark stare. A tremble shook his fingers as he clawed at my own, but rage locked my grasp on him tight.

I continued. "The Reaper hides in the shadows, knowing a person's fate. She knew mine until Olivia changed it. I was supposed to die down here, yet destiny now has me on the other side of these bars. But you…" A sadistic smile crept over my lips. "…you will die today. There will be no reprieve or escape. You will never feel pleasure again."

"If you kill me, you'll be signing your own death warrant, too," he warned.

"I don't care."

"All of this for some girl," he spat back, clenching his teeth.

"Yes, but it's not just her," I growled, digging my nails into his skin until his breaths shallowed. "You don't get to take away anyone's free will."

He struggled to force another word, but I didn't want to hear what the sack of shit had to say. "The Reaper is here," I continued. "I can feel Death in this room, and she's ready to drag your soul to the underworld."

"No," he spluttered, fighting to push back, but the poison they'd given him slowed his movements. I remembered the vile drink, which stole my strength. It was the only way I could get blood when I was imprisoned, by drinking the laced goblet with just enough to keep me from desiccating, keeping me too weak to escape. "I will make you pay for this. Even if it is in the underworld," he managed as he struggled.

I lifted my chin. "I no longer fear death or darkness. My fate will *not* be the same as yours."

His panicked pleas slowly faded, and he laughed as his blood ran like streams between his teeth. "Do you search for redemption?" he gurgled as I loosened my grip on his neck. "Sebastian Vangard, the first vampire to go to the heavens."

I shook my head, the cold seeping into my bones as death neared. "It's not my soul you need to worry about." As soon as I let go, he stumbled to the back of the cell, rubbing his throat. I pulled the key from my pocket, dangling the heavy thing from a piece of string. "I lied about why the guards left. They didn't believe me when I said Sargon was allowing me to see you," I explained, rebuking his assumptions earlier. "But there are ways to get even the loyalist of men to turn the other cheek."

"How did *you* manage that?"

"Everyone assumes Zach's wife is a nobody." I smiled to myself. "Anna prefers it that way. Who takes notice of a mere mortal in a castle of vampires? She's always been the best keeper of secrets, moving between immortals, invisible. She knows everything there is to know about everyone here, including the guards who were protecting you."

His nostrils flared, pressing his back up against the wall. "You mean keeping me here?"

"They were all that stood between you and me." I swung the key around my finger. "I don't want to be redeemed, Hamza. It's too late for creatures like you and me, but it's not for someone like Olivia, Anna, or Erianna. If the only good thing I do in my life is to take you out of their world, then I will die with a smile on my face."

"You took the key from them."

"Every man has a price. The guards have secrets Anna found out, ones we could use against them."

"What are you going to do, Sebastian? Kill me? Don't be so predictable." He wiped the last of the blood from his mouth. The wounds on his throat from my fingers had already healed. "I have connections, you know this. You're a smart man. We can come to an agreement."

"I will never make a deal with you." I unlocked the cell and strode inside.

He put his hands up as I closed the distance between us. "You don't want this life either. Being a prince consort means you'll be just as much of a prisoner as me. Ruling under Sargon's commands, with no power, forced to marry someone you don't want. It will destroy you. I can help you get away from here. My friends from the south are coming. I sent word after she melted me." His lip twitched, his nose scrunching as he relived the memory. "That's why I'm not dead yet. Sargon won't anger all those loyal to me. He doesn't know what to do, and if you kill me, they will hunt you for it. But if you let me go now, we can both escape." He nodded. "You are not my enemy. I know you'll make the smart decision."

Laughing, I ran my fingers through my hair and looked from the ground up to him. "I'd rather die than make a deal with you."

"You're not a killer." He balled his fists, and I stepped back, leaving a couple of feet between us. "You were always better than that."

"Those are the words of a desperate man, and you're wrong." I pulled Erianna's dagger from my pocket and ran my fingertip along the sharp blade. "This dagger is infused with magic. It ensures that wounds don't so easily heal, even on immortals."

"Wait! Don't! What are you doing?"

I spun the dagger in my hand, licking my lips. "Let's just say you'll wish you were dead when I'm done with you."

***

The hour Zach, Anna, and Erianna had given me was up. I slumped back against the wall, blood soaking every part of me and the cell. Some had dried, clinging to the rock. A pool of crimson surrounded Hamza's head. His still heart was discarded against the dirt in the dungeon's corner, a rat nibbling on the meat. I'd enjoyed torturing him—more than I wanted to let on.

As I sat, surrounded by body parts, I smiled. He would no longer hurt anyone else. The sick fuck took what he wanted, making others powerless against him, and it brought me great joy to take that from him in the end. His pleas for mercy still rang in my ears from when I cut him apart.

"Seb." Erianna stepped into view. Her brown eyes surveyed the scene. "You were supposed to make it look like a suicide. Remove the heart only."

"I got carried away," I said, standing slowly. "Where's Zach?"

"With the guards. They gave you an hour, but they'll hand us over once they see this mess. The king will kill them otherwise."

"Then kill them."

She gave me a look, concern etched in her strong features. "You don't mean that."

"If they won't stand with us against scum like this—" I pointed at what remained of Hamza. "—then they deserve the same fate. It is better if there are no witnesses, anyway."

"Seb." Her face crumpled.

"Don't look at me like that."

"Then don't give me a reason to," she said, her eyes swimming, reflecting the bloodied scene. "I won't kill the guards. They're innocent."

"No one is innocent. We're all dead if anyone finds out we were responsible for this. I won't risk any of your lives again. Not like last time. My family comes before anything."

"We made our own choices. Besides, we know the secrets they keep, thanks to Anna. It was enough for them to let you come down here."

I placed my hand over my chest, my heart thumping harder than ever. "No." My voice came out rougher than I expected, a growl lacing my tone. Rage bubbled deep inside of me, climbing into my chest like its own monster. "You are wingless because of me. Because of Olivia, too. I let my guard down."

"It's not her fault. Or yours."

I turned my back to her, pulled out a pocket handkerchief, and wiped the blood from my hands. "Those guards are too close to the king, even with their secrets," I decided. "If you won't do it, then I will." I stormed out of the cell, passing her the dagger. Voices carried from up the corridor to the locked door leading out of the dungeons. I recognized one belonging to Zach.

"Seb, I beg you," she called after me. "Don't do this. We had a deal with them. I can clean up the blood. We can still make this look like he ripped his own heart out. It happens all the time."

"And his head?" I shifted on my heel, halting us both to a stop. "How will you explain to the king how he took off his own head?"

She swallowed thickly, her lips parting, then closing again. I couldn't let the disappointment in her expression pull me down. Strengthening my resolve, I stood straight, flexing my fingers at my side. "Are we all done?" Zach asked as he walked to us with two other sets of footsteps. He wouldn't have brought Anna down here. Not when things were so unpredictable.

"Zach, he's going to—" Erianna shouted, but I'd turned already, both guard's faces unreadable as I plunged my fingers into their chest cavities, tearing apart their rib cages and muscle until I severed their beating hearts from their bodies. Blood seeped through my fingers, dripping down my arms and soaking my sleeves. The men crumpled and folded to the ground, and their hearts rolled, toppling from my hands.

The shreds of mortality left in my heart dissipated as I looked at their bodies. Erianna splayed fingers over her mouth, muffling a gasp. Zach remained still, his lips tight as he watched me. The concern in his pale eyes was too much for me.

The monsters that had come for me and my family three years ago, filled with bloodlust, echoed in the scene in front of me.

Stepping back, I pulled out a handkerchief once more, wiping my hands of their blood. It was one thing to become the darkness I'd always hated in flesh, fangs, and bone, but to give in to their nature was another.

"It's okay, Seb," Erianna said softly, as if she were coaxing a deer from the wood.

I cocked a brow. I must have looked dreadful if she was using her kind voice. A lump formed in my throat. "I'm fine, Erianna. It is done." I stepped over the guards, heading toward the exit, needing a breath of fresh air.

I'd gone further than I ever had, but some lines had to be crossed and if I had to play the villain to protect the people I loved, then so be it. It was true. I could have let them go. We had things to blackmail them with, but there was always a chance they'd fold. I couldn't risk it, especially when my family was involved.

Memories of first seeing the scars on Erianna's back flashed unwantedly into my mind, along with the screams of my family as they were ripped apart by Velda. I decided then that I would never let anyone hurt my loved ones again. No matter who I had to kill, deceive or torture to prevent it. Even if the people I cared for hated me for it.

SIX

Olivia

My father's crimson waves curled around a crown of gold and red. His green eyes observed me as I sat, shivering against my wet hair slicked around my shoulders.

They'd barely said a word since I left the bathroom. Sargon paced in a circle, his fingers flexing as he outstretched his fist. Guard after guard entered the room and muttered something to him. They quickly left after, their eyes trailing over me just for a second, fear in their gaze. I wasn't sure who they were more scared of. Me or him?

My mom sat next to me, the mattress dipping down, pulling me closer. She smelled like lavender, a scent I'd grown fond of over the years. I was glad some things didn't change.

Our last argument pricked fresh in my mind as I mulled over the words again and again. She'd forced me to wear the trailic, in some bid to win over the vampires. I wondered if she regretted it. Now that Hamza had used it as an excuse to take what wasn't his.

"Honey, it's okay," she whispered under her breath as I shuffled out of her embrace. The hardness in her stare softened. "It's just me," she consoled, as if fear of touch was the reason I was trying to get away from her. It wasn't.

"Where's Sebastian?" I asked, glancing at the open door.

"I don't know. He left after he found us and told us what happened." Her voice broke at the end, and she turned her head. I didn't say anything else. Neither of us could afford to be vulnerable right now.

A man walked in, whispered something in my father's ear, then gulped. Confliction threaded through Sargon's expression. He nodded at the man, then gestured for him to leave. The guard, wearing a uniform like Draven's, rushed out, closing the door behind him. Once we were alone, Sargon turned his back to us, looking out the window. "Hamza is dead."

My muscles tightened. "He was executed so fast," I stated, my heart galloping as I stood.

My father's blazer strained as his shoulders tensed. The blue trim clashed with his hair, the same red as mine and a dead giveaway of our royal descent. I almost wanted to hug my dad for the first time since I'd arrived. I had no idea he'd ordered Hamza's execution. From the back and forth, with guards and advisors traipsing in and out of the room, I'd assumed they were still deliberating on what to do, and worried Hamza wouldn't receive any punishment.

Sargon swept over to my mom, too fast for my mortal eyes. "Who did you order to kill him? Was it the boy guard? Answer me, Ravena," he boomed, his voice carrying through the walls.

I retreated a step, the hairs on the back of my arms standing erect. Her lips parted, but his hand was around her throat before she could answer. I opened my mouth to protest, but shock stole my words away.

His grip tightened. "I kept you alive!" he shouted, his fingers curling into her windpipe.

I pressed my lips together until they hurt. He brought his nose to hers, the tips almost touching as he pulled her up from the bed by her neck. I stepped forward instinctively, but she shot me a warning glare when I got too close. "You continue to disobey me after everything I have done for you." His eye twitched. "After all I've done for *her*," he spat. "This was too far. Even for you."

She kicked her legs, the tips of her shoes scraping against the stone floor as he held her above the ground.

I finally found my voice. "Stop. Let her talk," I demanded, although my voice wavered with a tremor.

When he jerked his head in my direction, I saw where the stories of the dark king had descended from. There was something insatiable and deadly in those eyes.

A muscle feathered in his jaw, the veins on his hands bulging as he threw my mom down on the bed.

He didn't look away from me. "You do not command me."

"You were killing her," I argued. She caught her breath, sitting upright.

"She can't die from that," he boomed.

"Sargon." My mom's voice came out far calmer than I thought possible. "Move away from our daughter."

He waved his hand, turning away from me. Pointing, he shook his head at her. "Seraphina has nothing to fear from me. I would never hurt my own blood."

She gritted her teeth, raising a perfectly arched, black eyebrow. "I did not order Hamza killed. I have been here with you this whole time."

Sargon shook his head. "Then it was the boy guard."

"Draven?" I asked. "No. He wouldn't have."

His voice rose, shaking as fury laced into his tone. "Then who?" he demanded. "Hamza was found without his head and his heart, along with two of my guards."

The sun set lower in the sky, splintering in orange hues throughout the room. The heat touched my exposed collarbone and shoulders. I couldn't think about who'd killed him. All that mattered was he was dead and couldn't hurt anyone again. My heart sank a little knowing my father didn't give the order. I guessed I should have expected as much. "Who cares?"

"What did you say?" he asked, as if he didn't have perfect hearing.

"I said, 'Who cares?'" I threw my hands in the air. "He was a sick fuck who deserved his fate. I'm only sad I wasn't the one to do it."

He paced again. "Do not misunderstand. I wanted him dead, too." He didn't look at either of us. "I've wanted him dead for years, but you can't remove someone like him."

My mom sat forward. "You're the king." Her nostrils flared. "And not much of one if you let lesser men lord over you."

I stepped between them before he could attack her again. A hint of a smile played on her lips, but it was gone before I could really tell if it had been there at all. "Please," I pleaded, glad I didn't have to grow up around this.

Sargon growled under his breath, moving backward. "I wanted him dead," he explained, "but he has substantial support in the south. Thousands of aniccipere are in his pocket, loyal to him. He's been gathering followers for centuries, and supporters in this castle, too. They will think I killed him once word gets out of what he did to you. There were enough witnesses. They've been searching for a reason to get me off the throne, and now you've handed it to them."

I clenched my jaw. "Am I supposed to apologize for almost being raped?"

He readjusted his crown, the wrinkles on his forehead deepening as he frowned. "No, but they will come for you,

Seraphina. They will blame you. There are many who want my brother on the throne, or the monarchy abolished altogether. They have made their traitorous thoughts known."

My mom looked from me to him. "What people?"

"A few of the lords, several business owners in the city, and other lesser people. I've had men in my personal guard keeping watch on them for years, tallying names."

Worry etched into her sharp features. "If they come for Olivia, I will kill them."

His fist clenched. "No. I will fix this. You will stay out of this." He paused. "Both of you."

"Wait," I shouted after him, but the door was already swinging open, and he was gone. I turned to my mom. "Don't let him hurt Draven. He had nothing to do with this."

"He won't," she reassured, but I didn't believe her. "Also…" She hesitated on the edge of words. "You don't need to wear the trailic anymore."

I let out a strangled laugh and pushed past her. "I shouldn't have been forced to wear it in the first place."

She lowered her head. "I know."

"But that's not the reason he tried to hurt me. He would have done it, regardless; he was just looking for an excuse." I thought back to when I touched him. I felt no depth of emotion that usually came with a person.

Instead, there was a void, a lack of anything of substance. As I peered into his eyes, I realized then he would have done anything to feel anything. Only extremes brought people like him to a high.

I balled my fists, lifting my chin. "He didn't get to do anything to me in the end, because I burned him to the ground. I stopped him. We're all the better for his death. As for who did it, I only hope I find out who, so I can thank them."

"Honey." She sighed. "This isn't you. I know he hurt you, but you're not vengeful."

I ripped my fingers away as she tried to hold my hand. "Perhaps you don't know me as well as you think you do. I'm going to find Draven and make sure he's okay. I won't have Sargon blame him for this. Then I'm going to bed. I expect you to be gone when I return."

Her gaze darted around me, her eyelashes fluttering as she held back tears. The emotion was gone before I could feel anything from seeing it. Replaced by a calm composure. "Be careful. If you need me, call the guards."

"I won't need you," I said, my voice as cold as her own. "Goodnight."

She paused by my side, sighed, then left the room. Once she was gone, I lifted my hands in front of my face. The magic pulsed under my skin, and I wasn't ready to let go of it. Not yet.

Perhaps never.

A soft knock sounded on the door as I climbed into bed, pulling the sheets up and over my chest. The windows filled with inky black, only the silhouettes of mountains breaking up the darkness. Draven walked in, his hand on the hilt of his sword as if a dead Hamza might still somehow be here, and a threat to me.

"Settle down, soldier," I teased to break the ice. "Come." I patted the spot on the bed next to me. "I've been looking for you."

"Same. We must've kept missing each other," he said, his tone strained. "I heard Hamza's been killed."

"You're correct. In fact, you were a suspect for a minute."

He sat on the bed, sending a pillow bouncing to the ground. "I wish I had been the one to do it."

I squeezed his hand, feeling his fingers link between mine. "I know. He didn't get to do anything, though."

He shook his head. "Don't make this smaller than it is."

"I'm not." I examined his calloused fingers as he tightened his grip. "My father's angry that he was killed."

"I couldn't give a fuck about what their king thinks."

I smiled. "Try to pretend to. I don't want you to get yourself killed."

"Are you worried about me, Livi?"

"Always," I said with a small smile, which dropped into a frown. "Sargon hurt my mom. He grabbed her by her throat."

"What did she do?"

"She let him," I said in disbelief.

He rolled his shoulders back, leaning against the headboard. My mom had never let anyone get away with anything, not even me. She was the strongest person I knew, but since she'd been here, that had changed.

"I don't want to become a vampire," I finally said aloud.

Draven sat upright, pulling me closer to him until we were face to face, our breaths matching under the flicker of candlelight. The smell of sandalwood drifted over as the intensity of his stare reached into me. "Then we should escape. I'll get you out of here now. Just say the word."

A part of me wanted to say yes. To let him take me into the night, and feel safe in his arms. But not even Draven could save us. There was no way out, at the least not for me. If I wanted to protect Draven, then I couldn't let myself think this way.

"I'll just miss my magic. That's all. It saved me today."

"Stop trying to help everyone," he pleaded, leaning into me. "Think about yourself."

"You know I can't. Sebastian also needs—"

"You don't actually care about him?" he asked, cutting me off.

I opened my mouth but closed it again. Did I? "It's not as black and white as that."

He let out a long exhale, lying back on the sheets. "Then what?"

"I made promises. Erianna, Sebastian, and Zach all risked their necks trying to save me. I owe them. Besides, we won't make it far. My father won't stop searching for me, and I can't have you getting caught up in that."

"We have to at least try."

"Please, don't." I pleaded, laying back, too. I closed my eyes against the flickering yellow and let out a tense breath. "Can we talk about something else? Maybe, tell me stories. Like you did when we were kids?" I paused. "I need that right now."

He half-grinned, softening his chiseled features. "Surely you don't mean ghost stories?"

I shrugged. "They're not as scary anymore. We're living in one."

"If it's what you need, then okay." His expression was swallowed by the blackness as he blew out the candle. "It was midnight when the woman heard tapping on her bathroom door," he said, lowering his voice. "Rap, rap, rap."

I smiled, recalling the memories of him making up scary stories when we were ten. I'd always thought they were so creative, even if I had been a little scared after. He always made sure he made me laugh before I went to sleep, so I wasn't as afraid anymore.

A loud knock sounded on the door three times. We both jumped, and I gasped, jumping to my feet. Sebastian walked in and turned on a lamp, wearing a mocking smile on his lips. "Evening."

"You heard us," I realized.

He gestured to Draven. "Please, continue."

I gave him a look. "Where have you been?"

"With Erianna, Zach, and Anna."

My heart leaped. "How are they?"

"As good as can be expected." He shoved his hands in his pockets. "I need to talk to you."

Draven rolled his eyes, then climbed out of bed. "Do you want me to come back, Liv?"

I shot him a small smile. "It's okay. I'll see you tomorrow?"

"You will," he answered and held his sword a little too tightly as he passed Sebastian. "Vangard," he acknowledged, his frown tight as he left, closing the door behind him.

I raised an eyebrow. "Vangard? He only calls people he doesn't like by their last name."

"I never assumed he would like me." He strolled to the bed. "I am about to marry you, after all."

"Why would that matter?"

He looked up. "Don't pretend you don't know how he feels about you."

"We're friends. It's not like that," I defended.

He lifted his hands, signaling surrender. "Okay, okay." He tapped a finger against the dimple on his cheek. "Anyway, I came to see how you're doing."

"I'm okay. Really," I added as concern etched into his features. "I felt powerful today, but at the same time power*less*."

"I know." He sat next to me. I noticed the dried blood speckled on the rolled-up sleeves of his shirt.

"Did you just feed?"

He blinked twice, his brows knitting together. "Oh." He glanced down at the stain. "Yes."

Something felt different. I touched his arm, and the usual pain was masked by a stark cruelness that threw me off balance. "Are *you* sure?"

"I'm fine," he lied. I could feel it in some unspoken bond between us. "I'm more worried about you."

"Don't be," I responded, my heart pounding.

Since Hamza, I'd gone through a rollercoaster of emotions. I didn't realize how vulnerable I felt until I was with Sebastian again. It was like he brought something in me to the surface. Something I wanted to keep buried.

I gazed at the lamp, then moved my eyes up to the painting of roses above the nightstand.

Breaking the silence, I licked my lips. "Sebastian." His tortured stare stole my next breath, the pained expression suppressed under a mask of restraint. Tears swelled in his eyes, and my heart ballooned. "You haven't come to see me, since everything. I know marriage isn't what you wanted. I'm sorry."

"Don't apologize," he whispered. "It's not that. I've just… it's been a lot. I was avoiding you," he admitted. "It was a mistake. Maybe if I hadn't, then Hamza would—"

"Don't you dare."

"What?"

"Blame yourself."

He pressed his lips into a thin line. "Hamza's dead now, so you're safe."

I recalled what he said, about wanting to murder him after he found out what happened. "Wait… did you—"

He shook his head. "No."

My stomach knotted. "Good."

"Good?"

"You're not a murderer. I wouldn't want you to become one for me."

He laughed. "I've killed before. You know this."

"I mean, you're not one in your soul. You're not like the other monsters here. You care."

His breath hitched, and he ran his hand through his dark strands. "I told you before, Olivia. Even demons can appear mortal. Hamza showed that today."

"You're not a demon," I snapped, hating what he was insinuating. "I understand why you betrayed me in the dungeons..."

"I didn't betray you. You've got it all wrong."

"You gave me up."

"To protect you. How else do you think we would have gotten out of there? The plan of turning you would've never worked."

"You didn't even give it a chance," I rebuked.

He rested his forehead against his knuckles. "Let's not argue." Worry coiled in my chest as I saw the defeated look on his face. "You hate me for making you marry me, don't you?" I asked the question I'd been dreading.

He shook his head. "I could never hate you. You saved me. I know that."

"It wasn't all that selfless," I admitted. "It was you or Draven, and I didn't want to submit his soul to that."

He flinched. "He's lucky to have you watching out for his soul."

"I care for yours, too."

Something changed in his eyes. "That's really…sweet."

"Of course." I flushed, but looked away. "I feel so lost," I admitted, the words leaving my lips before I could stop them. "I don't want to lose my powers just yet. Today has been… I wish you could, maybe, perhaps—"

"If you want me to stay with you," he said with a small smile, "just say."

I thumbed the side of my neck, moving my hair over one shoulder. "Just for tonight."

He climbed into bed after me, then wrapped his arm around me. "Is this okay?"

"Yes," I whispered, snuggling into his warmth, resting easily against the sound of his breaths and beating heart. "I didn't realize how much I needed this until now."

He pressed his forehead against mine and closed his eyes. "I needed this, too," he said before laying back down, and after a few minutes all the pain in his expression fell away. He looked so peaceful while he slept, Yet, as he fell into dreams, his grip never loosened around me.

I let the memory of Hamza slip away as I held onto Sebastian, as if daylight would come too soon and steal this moment away.

SEVEN

Sebastian

I could still smell her on my clothes. I breathed in the vanilla and jasmine scent, climbing my gaze to the arched windows overlooking the castle grounds. Icicles hung from the weathered fountain in the center of the courtyard, frost clinging to the gray stone. The first peaks of sunrise reached through the mountains, beyond the vast evergreen forest. My breath fogged the air as I caught my solemn reflection in the window.

Last night had been a mistake. It *had* to be. I couldn't continue to let her in, knowing any feelings I held for her would be her ruin. Her heart was too kind, and I would destroy it. I thought back to the guards I'd slaughtered. Olivia didn't think I was a killer, that I couldn't be. She was wrong, and once I revealed that darkness, she'd think me a monster like the rest of them.

I couldn't stop thinking about her, no matter how hard I tried to push her from my thoughts. There were moments where I felt myself softening, like last night when she'd given me most of the blanket so I wouldn't get cold. I didn't have the heart to remind her it didn't bother me like it did her.

Then there was the way she spoke about things; it was so mortal. So beautiful. When we'd gone to Laveniuess's Lake, she'd given me this speech about why he was the god she appreciated the most, and how embracing one's inner darkness was important. She even believed in redemption for the souls of vampires. Olivia didn't know it, but that conversation made me feel better about accepting what I was, although I was sure I was far past the line of redemption now. I still wore the dried blood from the hearts I tore out yesterday.

I turned and strode down the empty corridor. Baskets of wildflowers hung from hooks on the walls. Rose petals thrown from the various weddings over the last week floated from the wisps of air carried by my feet as I walked.

My heart skipped a beat as I walked into the throne room. I blinked twice, taking in the hundreds of unlit cream candles standing in alcoves, suspended from strings hanging from the ceiling. Several servants worked on one of the three archways over the aisle, entwined with ivy, thorns, and the red roses.

I walked the white carpet leading to the altar, looking out at the hundreds of chairs that must have only been erected this morning. I eyed a woman scrubbing the king's throne with a bucket and soap. She shot me a warm, but seductive smile. There was a twinkle in her sapphire eyes, and as much as I wanted to smile back, I couldn't.

My eyebrows furrowed, and I brought my attention back to the altar. This is where Olivia and I would get married tomorrow. The realization hit me like a punch to the face. I paused mid-step and wetted my lips. This was all too much. Even seeing the whole setup made me want to extend my wings and get the fuck out of there. But I couldn't. Erianna would never get away. Losing her wings forever marked her as a traitor to anyone who knew the laws of

Sanmorte. Who knows what would happen to Olivia? She'd likely be forced to marry someone else. There was Draven, and he was the safer bet out of the two of us, but she didn't want to submit his soul to eternal damnation. So she'd likely be set up with another, perhaps a lord. I thought about Hamza and half the monsters in this castle, and shuddered at the thought of any one of them ending up with Olivia.

"Getting cold feet?" Velda's sharp, clipped voice sounded behind me. "Don't worry. Marriage isn't forever. I mean, only as long as you're both alive, and accidents can always be arranged."

I didn't turn. I wouldn't give the bitch the satisfaction. "Feed your own ego, Velda. I'm busy."

"You're always in such a bad mood nowadays, darling."

"Believe it or not, when you're not around, I feel so much better."

She stepped beside me. I could smell the blood from her last feed on her breath. "We both know you miss me. Even if it's just to have someone to let all that anger out on." She dragged a finger down the sleeve of my shirt, sending a shiver down my spine.

I grabbed her hand, tightening my grip around her wrist. "If you want to keep your fingers, then don't touch me."

She ripped her hand from mine, latching her intrusive stare onto mine. "You're not usually this upset."

"What can I say? You bring out the worst in me," I snapped, venom coating every word. "What is it you really want?"

"I want you to protect you, Sebby darling. I always cared about you." The nurturing tone she forced through her words only made her sound all that more psychopathic. "If you marry the mortal girl tomorrow, she will be the death of you."

I turned to look at her. "Is that a threat?"

"A warning."

I arched a brow. "What do you know?"

A wide smile played on her lips, satisfaction filling her expression. I hated it. "I wish I could trust you to be on my team, but I can't. You still cling to some reminiscence of mortality."

"It doesn't mean I'm good," I remarked. "I can play both teams," I lied, trying to pry the knowledge from her deranged head. "Come now, Velda. Unless you don't have any plans at all. It wouldn't surprise me. Yet more empty threats."

She leaned in closer, twirling a lock of blonde hair around her index finger. "I'm not so easily manipulated." She curled her lips into an amused smile. "One day, you will embrace who you really are. We will never be like them, and you will never be happy with someone like her."

"It's pathetic how far you'll go for my attention," I baited.

She didn't bite. "It's your fate." She let out a long sigh, stepping back. I glanced at the slit in her dress, reaching up to her thigh, wondering how it would feel to stab Erianna's dagger into it. "Sebby," she said, catching me looking. "You don't need to imagine. We can still play like we used to."

My nostrils flared, and the corner of my mouth twitched. "No need. I've already had your daughter, not long ago, in the dungeons. Why would I settle for you?" Her smile dropped, and mine grew. I never wanted to push her too far. She was too powerful, but nowadays, I was tired of playing politics and had less and less to lose. "Goodbye, Velda," I said, and sped away from her and all the wedding things. Both of which were enough to put me off my breakfast.

"Sebastian!" Gwen called after me.

I repressed the urge to roll my eyes. "If it isn't blondie junior. What do you want?"

She hurried to me, her blonde braid bobbing against her shoulder. She stretched her painted, pink lips into a hard line. "I heard what you said to my mom, about *us*. Astor heard, too."

"I didn't see you both," I said with a shrug, and peered over her head. "Where is lover boy, anyway?"

"Gone," she replied, letting out a long breath. She wiped her forehead, as if sweat had gathered. "You promised you wouldn't say anything."

"She was irritating me. Also, like I said, I didn't know he was there."

"Since when you were so easy to anger?"

I balled a fist. "We all have our off days."

"No! You promised, and now he thinks I cheated on him!"'" she shouted, her voice echoing around the feeding room.

"You did cheat on him." Semi-conscious mortals emerged from the shadows as the full sunrise arrowed light through the windows. I saw one, a woman around my age, with olive skin and long, dark hair. There were hardly any marks on her neck. "Anyway, I'm about to eat," I said nonchalantly and moved to walk away.

She grabbed my arm, pulling me back to her. "My mom isn't the only one who you should fear. Don't underestimate me!"

"You're impossible to underestimate," I said simply. "And I'm not afraid of her."

She gritted her teeth. "Fuck you."

"I'm not that desperate."

Her cheeks reddened. "I might have lost Astor."

"Then I would have done you a favor."

"Are you going to hate me forever for what happened?"

"You mean how you tried to have Olivia killed, and me?"

She rolled her eyes up. "I told you already. I didn't know they were going after you too."

"It doesn't matter. The results are the same. Go cry to someone else who cares. I'm busy." I eyed the dark-haired woman and walked to the bench where she sat. The smell of the ocean still lingered on her hair.

I didn't turn, but heard Gwen race away, muttering some obscenity before disappearing back through the double doors. I walked to the mortal woman, lowering myself onto the seat next to her. "What's your name, love?"

"Does it matter?" Her voice was raspier than I expected. "You're going to feed on me whether or not I desire it."

"That attitude is going to get you killed," I warned, having seen a thousand girls like her come through. None I'd been able to save from the wrath of vampires who hated anything other than submission.

"So, I should get in line and submit?" She scoffed. "We were warned of your kind. Your lustful, dark desires, make it so you will do anything to get what you want."

"I wish I could tell you that isn't true."

She tilted her head, and after a minute of silence, she stretched her thick lips into a frown. "You haven't tried to bite me yet."

"How observant of you."

She looked at my shirt. "You still have blood on your, from your last feed."

"That's not from a mortal," I confided, but didn't elaborate. "Where are you from?"

"Asland."

"Ah, we've been having problems with a certain princess of yours."

"Penelope," she spat as if the name were one of a demon. "She always sympathized with your people. I was not surprised to see her here."

"The king is afraid there will be a war with your kingdom."

Fear threaded through her brown gaze. "I hope not. My people will be slaughtered here. I still have a family. Sisters."

"When did you arrive?"

"Four days ago. They kept us in these dingy places," she said with a thick, guttural accent.

"Blood dens."

"Yes, but they said I was pretty enough to be brought here." Her top lip curled in as she looked around the tall ceiling. Hundreds of tents were set up for private feedings. I noticed a spill of blood in the corner that the servants hadn't yet mopped up. Someone got carried away.

She continued. "This place is ancient. You don't even have any technology here. It's as if I traveled back in time, but the people are monsters instead."

My heart pounded heavily, the hairs on the back of my neck prickling. I saw my reflection in her eyes. I was the thing to be feared in the dark. I'd always put myself above that, but as I thought about my recent actions, I realized I wasn't any better than the rest of them.

Closing my eyes to the way she looked at me, I growled under my breath. I wanted to forget everything—Olivia, the wedding, the guards, and Hamza. Peeling back my eyelids to reveal the woman, I allowed for my pleasures to overtake me, hunger devouring my morals, drowning them as I looked at her clavicle.

"Better me than one of them," I told her as my fangs elongated, and I leaned in, holding her still. A scream erupted from her lips as her Aslandian blood coated my tongue, tangy but sweet.

The other man who'd come down for breakfast and was eyeing the mortal, moved on. After a few seconds, the woman collapsed into my arms. I grazed my thumb across her shoulder, filling myself with her blood. Her eyes rolled into the back of her head, a moan of ecstasy fresh on her tongue. The venom was hitting her. I remember that feeling. It was better than any drug, like liquid lust and elation. I couldn't feel bad for her. Over time, when there was no one there to tell me something was wrong, like back in the mortal kingdoms, it was easy to become numb to it all. Feeling just ended in more heartache, and I had no room for that.

The sound of bells snapped me back to reality as we lost ourselves in each other. Me in her blood, her in my venom. Those were the chimes of a war meeting.

Niall appeared next to us as I withdrew my fangs from her neck. I wiped the blood on the back of my hand.

"What do you want?"

"Where's the little redhead of yours?"

"Stay away from her," I snarled, my heart racing at the idea of his fangs on her neck.

He put his hands up in surrender. "Don't get touchy." He said as he moved closer. "I'm not going to hurt her."

"Where's your dad?" I asked, wanting to shift the topic away from Olivia. "I'm surprised to see your head so far away from his ass."

He laughed, a twinkle glimmering in his dark eyes. "You know, Sebastian, even as a prince, you still need to be careful how you talk to me."

"What the fuck are you going to do?" I laughed. "I have Sargon's favor."

He sped to me, closing the distance between us until I could feel his breath against my face. "And I have the favor of the one truly in power. We both know it. Sargon's nothing but a fucking figurehead."

I didn't step back; I wasn't going to give this asshole the satisfaction. "Such traitorous words. They can get you in trouble."

He shrugged, his fingers curling into fists. "You always pushed your luck. Go ahead, tell Sargon what I said. I'm not afraid of him or anyone else in this castle." He tilted his head, his brown curls dangling just below his shoulder as a glimmer of red flashed in his gaze. "Who's the brunette?"

My shoulders tensed. "She's no one."

"She's new." He licked his lips, pushing past and knocking his shoulder against mine. "Did she taste good?"

"Not really." I tried sounding bored. "Why don't you go terrorize someone else?"

I hated that he'd returned from wherever he'd taken a hiatus to. Every ounce of me wanted to rip out his heart before he could do any damage, but I knew better. Niall had support through the City of Nightmares and within the castle. Kalon adored him as if he was his own blood, even adopting him officially as his son. I also knew better than to back down from Niall. There was nothing he hated more than weakness, and I'd seen him exploit people's vulnerabilities in the cruelest ways in my first year here. My gaze trailed over the mortal I'd fed on, but I didn't linger. If he saw a glimmer of care, he'd snap her neck just to aggravate me.

"You know, Sebastian, I've missed this." He turned on his heel, an unnerving smirk on his lips.

My nostrils flared. "That makes one of us."

"I had no one to torture in my time away in the cities. They're all so—" He waved his hand lackadaisically. "—boring. You always gave as good as you got. Others, they submit so easily. So did Erianna. Where is she, anyway?"

"Not here." I walked away, gritting my teeth.

"Give her my regards," he called after me. "And Zach's. I'm sure I'll see them soon."

I was glad he couldn't see the muscle tick in my jaw. Pressing my lips together, I told myself repeatedly that turning back and punching him would only give him what he wanted. At least before this, I could have a break from this place and head to the city. Now I was stuck in this castle for good.

I looked around my new home as I strode into the throne room. A vampire hurried past me, carrying an enormous bouquet to fill some space still left on the wall. I spotted the goblets that Olivia and I would drink each other's blood out of during the wedding. Midnight was fast approaching. The wedding would be performed shortly after the clock struck twelve tonight. Such little time left.

Albert, the only aniccipere with social standing in the castle, bowed his thin torso as I passed through the double doors and out into the foyer to find Erianna and Zach.

EIGHT

Olivia

Niall ran his fingers through his hair, rolling back his broad shoulders as he approached me under the pale light pouring through the windows. "You are dazzling." He smiled, showing his pearly white teeth. The perks of immortality. Eternal beauty, and indeed every vampire here, were the definition of perfection—at least, physically.

"What do you want?" I asked, failing to keep the disgust out of my tone.

He grazed a finger over my cheek. "I'm here for the same reason you are. The bells were rung. We might have a war on our hands. I hope it's with Asland. They have the most delicious people."

I jerked away from his touch, pinching my lips together as I waited with him outside the king's office. "You're revolting."

He leaned down, whispering in my ear, "Everything I do, everything I am, is no different from your precious soon-to-be husband."

"He's nothing like you."

"We're more alike than he'd ever care to admit." He pulled away, an amused smirk playing on his lips.

"I strongly disagree."

His smile didn't waver. "He's lucky to have someone hold him in such high regard. Even if it is born from naivety."

I opened my mouth to argue, but the doors opened, revealing my father, his new head advisor, Penelope, Kalon, my mother, and Sebastian. Sargon leaned over his desk, digging his nails into the wood. He lifted his head to look at me, green eyes darting from me to Niall, then settling on me. "Sit."

I swallowed thickly, moving to Sebastian's side, who clasped his hands behind his back. The scent of his cologne lingered, and when I closed my eyes, I could transport my mind back to last night when his arms were wrapped around me, holding me tight. I had felt everything, as he struggled to withhold his emotions from me while asleep. The guilt, anger, pain, and confusion poured out between his dreams.

"My father will not come here!" Penelope shouted through the chatter, and I blinked twice, realizing I'd missed part of the conversation.

Sebastian didn't even look at me, as if last night never happened. He seemed calm when he stepped in front of the king, his hands now in his pockets. "Your Majesty, may I recommend we make this meeting more private?" Sebastian glanced at Penelope. "Where we may not be overheard by the very reason we are in this situation."

She scoffed, and a curl of hair fell from her perfectly pinned back golden locks. "Whose fault is that? I'm a vampire because you pushed me."

Sebastian growled under his breath, and before Sargon could respond, he was in front of Penelope, his hand on her throat. "Still sticking to that story then, you vicious bitch!"

She grappled at his fingers, but couldn't pry them from her dainty throat. Untamed power strained behind Sebastian's eyes.

"Get off me," she spluttered.

"Enough!" Sargon barked, but Sebastian didn't let her go. "Vangard!"

Niall finally walked over to them and patted Sebastian's shoulder, amusement lightening his chiseled features. "Penelope's on our side," he said smoothly, and tugged Sebastian's arm from her throat. "We are *all* on the same side."

My eyebrows furrowed. I didn't expect Niall, of all people, to play diplomat. I cleared my throat and tilted my head, watching Penelope as she glared after Sebastian.

I spoke up, "I'm assuming they found out about her new fangs?"

Niall shrugged. "It was inevitable."

Sargon's advisor spun the globe standing behind his desk, his finger landing on the large island I knew as Asland. A hot, exotic kingdom filled with the strangest animals and where the people worshiped a god far older than ours. The king's voice boomed over all others. "I have invited the King of Asland here."

My brows raised. "Is that wise?"

My mom's stare bore into me, and she shook her head.

Sargon's eyelids flickered as the corners of them twitched. "Seraphina, you are here as a formality as you will be the princess tomorrow. However, seeing as you don't know our kingdom, or anything about politics, it would benefit you more to keep your mouth *shut* and ears *open*."

Kalon grinned, and Niall poorly scoffed a chuckle. I sat back in a chair at the side of the room, pressing my lips together to prevent them from trembling out of anger. I'd never been good at hiding how I felt.

Sebastian stepped next to the king, turning his back to Penelope and Niall. He leaned over the hundreds of scattered papers and parchment maps covering the mahogany desk. "Speaking about her becoming a princess, I was wondering if it would be more prudent to postpone, at least until we know more about Asland's plans."

Sargon shook his head, then paused, moving his gaze to the arched, led-crisscrossed window. "We need not postpone. Their king will not arrive for three days. I need you and Seraphina with me. Family is important to them, and you will host them. Their declaration of war may yet be remedied with this visit."

The pieces clicked together. Asland had declared war on Sanmorte, not the other way around. My heart sank a little when I saw Sebastian. He was trying anything to get out of our wedding. While I didn't want any of this either, I'd at least accepted my fate. However hard it was. I wanted more than anything to keep my magic, even asking my mom if there was a way, but becoming a vampire was inevitable. Immortality waited patiently behind death as the clock ticked down my last hours. I hoped, at the very least, my newfound vampirism would make me powerful. Perhaps more than I ever was with my magic. Still, it ached for me to lose it, and I glanced at my mom, who seemed less than she ever was now, without her powers.

The king continued, and a servant entered the room, handing him a glass. Blood lapped at the edges as he took it in his hand, swirling the crimson liquid before drinking. "Asland has weapons far beyond anything we have."

Niall spoke up. "We are weapons."

Kalon nodded in his direction, pride sweeping his lips into something slightly warmer than the normal snide look she wore.

"They won't survive against our numbers. We have speed and strength."

I stood, placing my hands on my hips. "You're wrong." Every head turned in my direction. My heart pounded. "In Baldoria, we have a technology that can track any person. As well as missiles and guns which could destroy entire streets of houses. They wouldn't even need to come near us to kill us."

My mom chimed in. "My daughter is right. While Asland, fortunately for us, is further behind Baldoria with their weaponry and military, they still have technology far beyond anything we own. We must bring ourselves into this century if we are to protect Sanmorte."

Niall shook his head, glaring at my mom. "You haven't even been here for two decades."

I clicked my tongue. "She knows more about this than anyone in this room." I paused. "Except for my father," I added, hoping not to offend him further.

Sargon exhaled slowly, drumming his fingers against the wood. The crown in his red waves slipped forward as his shoulders slunk. "Ravena, you will lead a team."

Kalon stepped forward, his bony fingers clasped in front of his long, gray robe. "Brother, you cannot allow this. She is a traitor."

He slammed his fist down, jolting several papers to the ground. "She is my wife!" he shouted, and the room fell silent. "And your queen. I will hear no more objections. The king will come, and the new prince and princess will host them." He gestured vaguely to Sebastian and me. "Ravena will lead the forces and discuss shipments of weaponry to be brought over from Baldoria. Niall, you will ensure Penelope stays out of their king's way when he arrives. Initially, anyway. I want to gauge his temperament first."

She gave him a look, but he ignored her, looking directly at Kalon instead. My father and uncles' appearance was alike in almost every way, but the way they moved and spoke couldn't be more different. My father was more like me than I realized, reacting out of emotion, wearing everything he felt on his face. Whereas Kalon remained calm and unshaken, no matter what was said. He was utterly unreadable, even to me. Sargon twisted his wedding ring around his finger. "Brother, you will ensure the ceremony tonight goes off without a hitch. Everything must be perfect."

Kalon bowed, glancing at me for less than a second before leaving the room. Niall left too, and Penelope followed shortly after. Sebastian didn't meet my gaze as we walked out. Once outside, I turned to touch him, but he sped away before I got the chance to speak a word.

NINE

Olivia

Erianna was a vision in red as she stood at my door, wingless, broken behind her bloodshot eyes. "I had to come," she said quickly, glancing behind her. "Before the wedding."

I ushered her inside. "Erianna." I could barely get her name out when my voice cracked. "I'm sorry."

"Don't," she pleaded, then sat on the edge of my bed, placing her hands gently on her lap. Her red pants and low-cut top were far more modern than anything anyone else here wore.

I peered at her back, spotting the top of the scar from where her wings had been cut off. "I've wanted to see you. To see how you are."

"I will survive," she said simply, her tone colder than I expected. "I am here about Sebastian. He has not been himself, and with the wedding happening tonight, I supposed I should tell you."

"Erianna—" I softened my voice and stood in front of her. "I will protect him."

"It is not him who needs protecting."

"Then who?"

Her brows furrowed. "Do you know how Hamza died?"

It slowly dawned on me that my suspicions had been right before. "Sebastian."

"He took it further than I'd ever thought possible. I have seen many things in my immortal life, but seeing how he left Hamza made even me nauseous."

Pricks of cold crept up my back and arms, snaking a shiver from the nape of my neck down to the base of my spine. "Are you certain it was him?"

"Yes." She looked down at the ground. "Then he killed two guards. Innocents."

I laughed at the absurdity of her words. "No." I shook my head. "He wouldn't."

"I would have said the same thing a week ago, but he's changed. I'm afraid of how far he will go. I do not want him to lose himself. He's always regarded his morality highly, for a vampire anyway, and the idea of becoming mortal, I am presuming, kept him from straying too far from his morals. But now, he has nothing to lose. I'm hoping you can…" she trailed off. "I don't know."

My chest ached, feeling heavier by the minute. "I can't save him," I admitted, the truth stinging my mouth. "I chose him so he wouldn't die."

"I know."

"I wanted to save you, too."

She didn't respond. The sun set lower in the sky, casting red into the room, soaking the bed in an eerie hue.

"Erianna," I intoned. "I know I have a lot to make up for. Even if none of you will tell me to my face."

She almost smiled. "Zach might."

"That's true, but I haven't seen him."

"We are in hiding."

"For now," I promised. "As a princess, I will make sure I pardon you both."

"I am certain you will keep your promise," she said, with more regality than I had. If anyone could be a princess, it would be her. She lifted her head and looked at me with unwavering pride. "Please also watch Sebastian closely, and report to me on anything untoward. I've brought him back from the edge before. I can only hope to do it again. With your help."

I nodded, but seeing as he didn't want to be my husband, or a prince, I was pretty sure I was the last person he'd listen to right now. "I'll try."

"Your friend, Draven, has been most kind."

"I didn't realize you knew him well."

Her eyebrows lifted. "I thought you'd sent him to help us?"

"No." I sat next to her. "Honestly, it didn't occur to me. But he knew how bad I felt about what happened, and he's always been the type to help someone in need."

"He's been bringing us blood."

My lips parted. "That is *surprising*."

She inhaled sharply, a small smile hovering over her thick lips. "How long have you been friends?"

I counted back the years in my mind, remembering the day when a much shorter Draven walked into my life with honey-blond hair yet to turn brown. "We were ten."

"You seem so different to each other, is all," she replied, her dark eyebrow arching.

"I guess we are." I rubbed my wrist, hazily looking from Erianna to the window. "Our hobbies couldn't be more different, but we both have similar beliefs. He wears his heart on his sleeve just as much as I do. He's just better at hiding it. We always had that in common, and with his emotions, he needed someone to let it all out to."

She nodded slowly, her eyes widening. "What do you get from the friendship?"

"That's an intimate question," I teased, crossing my legs.

"I've found, over the years, there is little point in beating around the bush."

I licked my lips, my thoughts whirling. What did I get from Draven? Security, if I was being honest with myself. I could always depend on him. But it was more than that. He was gentle with my dreams and kind with my feelings. Unlike my mom or Astor, I didn't have to change anything about myself when I was with him. It was as easy as breathing. "He accepted me for who I was. I think he still does."

She pinched her knee between her fingers, her dark eyes drifting up to the chandelier. "I heard he offered to be your husband when he found out about the ritual."

My shoulders tightened, and my lips formed into a scowl. "I wouldn't put him through that. Draven hates vampires more than I ever did, and becoming one is the worst thing I could do to him."

She leaned forward. The afternoon sun arrowing through the window danced on her gold rings as she drummed her fingers. "Do you love him?"

Her expression told me everything. "Not in a romantic way."

"I had to ask."

"Why?"

"Curiosity." She didn't elaborate, but my stomach churned as she looked me up and down again, then stood. I felt naked as her intrusive gaze bore into me. I parted my lips, but the question hovering in my mind never formed.

Does Draven love me?

I already knew the answer; I had for the longest time. But I never confronted it, mostly because I couldn't bear to hurt him, and

I could never give him what he wanted. He was my best friend, and while I had caught myself staring a few times when he'd been training—because who wouldn't?—I never felt butterflies around him.

"If soul friends are a thing, then that is what me and Draven are," I added, hoping to rest any doubts in her mind.

Although, I had to wonder what her actual intentions behind this conversation were. Knowing Erianna, if it had anything to do with the heart, she would not spill easily. Perhaps she worried I wanted Draven over Sebastian and would hurt him.

"Do you—"

"You must prepare," she said, cutting me off. "The ceremony is in the morning, and your wedding is just hours away."

A lump formed in my throat. "I know."

"Have you spoken to Sebastian?"

"Barely," I admitted, my fingers flexing against the arms of the chair.

Even with the cuddling last night, we hadn't spent much time together. So there wasn't much to say, I guessed. I was dragging him down with me. He never wanted to marry, let alone stay a vampire. Because of me, any dreams of mortality were gone, no matter how unlikely they were to happen. But he was alive. "I'm just glad he's going through with this." My engagement ring glinted in the sun. It was handpicked by Erianna when we had to fake an engagement to carry out our plot to replace me as queen, one I didn't have any intentions of going through with. I just wanted to find my mom and Draven.

"You saved him. He's lucky it's this instead of..." She trailed off, and my heart hurt. Her long braid bounced over her chest with each step. The strands, blacker than night, somehow shone as she walked to the door. "I have some things to take care of. So I cannot come tonight. Not until you become princess, and I get my pardon."

I forced a smile. "I'll make sure it's the first thing I do."

She nodded once, and as she opened the door, my gaze trickled to her wingless back. My barrier lowered once she left, and a pinch of sadness shot through the air before she sped down the staircase. She had sensed me looking, and it only worsened the grief she felt from the loss of her wings. She hated pity, so I reminded myself not to stare. Even though all I wanted to do was hug her, cry with her and share in her pain. But Erianna wasn't like me—or anyone I met, really.

I hated my father for going through with it. He so callously took her wings, planning to take Zach's next, then throw them back into the dungeons as if it was a gift to me. That was before Sebastian helped them escape. I'd heard shreds of information, about how without Erianna's wings and both their jobs, they'd lost their dignities. Rumors reached me of how Zach walked around, barely an echo of who he once was with not even a snarky remark left in him. Erianna pretended to be fine, but I could feel her aching inside.

I only hoped I was there when she crumbled—so I could help take the pain away.

My eyes closed against the sunlight. I would become a vampire in less than a day, and while I could still feel others' emotions, I would lose the ability to manipulate people's feelings. My magic would be gone, and I would be a princess of vampires and the wife of a man who didn't want me. Yet, he'd torn out Hamza's heart because he hurt me, and as twisted as it sounded, that meant something to me. Even if it was reckless and stupid, because if he was caught, they'd have his head.

I closed my eyes, falling back on the bed. It was dark when I opened them again, and I realized I must have fallen asleep. My stomach grumbled, aching for food. I'd missed dinner. But nerves suffocated the hunger. A knock sounded at the door, and my mom walked in holding a long, black gown with lace sleeves—my wedding dress. "It's time, honey."

TEN

Sebastian

I adjusted my sleeves, smoothing down the front of my tunic. Silver silk threaded through the midnight-black creating constellation patterns, as if the fabric had been stolen from the night.

Roses harvested in full bloom entwined the metal arch over my head, with a tangle of ivy and thorns nestling between the pure white and crimson red. The fresh cuts intensified the floral notes hidden behind the musky scent of the roses, radiating a sweet smell.

An ache tightened in my chest as chatter flooded the throne room. Rows upon rows of satin-covered chairs were quickly filled with hundreds of vampires, many of who had traveled a great distance to witness the wedding and shadow kissed ritual of their princess. Mortal servants rushed to relight candles as the billowing cloaks of vampires swept the wind into the flames, putting them out.

I spied Astor, who kept to the shadowed corner of the room, occasionally glancing over at Gwen and Velda, who sat in the front row, wearing plunging red dresses. Gwen's glacier-blue eyes found mine, her jaw clenching as she rubbed a fallen, silk petal between her delicate fingers. Averting my gaze from her, I spotted several nobles who were fond of sitting in the middle section. Beyond them, strangers craned their necks to get a better look, each holding a wedding program. I wondered where on that piece of paper listed the time of Olivia's death tomorrow.

A trumpet sounded, and the room silenced, save for hushed whispers lost to the breeze. A loud voice boomed over us, jolting several vampires. "His Majesty, King Sargon of Sanmorte, and his queen, Her Majesty, Queen Ravena of Sanmorte."

Every vampire in the room stood, bowing as they stepped through the double doors, and made their way up the white-carpeted aisle.

Large rings covered Sargon's fingers, candlelight occasionally catching on the rubies and emeralds. I bowed when they reached halfway. Ravena was dazzling in red, her raven tresses flowing down her back.

She smiled when she reached me and placed her hands in mine. "Take care of my daughter." I could feel a thousand more words she wanted to say in them, but she couldn't speak freely, not here in front of her tyrannical king.

"I will." I forced as much conviction into my tone as possible, then folded my hands over my stomach. I would take my vows seriously. I peered over Sargon's shoulder, missing the faces of Erianna, Zach, and Anna.

"You will make a fine prince," Sargon said, and I lifted my eyebrows.

"Thank you, Your Majesty." I slipped into another bow, and they stepped past me, then took their seats upon their tall thrones.

Rich, melodious music signaled her arrival. Draven was the first to enter. He must have walked her downstairs. Goosebumps spread over my arms, pricking cold into the nape of my neck. A lump formed in my throat as the music loudened, emotion heavy in every key of the piano and violin.

Slowly, I turned my head, watching Olivia walk toward me. My lips parted slightly, my next breath stolen by her beauty. Sheer gloves covered her arms. Her off-the-shoulder, lacy, black gown flowed as if she was the goddess of the night herself. A diamond-encrusted tiara glittered from her red, pinned-back hair. She lifted her black veil, revealing her face in the light.

Her eyebrows knitted together, the corners of her eyes crinkling as she glanced around the room. Then, slowly, she lifted her head, her green gaze meeting mine. Relief flooded her delicate features, and the ache in my chest settled. A slow smile curved my lips, and the moment I'd been dreading for the past three days suddenly wasn't as soul-wrenching.

She closed the distance between us, her eyes darting around to the faces of Gwen, her father, and others. I didn't look away. No one else mattered in this room. I held her hands, steadying mine to still the tremble in hers.

"I'm scared," she mumbled, and a jolt of pain shot through me.

"It's okay." I wanted more than anything to reassure her. The desire to distance myself from her evaporated, leaving nothing but a desire to protect. But, no matter how much I wanted to tell her everything would be fine, it was a lie.

She studied me, her eyes narrowing. How could I protect her? She was damning herself by marrying me. There would be two death sentences today. She just didn't know it yet. As my wife, she would carry my sins and burdens with hers, and they were heavy. My smile fell into a frown, and I turned my attention to the priest, the heaviness returning.

"Repeat after me."

My mind raced as he spilled commands for Olivia to say. She spoke the words with such conviction. I could believe they were her own if I hadn't heard the priest speak them moments earlier. "I honor my pledge to my husband, to guide his light, and find redemption for his sins." She'd brought the vows spoken in Baldoria, combining them with our own. I didn't look at her. Not when I knew redemption was too far out of reach.

"In death, upon your execution," the priest continued, the words falling from his lips so casually, as if they were nothing, "your marriage will continue. The bond created here today is eternal and never to be broken. Do you agree to marry this man and take him as yours forevermore?"

She closed her eyes, and my fingers flexed against hers. "Yes, I do."

He spilled the same vows to me. I let out a long exhale as I repeated his words back to him. Then, for the first time in three years, I felt the cold chilling my bones as I muttered the words, "I do."

The priest said, "The gauntlets," and a man brought the two cups, placing one in each of our hands. I took mine, having seen it at many ceremonies before. Olivia fumbled with the knife they handed her and dug the sharp metal into her skin. She winced, and a hiss sounded through her teeth. Several vampires stood as the blood dotted through the skin, then settled into a steady stream.

I bit into my hand, filling as much of my goblet as I could before the bite healed. The sound of her heartbeat pounded in my ears.

She took the goblet and scrunched her nose as she lifted it to her lips. Slowly, I brought the cup to my mouth, wetting my lips with her blood. Closing my eyes against the bloodlust, a deprived, dark part of myself wanting the cup to overflow, or take more directly from the vein. "Sebastian?" Her voice cut through the lust, dragging me back. The goblet was dry. I'd all but licked it clean. *Fuck.*

"Congratulations," the priest said, and I blinked twice. The ceremony was done. We were married.

The crowd stood, their cheering overwhelming my senses. Olivia's grip tightened around mine as we were announced as husband and wife. It didn't feel real, but the anxiety in every squeeze of her hands anchored me to the real world. She needed me to be strong, if only long enough to get us out of there.

Her eyes widened as people called out to us, and the king and queen hugged us both. Once finished, I escorted her down the aisle. "Hold on to me. It's just nerves, love," I assured her as her arms trembled.

"Now I must die," she said, tears threatening to break through.

"Not yet." I placed my hand on the small of her back, hurrying us under the cloud of rose petals thrown in our path. "We still have time."

Kalon sped to us, paces from the doors leading us between further crowds swelling in the foyer. "Congratulations to the happy couple. May you enjoy your time together before the ceremony, Sebastian." He looked down at her, something dark dwelling behind that intrusive stare. "Seraphina."

I tightened my arm around Olivia, pulling her closer. Even with innocent words, he made them sound like a threat.

He arched a thin eyebrow, and I forced an amused smile. "You address her as Your Highness, now."

His frown pinched, a show of anger leaking through his stoic expression. "I'm a prince, so actually, I don't."

Kalon stepped out of our way, but strangers crowded us. Some booing at the princess they didn't want, most, fortunately, cheering, desperate for a look at her. "Prince Sebastian," one woman shouted, waving. I'd all but forgotten my new title. Two grabbed her shoulders, followed by others who danced their touches over her body, as if they owned her.

I held her tight against my body, cradling her head as my wings extended, forcing the vampires away from where we stood. Before they could bother us further, I kicked off from the ground, flying us up.

ELEVEN

Olivia

His thumb pressed against my chin as he lifted my head. I raised my lashes, peering at him. His breath hit mine, our lips only inches from each other. There was something primal behind his night-blue eyes as he landed us on the floor outside my bedroom. Our bedroom now, I supposed.

"I didn't think we'd make it out alive," I joked, but the feel of my subjects touching all over my skin made me shudder. "Thank you."

"Soon you will be able to do the same."

I wrinkled my forehead. The thought hadn't occurred to me before. "I'll have wings."

"You will. There's nothing quite like the freedom of flying."

My stomach knotted. I'd always been afraid of heights, but I supposed I had nothing to fear as an immortal. "Yes. Soon I will be a vampire." My breaths quickened, my mind speeding from one thought to another as a wave of numbness overtook me.

"It's not as bad as you think," he said gently, softening his tone.

I clasped my clammy hands. "Dying?" The word sent a shiver down my spine.

"Yes." He pushed open the door, and I walked inside. He sat on the bed, unbuttoning the cuffs of his sleeves, rolling them halfway up his arms. "It's as easy as breathing, and there will be no pain. Once you're on the other side, you'll be able to navigate your way back to the living. Although, with your royal blood, I have heard there will be a meeting there. Of the gods."

"Gods?"

"Yes. Apparently."

"My father mentioned something," I recalled, scratching the back of my neck. The thought of meeting gods—plural—made me want to throw up. I'd spent my life worshiping them, praying to them in my most desperate times, and now I was going to meet them. I suddenly realized I did not know how to act, or what the etiquette was.

"Don't be nervous. You'll be great," he said, as if he could read my thoughts.

I scoffed. "That's easier said than done." I wiggled my fingers, feeling my waning magic pulsing under the tips. "I'm going to miss being mortal."

"You will still be powerful," he promised, and ran a hand through his hair, disheveling the dark strands. "There's still time for you to enjoy your mortality."

I gave him a look. "How so?"

I'd never seen him appear so serious. "Come here."

"Why?" I asked, unable to tear my gaze from his.

He stood as I closed the distance between us. My heart pounded as raised his hand to my face. Feather touches trailed up to my bottom lip, his finger pushing into the plump skin, pulling it down. I closed my eyes, breathing in the smell of his musky scent, with a hint of warm vanilla, intoxicating my senses. I'd craved no one like this before.

"I want to lose myself in you," he said. "So we can both forget everything, for a moment." He divulged his truth against my neck, grazing the tips of his fangs over my skin. "I want your mortal heart before it stops beating."

"What about after?"

He whispered a kiss on my cheek. "Yes." He moved his kisses down my neck, stopping at my ear. "Tell me if you want to stop."

"I don't," I admitted.

A low growl escaped his mouth, reverberating against my skin. "Tell me what you want."

"I want you," I told him, the vulnerability of the truth almost stopping me. "More than I ever wanted Astor, or anyone else."

He ran a finger over my clavicle. "I'm going to fuck you," he said breathlessly, "until you forget every one of their names." He groaned against my neck, bringing his mouth to mine.

"I haven't done this for a while. I…"

"Don't think about it." He lowered me onto the bed, tucking a lock of hair behind my ear. Pausing there, he whispered against my earlobe, "Just speak to me with your body."

Some part of me recalled the door was wide open, but I didn't want to stop. He passed his fingers around my waist, tracing the curves of my body until he reached the top of my dress. The lace tore under his want, and he sliced the fabric down the center, exposing my breasts.

His breath hitched as his erection bulged in his pants, pressing against my thighs. I rocked against him, wanting to hold him closer. I gasped as his fingers tangled in my hair, jolting my head back. His lips dragged against mine with urgency. His sweet taste and the feel of his body quivering under my stroke heightened the desire building between my legs.

His tongue found mine, moving in unison as he deepened the kiss. My back arched to his touch, his lips frantic against me as he removed my panties.

I thrust my hips upward as he touched my wetness, his fingertips expertly playing against my clit. The pressure mounted, an ache begging to be satisfied.

He broke the kiss, my lips wanting for more as he moved his down to my chest. I moaned against his hot breath trickling onto my breasts, which bounced as his hips rocked against me.

I grasped the sheets, and my eyes rolled back as his tongue flicked my hard nipple. "Sebastian," I whispered his name like a prayer. A shock of pleasure rippled through my stomach as his dick pulsed under his pants. I moved my hand down to unbutton them, but he stopped me.

"Not yet," he ordered breathily.

He pushed his tongue against my nipple, rolling the other between his fingers. The slickness grew between my legs. His fingers danced down, sliding over my clitoris as he pushed two fingers inside me. I let out a high-pitched moan, and he groaned in response, sending a vibration into my chest.

Heat crept into my cheeks, pricking sensations sparking all over me as waves of pleasure rippled through my body, down my legs and into my toes. I licked my lips, and he took one nipple between his teeth, nibbling lightly.

"Harder," I commanded, my breath strangled as he flicked his tongue with caress. He obeyed, and his fangs grazed my breast. The orgasm built in my stomach and escaped into a scream I couldn't keep inside as he sent me to new heights.

Sweat beaded over my skin, the sheets rippling under my writhing body as he rocked the orgasm from me, slowing his tongue against my breasts with each pulse.

Dizziness encompassed every part of me, my mind numb against any thoughts as I came onto his fingers. Then, after I stopped, he pulled his fingers from inside me and brought them to his lips, tasting my arousal.

"Gods," he said, bringing his mouth back to mine, pausing to look into my eyes. His gaze darted around mine for a moment, a carnal need sharpening his features.

My mouth opened to his and nothing else mattered but us. I didn't care that I could taste myself on him.

Wild-eyed, he tore the little fabric of my dress left clinging to my body and threw it to the floor. I unbuttoned his pants, my breath hitching as his erection sprang free. His deep voice reverberated my name against me.

He pushed the tip in first, then his, long, hard length, thrusting himself deep inside me. Panting, I ran my hand over the muscles in his arms, holding onto him as he fucked me slow at first, then harder. Forcing my ass up the bed until my back hit the headboard, he then cupped my breasts.

Want rippled through me. He fisted my hair, and I brought my mouth to his, biting his bottom lip. I pushed my hips upward, and he enveloped us as one.

The bed rocked under our weight, wood slamming against the wall. The restraint in his features snapped when he looked at me. "Olivia," he said my name like I was his, only his.

He pounded into me harder, as a second orgasm built in the base of my torso. My toes curled against the sheets, fingernails biting into his skin. I wanted him, every inch of his toned, muscular body. I lost myself to the sound of the bedframe splintering under us, echoing into the wall.

Pillows fell to the floor as he pounded deeper, unable to stop.

He slowed, and kissed my neck, his fangs scraping against my collarbone. A trickle of blood slid down me.

Closing my eyes, I whispered, "Bite me."

He stilled for a moment and nuzzled into my neck. I readied myself for the initial pain, but it couldn't make its way through the pleasure. My blood seeped into him, and his venom coursed into my veins, sending me higher than I'd ever been.

My legs jolted, my arms shaking as the venom took over, stealing the second orgasm as if it were a whisper in the wind. Then, something hotter crept through me, like flames licking my body, an intense orgasm big enough it felt as if it could kill me. As if I wanted it to.

I ran my hand through his black curls, needing to feel every part of Sebastian. The animal in me recognized the animal in him, and something changed. It was as if we were one — his venom, my blood, were an obsession. An addiction—to each other.

"Mine." The word reached me through my venom-induced haze, and I screamed his name into the room as I reached the pinnacle, a fever sweeping my mind.

An orgasm unlike any other shredded through my body. He groaned, erupting hot cum inside me, and his legs stiffened. His mouth opened as he rocked slower until the orgasm finished with sparks vibrating through us both.

He lowered his forehead, resting it against mine. Then, catching his breath, he slowly moved from on top of me. I could only stare up at the ceiling, a satisfied smile on my lips.

Sex before him was nothing but a watered-down version of what I thought pleasure could be. I glanced at his body, every chiseled edge of it, and realized I didn't want anyone else.

My eyes widened. The realization of it hit me like a ton of bricks. He didn't want me to be only his. He married me because he had to, but he'd said 'mine'. I recalled what Astor had once said during sex, when he told me he loved me only weeks into our relationship that 'things said in the throes of passion weren't real'. Maybe that was the same now.

Sebastian's fingers locked with mine, and when he glanced over at me, he appeared just as surprised as I was.

"Stop thinking," he said again as if he could read my anxiety, and planted a kiss against my cheek.

My heart palpitated. "I can't help it."

He smirked. "I know."

There was so much I wanted to say, but I couldn't find the words and had no idea how they would be reciprocated. "Do you hate me?"

He turned onto his side, holding his hand in mine. "Did that feel like I hate you?"

I smiled. "No, but…" I held my breath for a moment. "What do you feel—for me?" I swallowed thickly, my stomach knotting.

He let out a long sigh, turning back onto his back. "It's complicated."

"I'm good with complicated."

He looked into my eyes, and something changed. "I'm not good for you. For us. This—we both needed this, and it was amazing. But I can't give you what you want. I can't be who you need me to be."

My eyebrows knitted together. "If you were that bad, I wouldn't feel this way."

He blinked twice, lips agape, then cleared his throat, averting his gaze. "I have to go." His eyes brightened. "We need to attend our reception, but I can always tell them you are feeling unwell if you'd like some time to yourself?"

"Wait." I stood, not really sure what to say. I couldn't admit the truth, that I wanted him to stay with me and that whenever I was around him, I wasn't as afraid.

He stared at me, eyes burning with knowing. It was as if he could read the unspoken words hanging between us, but ignored them anyway. "You're better off without pinning your hopes on me. We can fuck, be friends, and be husband and wife in name, but that's it. I can't be the one who holds your heart."

"Sebastian."

"Don't say my name like that," he pleaded, his voice pained. "Stay in bed. Rest. I will hold off the court."

"No. I'm coming."

"The Shadow Kissed Ceremony is tonight. You should enjoy your last hours as a mortal."

Regret seeped through his expression. He dressed and left the room without another word, and I looked at the clock. Time was ticking.

Only six hours were left until I was to become a vampire. He was right; I didn't want to spend my last moments dancing, surrounded by people I didn't know, or didn't like. So I stood, walking to the window, taking in the blackness. I gripped into the windowsill, still feeling the ache Sebastian had left between my legs.

Slowly, I pressed my hands over my chest, and closed my eyes. I clung to my mortality, to my magic, afraid of a life without it.

TWELVE

Olivia

Droplets of water ran down my curves as I stood in the tub, staring at the open bathroom door leading to the darkening bedroom. I wrapped a towel around my body and stepped onto the cold floor, leaving a small pool with each step.

The windows filled with purple and pink as the final of the sun's rays peeked inside. I looked out at the mountain spiked horizon, then down to the evergreen forest spilling out beyond the castle's walls. The sweet smell of honey clung to hair as I wrapped the strands into a towel, knotting it on top of my head. I wondered if the scent would overpower me once I was immortal, seeing as my sense of smell would be heightened.

The sound of the door handle pulling down sent goosebumps over my arms. I quickly turned, holding the front of my towel in case it was anyone but Sebastian.

My father entered the room and flicked on the light. "Good, you're here," he announced and closed the door.

"There's this thing we mortals do," I exclaimed, my fingers tightening around the top of my towel. "It's called knocking."

"Kings don't knock," he replied with a shrug of his broad shoulders. "You are not ready."

"I have an hour."

"You must look your best. Where are your maids?"

I didn't want to tell him I'd sent them away hours ago. "I can dress myself."

His green eyes shone when they met mine. "You are a royal, Seraphina. Therefore, you must relinquish these stubborn ways."

My eyebrows pinched down, wrinkling my nose. "Like dressing myself?"

"Precisely." His fingers interlocked behind his back, his posture straightening as he glanced around my room. "My brother is still bitter about my giving you this room."

"Yes. Kalon seems to have nothing but hatred for me."

He cleared his throat, admiring a painting of some landscape I didn't know. "You must try harder to get to know him." His shoulders tensed under the tassels on his jacket embroidered in gold. "Kalon is your uncle, and a prince of this kingdom."

"If only you knew," I muttered under my breath, and he sped to me, startling my hands so I almost dropped my towel.

"What do you mean by that?"

"Nothing." I inhaled sharply, stepping out of his shadow.

"I am not some mortal, Seraphina. No matter how quiet you are, I hear everything you say. So do not speak words unless you intend to clarify them."

Shit. I wanted to tell him, but as I gazed up at the man who might have looked like me, but could not have been more different,

I couldn't find the words. How could I know he would believe me? He and Kalon had centuries of memories between them, a bond far more substantial than anything I held with him. If he believed my accusations, he would have no choice but to kill his brother.

No. He wouldn't accept it, even if he thought there might be any truth to my words. I saw it in his fear-filled eyes and kept my mouth shut. I'd keep to my original plan, and deal with Kalon myself. "He's not trying to get to know me either," I said, hoping that would excuse my words. "I don't think he has any intention to."

"My brother will do what is asked of him, and I require you both to make peace. Don't think I haven't noticed your disdained glances in his direction. He is the prince, and the blatant disrespect you hold for him cannot be tolerated once you are officially the princess."

I swallowed my anger behind gritted teeth, my face flooding with heat. Night swallowed the sun outside the windows, and my time was almost out. "I'll try," I lied and white-knuckled my towel.

"Good. With that handled, I have other matters to discuss with you. Now that you will officially join the family, certain things are expected of you."

I sucked my bottom lip between my teeth and sat on the bed. "Can I get dressed first?" The cold danced over my arms, standing my hairs on end.

He waved a hand dismissively. "You can get ready while we talk."

My jaw clenched. "Boundaries."

The vein on his temple darkened, pulsing as he moved his incredulous gaze to mine. The room somehow felt ten degrees colder. I shuddered and swallowed the lump forming in my throat. There was something off in the way he stared. Behind the smiles, and the charm to the rest of the court was a possessiveness. It sliced through the room as my barrier lowered and his emotions crept in.

His tone sharpened, and his voice lowered to a threatening whisper, although no one could hear us. "Since arriving, you have done nothing but show disrespect for me and the kingdom. I have given you everything, and you continue to act with selfishness. Don't you understand what is on the line here? I have tried to be kind to you."

I blinked twice, attempting to recall this kindness. Maybe in his warped perspective he saw making me kill Draven after the ceremony and only taking Erianna wings instead of her life as a kindness. I did not. He didn't have to do it. As king, he could make a different choice, one not out of cruelty and punishment.

He continued, reining back some of the rage which thickened the air, an emotion so heavy it was suffocating. I flinched when he moved, and he paused, his fingers flexing. "The King of Asland is coming, as you well know. If we do not convince him we were not trying to turn that annoying bitch daughter of his into a vampire, then he will wage war on Sanmorte. Unfortunately, as you and your mother pointed out, we do not have technology and weapons. I do not have enough days to counter an attack." He looked over at the windows, as if recounting a memory that no longer existed. "This world has changed—for the worse. I remember when we were the ones to be feared, above all else."

Thank the gods that times have changed, I thought, but didn't dare say. I glimpsed his fangs under the dim, white light and shivered.

"They still fear us," he said, lifting his chin, "but not like they used to. We must play politics with them now. We will let Asland pretend they have power, treat them as equals if we must. You will charm the king."

"Would he not be more charmed by me…" I began, tentatively, "…if I remained mortal? For now. Like him," I asked, stalling the inevitable, but I wanted nothing more than to remain mortal for as long as possible. "We know they don't like vampires."

"What matters more is we present ourselves as strong, powerful, and unified. You will take your place as the princess, which you cannot do unless you have been Shadow Kissed. The gods must be the ones to crown you." His eye twitched, and he averted his gaze. "I cannot be worrying about what you may do or say. Asland is not the only threat."

"Hamza," I said slowly, recalling my father mentioning his followers from the south.

"Yes, but there are others, too. The little guild your mom was a part of has been sending spies here to find her."

I felt like my heart leaped into my throat. "Since when?"

"Since she returned home. She is Sanmorte's rightful queen. They have no business trying to return her to a kingdom she wasn't even born in. I have taken the heads of the spies I have found, but they send more." He shook his head. "Mortals. They never learn."

The screams from the night the vampires killed everyone in the guild, rang in my ears. I rolled my shoulders back, clamping my eyes to shut out the memory. "Maybe they see it as a kidnapping," I offered, which was one hundred percent true. My mom didn't want to come back. She'd killed to get away from here and hide me from his monstrous kingdom and his king. To keep me from the father I'd always been curious about, who I wanted to know.

How wrong I had been.

He cleared his throat. "We are being attacked from all sides. I am trusting you with the information. Sanmorte has never been so fragile. We are surrounded by kingdoms with armies growing by the week. One has put forward their intentions for war, which has never happened before. People are becoming suspicious of vampires, with more of my subjects leaving here and traveling the world, confirming rumors which are to the detriment of us and the mortals."

"They know vampires can be made?"

His nostrils flared. "Asland's princess has become one. How do we explain that? The Aslandian people have grown suspicious, and while it ails me, I understand why their king has declared war. I would do the same if I were in his position." He scratched the back of his head, then ran his fingers up to the crown. I wondered how heavy it felt, figuratively. "You and your friends committed treason, with your betrothed at the root of this. He killed Penelope, and now we will fall for his crimes."

"He didn't kill her," I snapped, unable to contain myself. "I know you won't believe me, but he is innocent."

He arched a brow. "She says otherwise."

"You will take her word over mine, over Sebastian's, who you once favored?"

His jaw clenched, and he paced around the room, thankfully at a normal speed. "It is true. I once cared for the boy. He is only three years into his vampire life, and even in his first year, he was smarter than the others. I saw a kindred spirit in him, and even trusted Sebastian. He was never afraid to approach me, and truthfully, he made me laugh. I enjoyed his company, which is why I made him Master of Travel." He inhaled sharply. "That is until he plotted against me, killing Penelope."

"Like I said before, he didn't kill her. His only crime was hiding who I was, and that was because I asked him to."

"You forced my hand when you chose him for your husband," he spat. "I cannot execute the man who is to be married to my own blood." He stopped pacing and faced me. "You may think me heartless, but you all committed treason. As soon as I learned who you were, I took you out from the dungeons even though you concealed your identity from me—which I will never understand. Not once did I try to punish you for your part in the plot against the crown. Then I only took the wings of your friends. I could have taken their lives, gods know the court wanted me to, but I showed mercy. All of it was for you."

Some of what he said tugged at me. I looked into his eyes and recognized the love he was trying to show. I just couldn't move past the image of Erianna wingless, knowing he gave the orders to carry out such a harsh punishment. Even if he felt like he had no choice.

Then there was Hamza, who would probably walk the castle as a free man if it wasn't for Sebastian.

"What do you need me to do?" I asked, mostly to get him out of my room.

"Obey my orders, try to fit in here, and help me clean up the mess you all created," he stated. "My hope is when you meet the gods and return to us, you will change your perception of us. We are not all as bad as you believe us to be. With immortality comes power, and you won't have to be afraid of anyone or anything again."

The memory of what Hamza tried to do hung between us, but neither of us spoke about it. "I will," I said and shivered against the cold. "I should get ready. Although I see little point in wearing such a nice dress when I am to get blood all over it from the dagger."

He hesitated on the edge of words, but quickly regained his composure, standing tall. "It's a transition." He pointed at the veil. "Make sure you wear that—it's a tribute to gods—and don't be late," he added and sped out, leaving the door slightly ajar.

Holding my next breath, I paced in a circle, unable to settle my emotions. I was expected to dress up and play some puppet role in his court. I could tell he loved me, but it was the dangerous, toxic kind, like he had for my mom. He'd forced her into her role and took her magic from her. He didn't even see me as my own person. Just the heir to the throne, and a daughter he can use to charm foreign kings. Not once did he ask how I was feeling.

Begrudgingly, I pulled on the thin, lace dress. The fabric itched my arms and stretched tight around my bosom. I dried my hair, not bothering to style it as I grabbed the black veil from the back of the closet.

A knock sounded, and I jumped. "Yes," I called, and Erianna stepped inside. I let out a sigh of relief, grateful my father hadn't returned with another lecture.

"How are you doing?"

Tears swelled unexpectedly in my eyes.

She rushed to me, wrapping her arms around my shaking body as the reality of my impending death overcame me. I didn't want to die. The thought of that and meeting all the gods tightened my chest. I touched her wingless back, and a pang of grief shot through me. It took me a moment to realize the emotion was not mine.

I rested my head against her shoulder. "I should be the one comforting you," I said, my heart aching at the thought of the stares she must get when she was seen, of how her pride and integrity were ripped away from her. "That's the only good coming from this—knowing I can save you and Sebastian. When I return, I can pardon you. Sebastian will officially be prince and therefore, safe."

She held me at arm's length, her frown tightening. "Do not worry about me. I am okay," she lied, because I could feel her pain. "I have come to warn you. The servants overheard Kalon and Velda discussing a plan. They're going to ensure you don't come back from the dead."

A wave of numbness ran the length of my body. I blinked twice, goosebumps covering my neck. "How. What—they can't do that."

"There is a way." She looked down at her feet, a sigh loosing from her lips. "In the forest, there is an herb. When ground and infused with magic from a sorcerer, it can block the spirit's ability to renter the body."

"Surely, Azia didn't help with this. He is the king's sorcerer?" I asked, remembering the bald man whose magic buzzed with electricity when he kissed my hand at the ball.

She raised an eyebrow. "You don't think they have their own sorcerers? They have an entire network of people under the king's nose. Olivia, you must eat and drink absolutely nothing they give you. Unless they have some other way of getting it into your system."

My throat felt like it was closing. I grasped at my neck. "What do I do?"

"I spoke to Draven. He agrees. You must get out of here. Even if they fail in killing you now, Kalon will not stop until you are dead."

The thought of running out of the castle flashed across my mind, followed swiftly by the image of Erianna, Sebastian, Zach, and Draven's decapitated heads. "I cannot." My eyes widened. "Sargon will kill you all, including Draven."

"Don't worry about us. I can find a way for you and Draven to get out safely."

My fingers were icy cold as the clock eased into ten o'clock. It was almost time. "I won't let anything happen to you."

"I will fight." She inched toward her dagger, and I froze. I believed it, and maybe they'd even take a few out, but they wouldn't win. Not against an entire castle of vampires. She had to know that.

"I won't let you die for me."

"It's not just for you." She let out a long breath, the smell of clove smoke thick in her hair. It was probably from the vampires in the ballroom, who lazed around puffing on their cigarettes brought back from others who'd got them on their travels. "If you go ahead, even if you eat and drink nothing, they will try to get the mixture into your body somehow. Then, when you do not come back, we are all as good as dead anyway. This way, we can save two lives." She paused. "Actually, three. Anna will go with you. Zach and I will cause a diversion. Sebastian will get you all out, then fight any that goes after you. He doesn't know yet—about any of this. We need to find him, but I know he will agree."

"This is insane." I stepped away from her.

It made sense now to why Zach was helping. He wanted to get Anna out. Sebastian had wings, so he could help fly us out if needed. Maybe he would agree once he found out about the plot against me. But it was unlikely that we would get far. Maybe with my mom's help, but even then…

"I'll take my chances," I blurted. "Even if I don't make it back. I will not have your blood on my hands."

"Olivia, I have lived many lifetimes—"

I raised a hand to stop her. "Don't. Please." I held the veil in my hands, smoothing my thumbs over the rough designs in the lace. "I will refuse any food and drink."

She shook her head. "It is too risky."

"This is my decision." I crossed my arms. "I am grateful, Erianna. Truly. You are a good person, and one of the few reasons I don't completely hate vampires. You were a friend to me from the beginning when I needed one most, and I will not abandon you now. I owe you and Zach for breaking your trust before and getting us into trouble. For not doing more to stop them from taking your wings." I didn't say Sebastian's name, but I felt the weight of his soul in my heart. I wanted to save him, too. "So, please. Let us believe I will return. In my last minutes, I need you to pretend nothing is amiss. I can't go into this scared. Please, act as if you believe I will survive this and their plan will fail," I begged, because I had to believe it, too.

She strained a smile, but there were no creases under the eyes to show any genuineness to it. "Of course, there's a good chance. As long as you don't eat or drink anything." Her voice was hollow.

"Thank you." I nodded. "I only wish I could remain mortal and still be the princess."

Erianna leaned against the doorframe. "Maybe you can. You should talk to the gods about it when you cross over." She said the words so casually, as if we were discussing what to eat for dinner.

My eyes widened, and I suppressed a nervous laugh. Gods. Actual Gods. And I would meet them. I glanced at the clock. We had minutes. I placed the veil over my face, glad for it so she didn't have to see the tremble on my bottom lip.

Sebastian entered the room. I felt his presence before he uttered a word. Turning slowly, I couldn't help but catch my breath from seeing him. Every touch we had shared last night was fresh on my skin. I could still feel his kiss against my neck.

He had no idea of the danger we were all in. I lifted my veil, shooting Erianna a pleading glare before lowering it again.

An amused grin spread across his face. "While you're there," he said to Erianna, "you can also ask them to make me mortal."

Her eyes narrowed, and the hue from the lamp caught a glint of darkness behind them. "Do not mock me. The gods will listen."

"I know they have no interest in what we have to say."

Erianna snorted. "You're right. They probably don't have any interest in what *you* have to say. You're not of royal blood. Just a prince by marriage."

"You wound me," he teased.

I sighed in relief. Duplicity came naturally to her as she acted as if nothing was wrong. Although, I supposed, she had centuries to master the art of lying. This probably wasn't the first time she'd had to remain calm in a tragedy. She was a warrior, after all.

Erianna tilted her head. "Be glad it's only with words." She unsheathed her dagger, rolling it around in her grasp.

He scoffed a laugh. "I am. I remember the last time I tried to spar with you."

Her expression softened, and a smile curved her lips. She put the dagger back.

Time was running out. I wanted nothing more than to grab the little hand ticking down the seconds until I was about to die and rip it clean off. Although it would do nothing to the time I had left, it might make me feel better.

"Olivia." A sigh loosed from Sebastian's lips. The laughter so ready in his mouth disappeared when he looked at me. As if he was remembering last night, too. "Are you ready?"

I nodded, wanting to be brave, but my knees almost buckled as I stepped toward the door. Erianna was by my side as the color drained from my face. I caught my reflection in the mirror over my dresser and placed the veil back over my face.

Sebastian kept his distance, unaware that we might never explore the connection we had together after tonight. But, I wondered, would he try to escape if I didn't make it back to the land of the living? Without me, my father would kill them all. I looked at them both, and the unsettling realization chilled my bones. They wouldn't.

Closing my eyes, I committed the pieces of Sebastian to memory; the way his touch felt against my skin, how his eyes twinkled when he laughed. I peeled back my eyelids, lifting my gaze to meet his. I studied how he watched me with the same intensity he had when we met. There was safety when I was in his arms, and I craved it more than ever. Slowly, I walked, and focused on only one thing: survival. I *had* to survive.

THIRTEEN

Olivia

It was genius really, not killing me before the ceremony. If Kalon had, fingers may have pointed back to him. This way, if I didn't come back, they would think I got lost on the other side, or the gods kept me there.

I'd underestimated him.

Erianna led me through the double doors, into the room where I'd married Sebastian only twenty-two hours ago. The clock chimed ten, and Erianna's hold on me tightened. She was risking everything. If she was seen by the king, she'd induce his wrath, but she didn't seem to care. She didn't even glance in his direction as we walked.

It was a stark difference from last night. The crowds were gone, dispersed by Sargon's guards and forced to attend celebrations elsewhere. But I could hear the thrum of the music in the distance.

This ceremony was far more intimate.

My mom bit her lip from the altar where she stood with my father, standing over the dagger that would end my life. Kalon watched from a few paces away, Niall next to him, a chilling look in his chiseled features. He held a goblet with both hands and approached me as I reached the altar made of stone, engraved with ancient symbols from a time long before any of us.

"This is for you." A twinkle danced those deep browns as he handed me the goblet. In it was a golden liquid. "It's venom."

I remembered I would need the venom *and* their blood to return as a vampire. Erianna shot me a cautious glance, knowing damn well what they must have put inside it. Then, before I could refuse the goblet, Niall stumbled, spilling the cloying liquid over my dress.

"Fuck, sorry," he swore, kicking a stone from under his foot, which must have made him lose his balance. I peered over his shoulder, finding satisfaction in Kalon's grimace.

However, I knew he would have a backup. In case.

Niall cocked his head and gazed beyond my veil, at my neck. "I would be happy to replace the venom, delivering it directly." He moved to bite my neck, but Sebastian sped between us, his fist connecting with Niall's jaw, knocking him backward. "The hell you will." His shoulders tightened, and his wings exploded outward, blocking me.

Niall laughed, wiping the smear of blood from his chin. "Someone has to." He pointed at the spilled venom.

Sebastian growled. "Then it will be me. Go back to your corner."

Niall snorted and returned to Kalon's side, who smoothed down a wrinkle in his hooded, jet-black robe. The corner of my mouth twitched when I spotted him watching me, his snake-eyes unblinking as I was forced to my knees in front of the altar by the executioner.

My father's shadow loomed over me as he approached, sliding the dagger over the stone altar. The blade glistened under the low, flickering light from the candles on the walls. Closing my eyes, my heart thumped faster as if it knew the end was coming. Adrenaline spiked through my veins, my survival instincts kicking in as the cold settled under my dress and veil.

My father's voice echoed throughout the room. "Sebastian, you will give your wife your blood and venom."

I straightened on hearing 'wife'. It felt strange to my ears, and my fingers prickled. Shivers took over my body, as the executioner—a masked man with white hair—took the dagger in his steady grasp.

My own trembled, and I felt a hand on my shoulder. Jolting, I swallowed my gasp, realizing it was Sebastian. "It's okay," he said, his voice strained as he lowered his lips to my neck. "I'm going to be right here when you come back."

Tears flooded into my view, tipping over and rolling down my cheeks. I wished I could stop myself from shaking. I hated knowing Kalon was watching me, and was only grateful that Gwen, Velda, and Astor hadn't been invited.

I inhaled sharply as Sebastian's lips grazed my neck, his fingers cupping my throat. Niall and Kalon disappeared from my peripheral vision as the executioner cpatured my attention, the dagger ready in his hands.

Fangs pierced my skin, sending a pang of pain down my chest and into the pit of my stomach. A scream left my lips, and his grip tightened, pulling me into his chest, cradling me in his arms. The searing heat in my veins calmed, turning to liquid ecstasy as I found myself in the depths of an itch nothing but his venom could scratch.

The feel of his firm hands on me and his body against mine ruined me for anyone else. "Don't stop," I begged, as he slowed the sucking of my blood.

His fangs retracted, leaving my skin, my hair wetting from blood as it seeped from the puncture wounds.

"Sebastian," I whispered his name, like he was my personal prayer. Nothing in the world mattered but him right now. Not even death. A small, rational part of me knew it was the effects of the venom, but his touch did something different to me. My thighs fell apart as arousal slicked between my legs, an ache only he could satisfy.

"Later, baby girl," he promised as I laced my fingers under his shirt, tracing the deep muscles forming a V down to his groin.

He lifted his wrist against my lips, and blood wetted my mouth. I ran my tongue over the bite marks he'd made and took his blood. The taste should have made me shudder, but I craved more of it. *Of him.*

"Don't let him kill me," I asked as his hold on me loosened. The thought of my death made its way through the venom-induced haze, and I stiffened. "I want you to do it."

His breath hitched, and voices sounded from beyond us. They were discussing it, but Sebastian didn't care. Before they could come at me with the dagger—as was tradition for a royal—his lips were back on my throat.

His venom quickly numbed the pain, and my head tipped, my eyelids closing on the view of the high ceiling. Tingling pricked over my arms and legs, and my breaths quickened. My lips fell open as I tried to say something, but I was too weak to speak. My heart slowed drastically, skipping a beat as I succumbed to the dizziness.

Hot flushes ran the length of me, yet I felt cold, shivering against his body. Tiredness came in waves, and before I knew it, I couldn't open my eyes. Consciousness lost its grasp, and I was blacking out.

I understood now why they called it being Shadow Kissed. Shadows crept through, spilling into every corner of my mind, coiling around my soul. His hand clinging to mine as I took my last breath, and death swept me into its arms.

***

There was no pain in the afterlife, only darkness. I could hardly catch my breath as I sat up, emptiness hollowing through me. The taste of ash hit my tongue when I gasped, drawing in the thick, hot air. Endless black surrounded me as I laid on rubble.

"Hello?" I found my voice. Slowly, I stood, ready for the wooziness that never came. I wiggled my fingers which were no longer grasped by Sebastian's.

I touched the skin where Sebastian had bitten me, but the flicker of touch sent no sensation into my skin. Everything felt less here. My breaths and steps were all lighter, and the sensations that generally accompanied them were gone.

"The gods," I whispered, hoping they could hear me in this dark place, unless… Had I accidentally gone to the underworld? Or perhaps Kalon had given me the poison to keep me here. Maybe he'd fed it to Sebastian, and it was in his blood?

I looked around, my mouth drying as I realized this might be the hell that awaited me.

"Seraphina," a voice cut through the emptiness, icing into me. No one called me that except my father.

"Yes." I swallowed thickly.

The horizon transformed. I stumbled back, hitting the trunk of a tree. The bark of the branches glimmered like gold under the now blaring sun, spreading warmth and light over me. Grass stretched out to rolling hills, the sky the brightest blue. A babbling brook sounded close by, and birds tweeted in the trees. I recalled seeing this place before, but where?

It flooded back to me. This was like the scene depicted on the stained-glass window in the chapel in the castle.

"Welcome, Seraphina," a woman spoke. She stepped out from nowhere, as if she was space itself. "I am Vaneria."

I froze on seeing her, feeling like I was trapped in a dream. Her blonde waves fell like silk down to her naked breasts. Looking into her eyes was like staring at the night sky, crafted from stardust. Her skin shone as if she was bathed in moonlight. I'd never seen someone move with such grace, and I couldn't tear my gaze away. A thin piece of fabric hung from her wide hips, slitting down one leg.

"You're beautiful," I said, blinking slowly.

Her smile was infectious, and I smiled back with a lightness in my heart, as if I'd known her forever. Then I realized—my soul knew her. She was a goddess, and in my blood ran hers.

She reached me, her delicate fingers lightly touching my chin, lifting my face as she examined me. Nothing in her expression evoked fear. In fact, I was quite at peace standing in these gardens with her.

She is a goddess. My brain reminded me, and I dropped to one knee, bowing my head. The grass cushioned my legs, the smell of wildflowers faint, but pleasant in the warm air.

"It is an honor," I managed, through a raspy breath.

"Rise." Her melodic voice was the pleasant sound I had heard in a long time. "The last time I saw a mortal was your father."

"You don't see them often?"

She glanced at the sky, a small smile spreading over her full, pink lips. "Mortal souls move on. We do not disturb their peace. Vampires go to the underworld. We remain here."

A familiarity settled in my stomach. Her scent, floating between cinnamon and vanilla, intoxicated my senses, and I could see why she was referred to as the goddess of love. Everything about Vaneria made me feel warm, like butterflies were swirling in my torso.

"Don't worry," she said with a knowing smile, "it's a normal reaction. Any mortal would feel the same way."

I gulped, feeling a little unnerved by how easily she read me. "I don't know what to say," I admitted, forgetting every scenario I'd imagined in my head of what this would be like. No fantasy compared.

Several paces behind her, two men appeared from nowhere, stepping out from a slit in space. The first thing I noticed about the taller of the two was his size. He was a mountain of pure muscle, his body rippling as he approached me. My jaw dropped, and I tilted my head.

Long, dark hair hung down to his chest, glistening as if he had just stepped out of a river. Eyes which reminded me of midnight met mine. I couldn't help but stare at his tattooed arms and the sides of his torso, depicting various scenes cemented in ethereal history.

I'd heard so many stories of the infamous Laveniuess, and now here he stood, in front of me, his shadow casting over Vaneria and me. Next to him, Jaiunere moved with a quick grin, a twinkle of mischief in his golden eyes. His skin appeared as if he had been kissed by the sun, his hair a tangle of tight curls. It was as if he had been crafted from the beauty of laughter, music, and art.

Laveniuess moved differently, slower, with purpose. His melody was different, crafted from a place of deep longing and loneliness. Being in his presence was like looking at a mirror, my inner demons reflected at me.

Each of them evoked a different concoction of emotions. Laveniuess was the first to speak, his voice a low, husky growl. "You are Seraphina, the future of Sanmorte."

I bowed to him and then Jaiunere, my heart feeling like it was in my throat. "I cannot find the words to express how honored I am," I repeated similarly, because I genuinely did not know what to say. They were the embodiment of everything that drove me as a mortal; desire, love, kindness, humor, happiness, anger, vengeance, and every other feeling.

Vaneria placed her hand on my shoulder, sending a ray of heat into my body, calming my nerves. Around us, chairs materialized, as if they'd been there all along. I sat on one, crafted from gold, and basked in the serenity Vaneria had given me.

"You are an Empath," she stated, and I nodded. "It is a beautiful gift."

"I am grateful for it," I said, although that was only partially true.

She ran her hand over her knee, taking the chair across from mine. Laveniuess' and Jaiunere took their seats either side of her. "It is more a gift for others. You are a healer, sent to take away pain. A light bringer."

I forced a smile.

Jaiunere leaned forward, his tone light. "You are allowed to both love and dislike it."

I flushed and clasped my hands in my lap. "I have spent most of my life building a barrier against others' emotions," I admitted, shame creeping through me as I felt the rejection of such a god given gift.

Laveniuess spoke, his voice commanding attention. "It is normal to desire to rid yourself of a gift to humanity if it causes you pain. However, it is up to you what you choose to embrace, Seraphina."

I sucked in a deep breath, squinting at the sun's rays. "You are nothing like I thought you'd be," I said, my gaze passing over each of them.

Vaneria touched her clavicle, and I couldn't help but glance at her perfect chest and neck, just admiring the beauty in her. I moved my gaze to meet her starlit eyes, a smile forming over my face. She opened her mouth, tilting her head. "So, Seraphina, tell us, what has become of our beloved Sanmorte and your father."

"You don't know?" I asked. "I apologize, I just mean, I thought you knew everything happening in our world."

Laveniuess shook his head, the muscles in his shoulders tightening as he sat back. "We have existed in this plane, far from the world we once inhabited, for many centuries now."

Sadness laced Jaiunere's soft features. "We have been distant from our descendants, cut off from our physical forms."

My eyebrows pinched downward. "Excuse me for my ignorance, but I see you in your physical forms now."

Jaiunere chuckled, a sound as light as the breeze passing through us. "All this is an illusion we have created for your comfort."

"Oh." I touched the back of my neck, my stomach knotting. "Thank you." I looked at Vaneria, her question of Sanmorte playing in my mind. I was unsure how to answer, because there was nothing good about the vampire kingdom.

The sky darkened as concern threaded through Vaneria's expression. "I command you to speak the truth, Seraphina."

"From what I have learned in history books," I explained, recalling the origin stories, and what Draven had told me about the gods anointing the kings of vampires. "You chose our bloodline, and one before ours, to instill a fairness and control to the creatures your sister created. Is that correct?" I asked, unsure if what I had been told was true.

Vaneria answered, "Yes."

"I'm sorry to tell you this, but we have failed you all."

"How so?" Vaneria asked.

I hesitated to find the words. Sanmorte was a place of deceit and unleashed terror. "I'm not from Sanmorte. I was born there, but I grew up in a different kingdom. Only recently did I return and… it's terrifying."

Vaneria gestured for me to continue. "Please, tell us everything. We only know about your birth. Whenever any royal is born from your bloodline, we can feel it, but we know nothing beyond that."

"There's…a lot to say."

Vaneria understood and approached me. Softly, she placed her fingertips against my temples, closing her eyes. I felt her presence run through me like a river. It took me a minute to realize she was in my head, seeing everything I did. She flicked through the chapters of my life, as if she were reading a book.

Every suppressed emotion came to the surface the deeper she dove into my subconscious. The vampires destroying the guild flitted into my mind. My head ached as she forced me to remember it all in painful detail.

I was taken back to Draven protecting me, leading me through tunnels until he was taken by one of the creatures. Then Sebastian stealing me away, and every moment that lingered between us after. She skimmed over those moments, only pausing at the details of our conversations regarding Sanmorte. Pictures formed in my mind of the dead mortal on the streets in the City of Nightmares, the auction rooms where I was sold to Hamza, and the aniccipere, devouring souls.

Everything fell into slow motion. The blood dens, the castle, my mom as a vampire, the feeding room. Even the stench of the bodies burning in the courtyard seemed to materialize, sending the smell into my nostrils.

Vaneria experienced it alongside me, while her brothers watched. Finally, after what felt like an eternity, she let go of my head, and my eyes snapped open.

Laveniuess was the first to speak. "What did you see, sister?"

She lowered her long lashes, stepping back. "The world has fallen into darkness." Then, closing the distance between her and her brothers, she showed them what she took from my mind, and before I could part my lips to utter a word, they'd decided what to do. "Seraphina," Vaneria said softly. "I have seen your heart, and we have chosen you for what will come next."

Goosebumps spread over my arms and neck as she uttered the words I would never forget.

"You must take your father's place on the throne."

FOURTEEN

Sebastian

"She should be back by now!" I stormed over to Sargon. "What's happening?"

He pointed the Cane of Cineris at me, pulling from under his cloak. "Know your place, Sebastian, or I will return you to ash."

Ravena patted his hand, lowering the cane. "I have the same question." Her voice broke. "Where is our daughter?"

Sargon glanced at Olivia's lifeless body, a tinge of gray covering her skin. My stomach was still full of her blood, and I wanted to throw it all up. "Tell me she isn't dead."

"Don't pretend you care." Kalon snarled from the shadowy corner of the throne room. "We both know you only married her because death was your only other option."

"You," I snarled, rage searing under my skin. I'd bet my wings he had something to do with this. He'd wanted her dead since the moment he learned of her existence. "You did this."

He snorted, but I saw the hint of amusement on his thin lips. "Careful where you shoot your accusations."

"I will fucking end you if you did!"

"Enough!" Sargon boomed, his hand around my neck before I could react, slamming me into a wall as his gold wings expanded from his back. "Know your place now, or I will have you thrown back in those dungeons. Prince or not."

Erianna spoke up for the first time, moving to Olivia's body. "Seb, calm yourself. Please. She may still come back. She would meet with the gods. This isn't a normal Shadow Kissed ceremony."

Niall gritted his teeth, a hiss in his words. "Listen to the traitor."

"Don't," Erianna warned as a growl sounded low in my throat, and I aimed my anger at Niall. "I don't care what he has to say about me."

Niall clicked his tongue and sped to Olivia's side, lifting her hand. I wanted to stop him, but Sargon's grip tightened around my neck, lifting my feet from the floor. If he wasn't the king, I'd have torn his head off. He let me go, landing me on the ground with a thud.

Clenching my jaw, I stood, my fingers flexing. "It's been two hours."

Ravena covered her mouth, a gulp bobbing her throat as her brown eyes glossed over with tears. It was the first time I'd seen genuine emotion from the woman. "She's with the gods. That has to be it. She isn't dead." Her voice cracked at the end. "She can't be."

There were a thousand things I wanted to say to her, and Sargon. They were responsible for all of this. Olivia didn't have to go through this bullshit ceremony. He didn't need a princess. Only a daughter. Ravena should have done more to stop him, especially considering she was partially to blame for what happened. She had forced Olivia to wear that trailic when she didn't want to. Servants heard everything these days, and the truths they whispered were sickening.

Instead, I stayed quiet, knowing I couldn't help Olivia if I was dead. I pressed my hands together, as if in prayer, and placed the tips against my lips. Erianna had to be right. She would return.

That had to be true because the alternative couldn't be. I didn't have time to tell her about the burning connection I felt with her, not only when we were in bed. She was so beautifully mortal—in every way.

Yet, I was a murderer who tore out men's hearts, tortured enemies and enjoyed it. I'd fucked my way through more women than I could count over the last three years, allowing my lust to steal my morals. Even in my final moments, I'd let Gwen suck my dick, if only to feel anything but the looming presence of death.

Then Olivia was there, growing on me. Caring for her happened like falling asleep. Slowly, then all at once. There was a tie to her I could not understand. It settled my heavy heart, holding her close to me. Yet, I couldn't shake knowing I wasn't good enough for her.

She took away people's pain with one touch. While I caused it.

I admired the freedom in her smile and felt almost mortal when I was with her. It was the closest I'd come to gaining back any morality for myself.

Azia walked in holding his staff, wearing velvet robes flowing out around his feet. "Your Majesty."

He was the only one who didn't bow to the king. I respected him for that. Because he knew what Sargon hated—that Azia was far more powerful, even more so than a vampire king.

Sargon rubbed his forehead, ironing out the wrinkles forming from his frown. "Olivia has not yet returned to us. I need you to see if she has been tampered with—magically."

Niall instinctively moved toward her when Azia touched her. What the hell was his problem?

Her gasp jolted all of us. Olivia sat up, before Azia could have time to do anything. Her eyes fluttered open. She was beautiful, Immortal, and most importantly, alive.

Her eyes pinned me across the room. She was different, not a vampire, but no longer mortal. My eyebrows creased, and jaw slacked. It was impossible. Of course, I heard the stories but put no thought into them.

I felt it, like a tangible pull between us. It explained why I couldn't stay away from her when she was mortal, even when I tried to. Everything in my heart and soul wanted to protect her, to hold her close and take her as mine. The startling revelation sank into me, and I stilled.

She's my soulmate.

FIFTEEN

Olivia

Flicking my eyelashes up, I peered at Sebastian. Everything about him was suddenly all-consuming. The smell of his warm, musky cologne filled me, flooding memories of when we'd made love. Arousal slicked between my legs, my thighs clenching together as I recalled the feel of his lips against mine. I walked slowly, as if I was being guided by invisible strings.

Something changed in how he looked at me, eyes widening in surprise, his expression the only movement on his body. A lump bobbed in his throat, bringing my gaze to his tattooed neck. Stepping into his space, I lifted my chin, his intrusive stare capturing my soul, as if he could see into all the dark places I buried.

My heart pounded as I waited for him to speak. *Say something. Anything.*

Inhaling sharply, I pulled my eyes away from him. The compulsion was too intense, and I could absorb his emotions without even touching him. Shock tore through our connection, bringing with it everything hidden. All the secrets and lies surfaced, coiling around me in a desperate heartache, a clawing for redemption, enveloped by the desire to do the right thing. It was as if I was him.

Shaking my head as if to scatter the thoughts of him, I let out a small sigh. I had work to do, and I was clearly experiencing heightened emotions with my immortality. That had to be why I was so drawn to him. Why I could *feel* his soul. It was the empath in me, enhanced.

Magic pulsed through my core, matching the energy of Azia, who stood across the room. His gaze bore into my back, as if he were trying to reach inside of me to figure out what I was.

Because now, everything had changed. The gods had given me a new purpose and with that, the greatest gift of all.

I glanced behind me, fear swelling in my chest as I glared at my father and his crown. I spotted Niall watching me, his brown eyes widening as he took me in. He had spilled the venom, supposedly by tripping, but everyone knew vampires seldom made such blunders. Even Kalon had to know. Niall saved my life. I just wanted to know *why*.

SIXTEEN

Niall

It was torture watching her come to the slow realization that Sebastian was her soulmate. Seraphina glanced at the venom, before turning her attention back to Sebastian.

The corner of my mouth twitched as I watched them. He just stood there, looking at her, his eyes just as wide as hers. *Do something.* If I were him, my mouth would have been on hers before she could take her next breath.

Fucking soulmates.

I had planned on killing Sebastian, but now it would destroy Seraphina. No matter, I was patient. I'd waited this long for the crown, and if becoming a prince meant I had to wait for her to grieve before charming her into marriage, then so be it.

We had forever. That was the beauty of immortality.

Father was annoyed. I could see it behind the restraint in his eyes as he forced a smile. He couldn't get mad yet. Sargon was watching us, after all.

I stared at the spilled venom on the stone by the altar. It was a brilliant plan to lace the venom with the herbs to keep her trapped in death. The king would never have figured out we were behind it. People often got lost between the living and dead. But I couldn't let my father kill my future bride. Seraphina was the very thing I'd been waiting for. Her coming back was an opportunity to take the crown I deserved.

I tilted my head, watching after her as she glided over the ground, her red curls dancing down her back. She was a prize, and Sebastian was so ungrateful. He had *everything*. A crown. A princess. Power. Yet he moped around, brooding as if his life was so difficult. *Please.*

The hallowed glow from the candles soaked around her as she swayed her hips, her gaze lifting to Sebastian as she moved past him. Immortality suited her, but there was something different about the princess. From her skin's subtle but translucent radiance to the sudden grace in every elegant step, it was as if the bloodlust didn't affect her. She raised her gentle hands to her teeth, searching for the fangs, blinking slowly as a wrinkle formed between her brows.

Something was wrong.

She left the room, leaving Sebastian staring after her, rooted to the spot. Father placed his hand on my shoulder. I'd forgotten he was standing next to me for a moment. "Clean that up." He pointed at the venom glistening over the smooth stone. "Now."

Restrained anger laced his words, but he didn't need to worry. I wasn't about to let Sargon or his righteous sorcerer touch it, to find out what else was mixed in. Else we'd all have been screwed.

Sargon grabbed Ravena's wrist, tugging her to follow their daughter. Her expression darkened, sharpening her bold features as she glared at him with as much hate as I had. As Kalon did.

I wondered if he knew so many in this room, people he believed loved him, would instead enjoy killing him. Father's resentment had hovered over us like a black cloud for years. He was the one who took care of all political matters, including slipping the idea of inviting the King of Asland here.

After all, he believed if Sanmorte was to one day become his, then he needed to ensure there was a kingdom left. A war with Asland would destroy us all, and if Sargon had any sense, he would have listened to his wife. She was the one speaking the most sense. Even his daughter had more than him.

Sargon disappeared through the tall, arched doors with Ravena and Azia. I was glad to be rid of them all, including that sorcerer. He thought himself better than any of us. My fingers flexed on seeing his pompous stride. Just because he had magic. But he didn't have fangs, like me. I'd enjoy sinking them into his throat if I could get away with it.

One day I would.

Father grasped my shoulder, my skin slicing open under his nails before I could put enough distance between us now the room had emptied. "You spilled it on purpose. Why?" He pulled me back to his side, toppling me farther until I hit the wall behind us. His snake-green stare latched onto mine, the low light enhancing the burning rage behind his eyes. There was little point in lying. To his frustration and benefit, we were too alike, as if we were blood.

I lifted my chin at the man who'd adopted me seventy years ago, when I was nothing but a washed-up merchant clawing my way out of the shipwreck. I was a good man then. It's a good thing he was dead.

"I saved us," I said in a hiss, digging my nails into his wrist until he removed his grasp. "You refused to listen before, so I took matters into my own hands."

"That," he spat, nostrils flaring, "was our only chance." His voice lowered, a shaking in the raspy deepness as he tried, but failed to contain his anger. "You foolish boy."

"There will be other chances." I stepped out of his shadow, my shoulders tensing as I looked around the room, smelling the sweet lace of Seraphina's blood that had dripped as Sebastian fed on her. Closing my eyes, I imagined my mouth on her, filling myself up on the blood of a sorceress. It was the highest of highs, a luxury to be sure.

"Niall."

I'd launched into the speech I'd prepared in my head while she was on the other side. "Azia would have known, when he touched her. He'd have sensed the magic in the mixture still in her veins. Besides, Sebastian ended up sucking her dry, anyway. So it wouldn't have worked."

His eyelashes flickered, the skin under his eye twitching his stretched skin. He knew I was right, not that he'd admit it, but we couldn't have known she would die that way. She was supposed to use the dagger.

"You have the power of foresight now, I see?"

I composed my emotions, blocking his attempt to feel them. He couldn't manipulate them, but he was an empath, like Seraphina, only he had better control than anyone I'd seen. They didn't affect him because his heart was stone cold after his centuries. "I thought of every eventuality, and it's a good thing I did. Else we'd have been the prime suspects. You sent *your* servants to fetch the ingredients instead of using others."

His jaw clenched, his robes swaying around his thin legs as he paced the length of the room. "I do not believe you." He tried to feel my emotions again, but the wall I'd built since learning of his ability was strong. "But I suppose you're right."

The corner of my lip lifted. I wondered how much that pained him to say.

"Clean that up," he ordered, turning his back to me and speeding out of the throne room. I glanced at the venom, deciding to send for one of the mortal servants to do it. I was no one's fucking housekeeper.

My stomach tightened as her blood's aroma reached through the venom's stench. Crimson blotted my thoughts, and I headed to the feeding room.

***

Fuck.

Gwendolyn spotted me as I walked into the feeding room. She wiped her lips of the mortal she'd eaten, slumping him against the table as he lost consciousness. She always overindulged. We at least always had that in common.

My heart raced as I let out a breathy sigh. The blackness lifted from the sky, sending a pink light through the tall windows, blending with the flames from the torches on the walls.

I'd successfully avoided her since I came back. We hadn't seen each other in a year. I'd hoped to continue evading her presence, but this had to happen at some point.

I'd hoped she'd returned to the City of Nightmares after she sent me flying from the castle after her little games. But she was still here, torturing me with a purposeful smile as if we didn't share a history tangled in darkness and hate. She slowly made her way over to me, fluttering those damn eyelashes when she reached me.

"We haven't had the chance to talk yet," she said, her voice smothering me like silk, flooding back the obsession I'd spent twelve months sedating. "I've missed you, Niall."

My name on her lips unexpectedly dipped my stomach, swirling bubbling anger, singeing my veins. "We both know that's bullshit."

"Oh, come now." Her face split into a grin. "I speak nothing but the truth."

I scoffed a laugh. "You're a good liar, sweetheart. You've been learning." I couldn't tear my gaze from hers, the intensity of it burning into me.

"I had a good teacher." She winked, and moved a pace closer, her lavender-laced scent just as intoxicating as I remembered.

The urge to run from the girl who'd destroyed my life, was overcome by the magnetism rooting me in place. Tension thickened the air, the words cutting into a place I kept buried.

"Niall, speechless…" She raised an arched eyebrow. "That's a first. What happened to the man who had a quip for everything?"

I wanted to say it was torn out by you, along with my heart, but it would only widen that satisfied smirk. "Where's that vulture mother of yours?"

My gaze ran to her chest, pausing at the contours of her breasts under her silk top, her nipples visible through the fabric. She tilted her head, biting her lip. "Around somewhere, probably cozying up to your father." Her nose wrinkled.

"You still hate her," I observed, finding my resolve after the shock of seeing her again dissolved. "Some things never change."

"She's my mom."

"That's not an answer."

Her long lashes lowered, her gaze flitting from my lips to my eyes, opening an ache in my chest. "Speaking of parents we don't like, I see you're back to sucking up to Kalon."

The corner of my lip twitched, a tell she would have noticed. "He's my father," I repeated her words back. I refused to be a part of this game again. "I heard you have a boyfriend now. Astor." I spat his name like venom.

She licked her lips, flashing her pearly whites. "So, you *have* been asking about me."

"Don't flatter yourself, sweetheart. People talk. It's hard not to hear about the pandering idiot you turned. Wasn't he Seraphina's man before yours?"

Her expression hardened. "She was nothing to him. He chose me."

"I suppose we all make mistakes."

Her eyes narrowed, her full lips parting as the softness which once melted me returned to her gaze. I wouldn't be pulled back in.

I couldn't. The thin boy I'd seen around the castle with a mop of honey-brown hair walked over to us.

I almost laughed, but caught myself. "That's him?" I asked before he reached us. "I see now why you missed me."

She opened her mouth to argue, but he was already at her side, extending his hand. I laughed at his gesture, forcing a puff of air through my nose. Then, before he could speak, I gave her one last glance and walked away. So much for her stance on monogamy and how it wasn't in our nature. It took all my restraint not to turn and look at them.

Knowing he was fucking her was enough to make me snap, to carve his heart from his chest and eat it in front of Gwen, but I kept moving. Doing that would only show I cared, and I couldn't, not after all this time.

We'd both moved on, and it was a good thing. I had a new prize to turn my focus to. The princess—and the crown that came with her.

I searched the feeding room for a mortal to fuck and feed on. Anything to erase the image of Gwen and Astor forming in my mind. Images of them enraptured in a mess of limbs plagued me, balling my fists. What did he have? Apart from someone she could boss around?

The room filled with soft, humming music, vibrating the tables slathered with wanting mortals, begging for another hit of my venom—and who was I to not oblige them?

A new batch had been brought in, and one caught my attention with sapphire eyes and thick, supple thighs. The lacy fabric clung to every curve. Her eyes widened as she basked in my appraisal.

She would do.

Sliding her hair over one shoulder, she bared her neck to me. Her siren stare lured me to the nook she sat in, her body draped over a cushioned sofa. A thin sheath of net hung over the alcove, an illusion of privacy. The smell of blood mixed with arousal thickened the air, and I pressed my thumb against my lips. Moving the net curtain back, I towered over the mortal.

"Your name," I commanded.

"Alana," she said back, her voice cracking.

"I'm Niall."

"They rarely tell me their names," she admitted, her hand dancing below her navel.

I let out a low chuckle, tilting my head to take her in. "I want you to know what name to scream when I take you."

She tensed, and I touched her neck, my fangs elongating as the thrum of her heartbeat sounded in my ears. Then, wrapping my arm around her waist, I tugged her closer, sliding her form against mine. Thoughts of Gwen shoved unwantedly into my head, muddying it as I glowered at Alana. She was beautiful, enough to pass an afternoon, but Gwen kept fucking up my process.

"I'm not going to hurt you," I said, suffocating the silence. "Well, only a little."

Cupping her cheek in one hand, I forced her head to the side, revealing her throat. I closed my eyes as I sank my fangs into her skin, relishing in the familiar gasp that usually escaped their lips before they were overcome with the effects of venom.

The heavenly nectar of her life source coated my throat, trickling deep into my stomach. This one ate well, altering the usual tang found in the mortals' veins. She was a perfect specimen to feed on. I would ensure I kept her that way, and maybe move into a room under my lock and key.

My gaze moved down to the fingers clasped between her thighs, running under her dress. Her eyes rolled to the back of her head, her dark hair spilling down her back as she leaned back against the sofa, a sweet moan escaping her lips. I knew the type. She was a volunteer, because she was far too wanting for a mortal who'd been kidnapped, brought here against their will. No, this one came without protest. They were always my favorite.

A surge of euphoria rushed through me. I closed my eyes, sucking harder, gulping down a mouthful too much. Reluctantly, I pulled away, my erection growing under the touch fabric of my pants. I wanted her conscious, especially with the obsession of Gwen slowly burrowing back into my soul.

Licking my lips, I stood over Alana, turning her onto her back. Her supple, round ass lifted. "Very good," I praised, imagining how Gwen's would feel under my grasp.

Ignoring the whispers of Gwen echoing in my head, I rolled my shoulders back, basking in the power from the feed, pulsing adrenaline into my veins. I laced a finger around the curve of her cheeks. Then, raising one hand, I spanked her, feeling the sting under my fingertips.

She yelped, biting into one of the velvet cushions.

"Don't do that. I want to hear you."

She nodded, and I smiled as she obeyed. Guiding her movements with my hands, I pressed her deep into the sofa cushions. The taste of her blood fresh on my lips tingled my tongue as I brought my mouth between her legs, breathing hot air against her pussy, glistening with wetness.

My eyes widened as she pushed herself against my waiting lips, easing them against her desire, coating my tongue in her invigorating lubricant. Bringing her swollen clit between my lips, I flicked the underside, tugging on her thighs. My eyes closed as I appreciated her moans with each caress of my tongue.

When I felt her hips quiver, the slide of her form as she glided up against my chin, I smiled, wide lips spreading over her. In exploring the folds of her, the echoes of Gwen dissolved. Nuzzling deeper, I thrust my tongue inside, holding my breath as she rocked herself over my nose and mouth. Her thighs clenched around the sides of my face, and I darted in and out, bringing my hand down, cupping her ass, guiding our rhythm, perfectly in sync.

My dick pulsed under the tightness of my pants, the heat of her peaking forcing a groan from me, the sound vibrating as she tightened around my tongue. The pillow muffled the broken scream of pleasure. I wished she wouldn't have tried to keep quiet; I wanted to hear her every sound, but never mind. I'd punish her for it after.

Forcing my tongue in deeper, I pulled her further back into my face, letting her know she needn't restrain her strength against me. Her moans turned to whimpers as she rocked slower, the rush of her juices over my tongue as I coaxed the last of her orgasm into my mouth.

Running my hands over her curves, I gripped her hips. "I told you not to use that pillow."

Her eyes widened in surprise, her cheeks flushed pink, beads of sweat gathered on her brows. "I…"

"Don't apologize, just bring your ass closer. This time," I warned, unzipping my pants, "I want to hear every fucking moan."

"Yes," she said breathily, her glassy eyes finding mine. I basked in the glow of her sweat slicked body, like liquid gold. Then, letting out a low rumble of a groan, I grasped my aching erection, and her legs fell apart.

"Good girl." My ass clenched as I pressed the tip into her, my hands moving up to her full breasts, lingering a touch over her hard nipple, before moving them up to her throat. A satisfied smile tilted her lips as I strengthened the grip, waiting for the breathy gasp before thrusting into her, pressing my free hand into the cushion as our bodies clashed together.

Forcing her head back, I pressed harder, hearing her shallow breaths under the weight of my hand. A part of me hoped Gwen had come back, that she was listening to us fuck, knowing that she could never have that with her boyfriend.

My nostrils flared, anger thrusting me harder as a mix of hate and want for Gwen tangled into pure desire, and I took out on the mortal, her high-pitched sounds making their way from under my hold. Time disappeared as I fucked her harder, forcing us deep into the pillows, aware of my strength as she could barely catch her breath.

That's what she got for not obeying me.

I loosened my grip on her throat as my thighs tightened, muscles spasming as the abrupt rush of my cum spilled into her. My eyes rolled back into my head as I continued to rock, feeling her orgasm throb over my dick.

I pulled out, leaving a trail of semen behind as I buttoned my pants, my breaths heavy.

A chorus of 'Your Highness' erupted outside, and my muscles tensed. She was here, Seraphina. It had to be her, or my father. I hoped for the former.

Licking my lips, I moved the curtain back, and there she was, beautiful, like a goddess, the ultimate prize. Everyone dropped to their knees, including me. I'd never gotten on my knees for anyone. I only hoped she saw.

SEVENTEEN

Olivia

I cast my eyes over the feeding room, their whispers crawling over my skin. Vampires bowed their dropped to their knees, for me. Before, I hated them, but now, I saw vampires for what they really were—slaves to their darker nature. They needed my help. Centuries of poor leadership from a man with a crown tainted in sin had given them the freedom to do whatever they wanted without consequence. Without laws to dictate between right and wrong, it was easy to blur the lines of morality. I understood that now.

Breathing in the thick, musky air, I licked my lips. I had been living a muted existence before, but now I could hear everything. For a moment, it was overwhelming. Then, steadying myself, I focused on the exhale of a breath from the man in front of me, narrowing my senses to him. Slowly, the rest of the noise fell away.

I looked around, and it was as if a film had been lifted from my eyes. Everything was sharper, more vibrant than I could have imagined. Sunlight arrowed through the windows; in them, I watched dust dance in an illusory swirl. I wanted to capture its beauty, but no photograph could do it justice.

My pupils dilated, and excitement sent goosebumps over my arms. I'd never felt power like this; it thrummed alongside my racing heart. Magic sizzled beneath my fingers, submitting to my will. I moved it inside myself, adjusting the sorcery to expand from my body, searching the energy of the room.

Erianna came into view, and relief settled my nerves. She was okay, along with Sebastian and Zach. Their empathy overshadowed their desire to give into temptation, and I admired them. I'm sure there were others like them, too. But as I slid my eyes from the tents to the half-conscious mortals lying across tables, the gravity of the momentous task awaiting me grew heavier in my chest.

How could I guide those with centuries of bad habits to change? A lump formed in my throat, and I swallowed to remove it. But, the gods believed in me, and their faith was all that stopped me from running to my room and locking myself away from their curious eyes.

What is she?

I could see the question burning on each of their faces. My father swept to my side. My mother remained a step behind. I could sense her anxiety rippling through the space between us. Her barriers were low. She wanted me to know how she was feeling and tell her what happened with the gods, but now was not the time. I had promises to keep, and a kingdom to rule.

But the next part was going to be the hardest. I knew what was required of me, a command by the goddess Vaneria and her brothers, yet it pained me.

I spotted Niall as I took a step forward. His long hair fell over his chest as he bowed deeper than the others. Then, slowly, he raised his head, his blood-slathered lips lifting at the corner.

He'd saved me. *Why?*

Shaping and carving my gift, I darted it to him. As it reached him, I jolted back, feeling the power thrum against the wall he'd formed. He had a stronger barrier shielding his emotions than even mine.

Kalon.

Of course. It only made sense to construct a strong defense with a man like that for a father. "I wish to leave," I stated to my mom as she hurried beside me, her fingers grazing the top of my hand.

She glanced at my father, who'd barely nodded when she grasped my arm, pulling me out of the room and away from their prying eyes. We glided through the foyer, my senses capturing every slice of light that came with the rising sun blotting pink into the indigo sky. I didn't move from the arched windows, even as she tugged at me again. "Olivia."

"Stop." I ripped my arm from her grip, raising my tense shoulders. "It's Seraphina now."

Her raven eyebrows pinched downward, scrunching her nose. "Since when did you want to be called that?"

"It is my birth name." A pang of regret shot through me, but the only people I wanted to call me Olivia were people I was close to. The distance between my mom and I was so far now, and I couldn't help but resent her for her choices, especially for forcing me to wear the trailic.

I listened acutely to every step as my father's shoes clicked against the stone. The mix of orange hues from the lamps and morning light through the windows brought out the colors in his auburn waves.

"Daughter," he said, leaving behind the muddied chatter of the feeding room. "We will go somewhere more private to discuss your—" He paused. "—situation."

I exhaled forcibly through my nose, suppressing a scoff. This was no situation; the greed widening his eyes told me everything I needed to know. He was jealous. Unsure why I had been given true immortality while he was just a vampire, even one with gifts others didn't have.

"Do you want me to fly you up?" he asked, extending his gold wings.

"No, you go ahead." Before either of them could respond, I took off, expecting a blur of my surroundings, but instead finding sharpness and clarity of every vase and decorated tapestry.

I didn't need wings. I had speed, and I was much faster than even a vampire. Instinctively, I turned left at a stairwell, breathing in the smell of sulfur and cinnamon on my father's clothes, and listened. His short, shallow breaths guided me in his direction, the flap of his wings beating against the air.

I met him in the gardens, the cold sinking into my arms, snaking a shiver down my spine, but I quickly adjusted, finding warmth within myself. Becoming immortal was invigorating, and I finally understood the allure.

Mist followed me as I strode over to him and heard my mother land behind us. The smell of rain hung fresh in the air. Leaves crisped under my feet as I walked to the stone bench. I smiled, delighting in the sensation from each crunch. Wind whistled through the stark trees, catching wisps of cobwebs and creaking branches.

My father's voice cut through the daze, his tone guided with unease. "You are not a vampire."

I smiled, looking him directly in the eye. "A keen observation, Father."

His jaw clenched, the muscles in his forearms bulged. "Do not take that tone with me. I am still your king."

Not for long.

My mom sat beside me, crossing her legs under her black dress. "What he means to say is, well, what are you?"

"Can't you see it?" he snapped, pacing in a circle, his hands clasped behind his back. "They gave her the elixir of immortality—without the curse of vampirism."

He was more intelligent than I gave him credit for. "Yes," I confirmed.

Only one question threaded in his expression, his lip twitching. "Why?"

"The gods wanted a true leader. You've not done a good job as king. They want me on the throne instead."

His nostrils flared, and he sped to me, arms outstretched. I darted out of his way before he could reach me. My mom's wings expanded outward as she forced herself in front of me, but I stepped out of her shadow. "You don't need to protect me. I'm stronger than him."

A trail of saliva glistened on his lip as he bared his teeth. "You are lying."

"I am not," I said simply. The shift in power filled me up. Never again would he lay a hand on my mom or tell me what to do. Challenge burned into me as he poised himself to fight, and I simply stood, unbothered by his stance. "The crown is rightfully mine, and you will hand it over, or…"

"Or what?"

"Or you'll die."

He stilled; even my mom tucked her wings behind her back, her jaw slack. "Olivia."

I whipped my head in her direction. "I told you not to call me that."

Sadness laced her features, softening them. "Seraphina, then," she choked out. "You wouldn't. You are no murderer."

"I am carrying out an order from the gods." I pressed my hands together, pursing my lips, trying not to show the regret bubbling inside. Killing was not something I was sure I even knew how to do or wanted to learn. It was commanded of me, but now that the time had come, I hesitated. He was my dad, after all. But the gods wanted this. Yet, my heart ached as I said the words.

He flung his arms out, hiccupping out a mocking laugh. "You can try, but what will you tell the court if you even succeeded? What makes you think they would take your word on behalf of the gods? The gods are not here and cannot hurt me, which is why they sent you. While you may be immortal, I have centuries of experience in the art of death, and you will not best me."

My mom looked from me to him, and back again, her eyes widening. "Stop this. Neither of you will hurt each other. This is ridiculous. It has to be a misunderstanding. Perhaps you heard them wrong."

"Why would you assume that?" I tilted my head at her. "Because I have been weak in your eyes my whole life? Because finally, I have more power than you—or him?" I pointed at my father, the tip of my finger shaking as my heart galloped. "They want me to rule Sanmorte, and you insult them and me by thinking there could be a misunderstanding. I was born into royalty, a secret you kept from me, and now I'm willing to accept my fate and rule."

He shook his head, the crown sliding down an inch. "You are almost twenty, naive to how the world or politics works, and disliked by most of the vampires in this castle. The gods may want you as queen, but the people of Sanmorte do not, and do you know what makes a king? Do you think it is just an anointment or a royal bloodline? Kings have risen from less. It is the people. They enjoy me as their ruler because I offer them what you will not." He clicked his tongue, glancing up at the lightening sky. "You may be strong, perhaps even stronger than me, but not even you can take on a kingdom of vampires and live." His eyes squinted, his nose scrunching as he closed the distance between us. "The world with gods is forgotten."

I clenched my teeth. "You worship them."

He wetted his lips. "It is an illusion. They can only reach us in death, but it is the realm of the living in which we live. Here, I am king and will not hand over the crown. Not even to my daughter. What you have done is high treason," he seethed.

"Sargon." My mom turned on her heel. "You will not threaten her with that. She is still our daughter and clearly is only following orders. It has nothing to do with her love for you."

I balled my fists. She was still trying to protect me against him. The gods gave an order, and he thought himself above them. They created this entire world, and all he had done was destroy what they had tried to mend.

Their sister's mistake had cost mortals. Salenia created the curse to punish her lover, and by doing so, had punished millions. How many families had been torn apart by vampires? How many lives ruined by being forced into this darkness without redemption—like Sebastian, who never wanted to become one? Now she was in the underworld, trapped in a prison she had made, and the gods were in another realm.

And I was alone.

I wasn't sure what I expected, but it wasn't this. Why would the court—or anyone else—believe me? Even if I could persuade some, it wouldn't be enough. Becoming queen would take away their ability to traffic people, something I was planning on putting an immediate stop to.

I hated to admit it, but my father was right. No one would accept me even if I did kill him. Why did I think they would care about the gods? They only worshiped them while they could live the life they wanted, and if that worship required sacrifice and discipline of their darker nature, they would throw those beliefs out.

Father spoke after letting out a long exhale. "I will not have your head, because they have clearly filled yours with nonsense. However, if you speak of this again or try anything stupid, I will lock you away and allow you an eternity of loneliness." He looked at my mom. "I won't kill my daughter, but I *will* punish her."

"Please," she begged. "Oli—I mean, Seraphina won't. I'll talk to her. This is a mistake. She'll be a good princess." She glanced at me. "Won't you, honey?"

I gritted my teeth, the rage in my fingers blending with my magic, wanting nothing more than to melt him into a puddle of skin and blood. But I couldn't be hasty. He made some excellent points, and I needed a pause. To stall a little. "Yes. I won't try anything."

He didn't respond, and I knew he didn't believe me, but he didn't call for me to leave and that was enough. I did not know what to do from here, and realizing I was in over my head, hurt. Suddenly, standing in the brisk air, I only cared about finding Sebastian.

EIGHTEEN

Sebastian

Howling wind tore through the mountain paths as I glided over them, my wings carrying me to colder heights. Glancing over my shoulder, I watched as the castle disappeared behind an ocean of evergreen and rocky peaks. Blinking away snowflakes, I exhaled sharply.

Pockets of air hit the insides of my wings, swerving me sideways. I propelled between mountains towering into the clouds, misting the tips from view.

Steadying myself, I flew with the gusts from the south, basking in the warmth of the sunrise. Glacier-blue lakes shone from below, carved between jagged edges and smooth rock, a deadly trap to any mortal who dared to try and escape the castle.

There was nothing but death behind the deceptive beauty of the deep waters below. Caverns carved from stone held rogue vampires—those who had left society, neither wanting to brave the aniccipere-ridden towns of the south or be a part of the debauchery of the City of Nightmares.

Stretches of undisturbed scenery continued for miles, bringing a false sense of freedom as I dipped, slowing before I hit a curve at the base of a mountain. Then, drifting down, I landed in a flurry of white.

Clenching my teeth, my gaze climbed the towering peaks. A shiver danced down my spine, but it wasn't the cold that bothered me. Thoughts of Olivia echoed in my mind, questions relentlessly poking unwantedly into the peace I craved.

She had gone with the king. But, of course, he wanted to show her off now that she was immortal, bestowed a gift from the gods that no one alive had ever seen before. Neither vampire nor sorceress of a god, but a mix between them. I recalled the smell of the cloying elixir—which the goddess had once given her lover to make him immortal—clinging to Olivia when she approached me after awakening. It was in my veins along with every other vampire. Except ours was mixed with a curse—an unending bloodlust, heightened emotions, and the allure to delve into the darkness.

The gods had removed the threat of death, giving her an eternity of life. They allowed her to keep her magic, along with other mortal luxuries. I half-expected to envy her, but I only felt relief. Suddenly, all I cared about was her. Her soul consumed every part of me, feeling unlike anything I'd ever experienced. It was as if I was wearing my heart on the outside of my body.

I sucked in a deep breath, tucking my wings behind my back as ice crunched under my shoes. Finally, I found an edge to sit on, surrounded by nothing, and loosed a sigh.

She was my soulmate. There was no other explanation, no matter how much I tried to find another. She deserved better than that, and yet, I was her soulmate. Destined long before either of us ever came to the world.

Closing my eyes against the stark white, I focused on the threads of uncertainty and shock coursing through me. My shoulders tensed as the flap of wings sounded through the whistles of wind. Jumping to my feet, I looked up, blinking away flakes of snow resting on my eyelashes. A bold silhouette blocked out a ray of sunlight dappled by the clouds. The figure slowed their flight, drifting down to where I stood.

A mess of silver hair flung behind him, and I breathed a sigh of relief as Zach landed in front of me. "I thought I might find you hiding out here."

I rubbed my forehead, settling myself back onto the iced mountain edge. "I needed a moment…"

"To think?" he finished. "Yes, I figured."

"Alone," I said, my tone harsher than I wanted. His silver eyes shone as they reflected the blanket of snow under our feet. "Olivia," I said breathily. "I think she's my soulmate."

"I could have told you that, brother."

My lips curved a hint. We weren't siblings by blood, but there was no other word to describe what Zach was to me. "How long did you know?"

"It was obvious. You were both so absorbed with your schemes and brooding you couldn't see it." His expression remained stoic, but a glint of humor danced on the edge of his lips.

"I wasn't brooding."

He arched a thin eyebrow, a smirk creasing his skin. "Let's call it self-loathing then."

I buried my head in my hands, removing my gaze from his incredulous stare. "How did you know Levian was yours?" I asked, recalling the stories of Zach's former partner before he died.

"As you know, I didn't before he was turned. Immortality heightens everything, especially a soulmate connection. Looking back, I knew he was special while he was mortal, and had I known more about soulmates, I might have guessed. But after he became a vampire, it was unlike anything I'd experienced before." His eyebrows pinched together as he looked at the snow, glassy-eyed. "He felt like home. I could no longer deny the pull between us. At first, he consumed me. It wasn't always easy. He challenged me unlike any other."

"That's how I feel," I admitted, my heart hollowing. "She deserves better."

He scoffed. "Brother, you think so little of yourself, I can't stand it. While she may be kind, Olivia isn't without her many flaws."

"You've never liked her."

"It's not that." He fumbled with his fingers. "She's just young. Barely twenty. She doesn't know the world yet, and you know how I feel about dramatics."

I opened my mouth to argue, but smirked instead.

"She's growing stronger," he intoned. "I've been watching from the shadows."

"Of course, you have." I glanced up at the sky. "And yes, she is. Especially now that she's an immortal."

"The gods saw her worthy. That's good enough for me."

My eyebrows flicked up. "I'm glad, and she has a good heart."

"She does, but please don't discount yourself. You're fiercely protective, loyal, and you know, sometimes you make people laugh."

"Ah, so you finally admit I'm funny."

He chuckled softly. "I said sometimes," he pointed out, then sighed. "She's lucky to have you."

The thoughts of how I ripped out those guards' hearts, still haunted me. She'd hate me if she knew what I did. I was a murderer and had given into my darker desires too many times. She didn't see that side of me. The part where I'd attended sex parties, and fucked my way through half of Sanmorte to avoid feeling anything after my family was killed.

"I don't even know how we found each other. There are millions of people in the world, and she was…"

"The girl you kidnapped?"

I laughed. Gods, it sounded terrible when he said it like that. "I mean, yes."

He shook his head with a small smile. "It was fated to happen. You both hide from the same destiny, forced into a life you don't want. You live in the same darkness, and your souls were going to find each other."

"*Soulmates.*" I let out a long exhale, fogging the air in front of me. "What does it even mean?"

"I researched everything I could about it after I met Levian. I sought sorcerers, read old books. From everything I gathered, soulmates recognize each other from another realm. Wherever it is our souls reside before this place."

"With the gods?"

"Beyond that. Even in my old age, there's still so much that remains a mystery to me. All I know is there are so many planes in the afterlife, but the wheres and whats, I could not tell you."

"So that's it?" I arched a brow. "We were together before this life."

"Sort of. There are shadow parts of ourselves we must learn to embrace and heal before we are whole. It's called shadow work, and your soulmate is the person who will travel alongside you while you navigate life. They agreed to help you grow and become the best version of yourself. Imagine shadow work as a dark ocean. It's easy to drown. Your soulmate is that small boat you can seek refuge in. It doesn't mean the water from the ocean won't get in, but they will give you peace in the storm. It's a mutual contract made in the stars of love, unity, and growth."

"Fuck. I wish I had the amount of faith you do in all of that."

He snorted a laugh. "You don't have much choice but to now, brother."

NINETEEN

Olivia

I curled my fingers around the edge of the smooth stone edge of the wall and glanced at the drawbridge as it was lowered. Creaking wood screeched into my ears, and I refocused my senses onto the steady droplets of rain crashing against the grounds.

I let out a tense breath, peering out to the mountains silhouetting against the sun, blocking any warmth trying to make its way to the castle.

It was strange to see buses coming up to the castle, a reminder of the modern world I'd left behind. Sanmorte was stuck in the Middle Ages while the rest of the kingdoms had technologically advanced, leaving us vulnerable to threats of war. Sometimes, the two met, I found missed things like watching movies and scrolling through my phone.

Wheels growled over the leaf-carpeted winding road, and I craned my neck to see through the grimy windows. My father sped up next to me, his hands landing inches from mine on the wall.

"Good. The mortals are here," he stated, answering my unasked question. "We need to replenish our supply."

My fingers flexed, shoulders tensing, but I didn't dare refute him. I'd threatened to dethrone and kill him less than an hour ago. I was lucky to still have my head. Apparently, even having the gods on my side didn't mean shit in this wasteland of blood and sex. I wanted to scream at him; if we had to have mortals here, why not instead command the vampires to feed and then heal, instead of killing them?

I stepped back, snapping a twig under my foot. "Are they from the City of Nightmares, or were they brought in from another kingdom?"

Kidnapped is what I wanted to say.

"They're from the city. I need mortals who are already familiar with us and know the rules. They can work in the kitchens and play the part. The rest can go into the dungeons until the Aslandians are gone. The king arrives tomorrow, and I won't have us looking foolish."

That would be difficult with you as our king.

I glanced sideways at Sargon. His jaw was set, the vein in his temple throbbing. Tentatively, I reached my powers out and felt the sting of anger pulse into me. I couldn't leave things like this, not if I wanted to do right by the god's wishes. I, unlike him, worshipped them. Especially considering it would be their realms I walked in the afterlife, once I was ready to leave immorality behind.

I'd never been one for the long game, always rushing into things without thinking, but I couldn't succumb to impatience this time. He was right; I wouldn't be able to persuade a kingdom of unruly vampires to accept me as their queen if I killed their king, and made them agree to new laws.

Swallowing my pride, I pressed my lips tight, and entangled my fingers together. "I've reflected on what you said." He arched an auburn eyebrow, but said nothing, so I continued. "What they were asking of me was unfair. Sanmorte has flourished under your leadership."

"Don't lie." His words cut through me like a knife. I stilled, my hair waving in the breeze as we stared out over the long road leading through an ocean of trees up to the mountains. "Nobody changes their mind so easily when you had much to say an hour prior about how awful a king you believed me to be. You are my blood, and I know when I'm being manipulated."

Rage consumed each word, smothering anything else I'd planned to say. What is it he wanted? What would he believe?

I reached out again, my magic spreading like arms outward, curling into him, feeling his emotions. Closing my eyes, I found the thing I was looking for.

It matched the pain I'd felt countless times when Astor and I were together, and I would catch him betraying yet another promise. It lowered my self-esteem, and I felt the same ache in my father. I'd hurt him.

Opening my eyes to the stark white, I breathed fog into the air. "I'm sorry." Droplets of rain clung to my dress as dark clouds formed overhead. A storm was coming, and I could see two sets of wings in the distance as vampires made their way back to court. "I wouldn't have been able to kill you. It's why I didn't attack. It felt wrong because, despite everything, you are my dad."

A pang of something shot through him, but I was pushed out before I could feel it properly. His expression softened a little, and I noticed a gloss in his eyes I hadn't seen before. Neither of us moved, standing like statues. The bus of mortals finally reached the drawbridge and let out a deflated whoosh as it pulled up and braked.

"Let me teach you." He gestured for me to follow as he strode to the opening doors of the bus. "You're the princess now and need to know how things work."

My heart swelled as relief took over. He may not have responded, but his silence was answer enough. For a man with little compassion, there was love in there. It was just tucked away, and it was for me. Sebastian had told me that Sargon became obsessive, to the point of frantic paranoia with my mom and me as an infant. It was toxic, scary, but it was driven by love, and on some base level, I could understand it. Even if I didn't agree with his actions at all.

It was going to make it harder to murder him one day.

"This is the latest crop," a beefy man with a thick mustache told my father. One by one, people emptied through the doors. Chains dragged over the uneven ground as cuffed mortals trudged into the castle, the liquor-tainted scent from blood dens still on their skin.

Sargon stepped forward, evaluating each of them with a tilted head and a bored expression. He pointed out a gaunt woman and a man with a thick mop of brown hair. "Those two can go straight into the dungeons with the others. Lead the others into the kitchens. We need more staff with the King of Asland's arrival tomorrow."

The man nodded and grabbed one mortal's arms who'd paused for breath against a wall. "You're slowing the others," he growled, and my heart skipped a beat. Their accusing eyes glided over me as the last of them made their way through the doors.

Draven stepped out, the muscles in his arms bulging as he balled his fists, staring after the mortals. Erianna walked out after, bowing her head in our direction, whereas Draven just grabbed the hilt of his sword.

The king glanced away from them, his disapproving gaze moving to mine. "Do not stay long with your friends. We have work to do."

I nodded. "Of course, Father." I tried but failed to keep the clipped tone from my voice.

He paused, unsaid words teetering on his lips, but left before he could express them.

Once they were gone, and the smell of disappointment and depression had disappeared with them, I sucked in a deep breath. Draven walked to me slowly, his eyes unblinking. "You're not a vampire."

"Just immortal," I said with a small smile. "I was given the same elixir from the story you told me about Salenia and her lover, Vener."

He looked me up and down, pausing on my lips, his brow lowering. "You seem the same, but there are differences."

I shrugged, a tendril of regret coiling around my core. "All my imperfections are gone."

His frown deepened. "They weren't imperfections."

"Draven…" I hesitated. Sargon said I would need to kill Draven after the ceremony, to turn him into a vampire. It was an agreement I had no plans on fulfilling. "I've been thinking, and you need to leave," I said, lowering my voice to a whisper. I raised a brow at Erianna, and she nodded. "The king will not wait long before he expects me to fulfill my obligations."

"No." He stood taller, the muscle in his jaw feathering. "You are not a vampire, and therefore cannot turn me. He must understand that."

"He will still want you to be a vampire, even if it is done by someone else."

Erianna's breath hitched. Knowing threaded between us, and she turned to face him. "Olivia's right. The king will not want a mortal in his guard. So unless you want to become a feeding bag, you should go. We can help you escape."

Concern wrinkled his forehead. I closed my eyes, breathing in the scent of his honey shampoo. He had been a part of my life for so long, and I'd hoped I could keep him here if I became queen, but that was no longer an option. Even if I somehow took the crown, he would still be a mortal amongst evil. I was only surprised he'd made it this long without dying.

"Liv."

My stomach dipped. "Please don't argue. You know I'm right. It's only so long before one of them gets hungry and decides you're the closest snack. I couldn't bear it if they…" I trailed off as disturbed images of his broken, blood-drained body floated in my mind.

Erianna chimed in. "Sebastian and Zach can fly you out of here. We can get enough stagma to buy you passage back to Baldoria. The guild will take care of you from there. They've been searching for you, and Ravena."

I pinched my eyelids shut to prevent the tears from forming. His leaving was the right thing for him, and my care for his safety far outweighed my selfish desire to keep my friend with me. "Please, Draven."

He closed the distance between us, grabbing my wrist, his pleading gaze boring into mine. "We can go together." He glanced at Erianna before looking back at me. "All of us. Let's get out of this place."

A sob hiccupped in my throat. "I have to stay."

"You don't."

"I do." I pressed my thumb against his hand, loosening his grasp, easing a pace back. "The gods have given me a task. One I must remain here to do."

A laugh of disbelief fell from his mouth. "You can't be serious? We are surrounded by monsters." He arched a brow at Erianna. "Except for you."

She rolled her eyes and focused her attention on me. "He will leave. I will ensure it. It is for the best." How she remained so determined in the face of everything strengthened my resolve. I could taste the desire she held for Draven, but I didn't let on that I knew.

He looked from me to her. "Don't I get a say in this? I've always protected you, Liv. Now what? I'm supposed to leave you here to fend off these monsters?"

I threw my arms around him, capturing his every scent, and committed them to memory. "You've always been there for me, but it's time for you to start your own chapter now—without me."

"You don't understand. There are things I need to tell you."

Goosebumps spread over my arms as he held tighter. His hot breath hit my temple, and I leaned into his shoulder, tears forming. I knew what he wanted to say. I'd felt it for years, but ignored it. Now was not the time for confessions, and I wouldn't permit him, or Erianna, to any unnecessary complication of feelings. "Sebastian is my soulmate," I admitted, saying the words aloud for the first time since I thought them. "He will protect me."

Draven's shoulders slumped, his whimpered sigh sending a ripple of sadness into me. He pulled back, taking me at arms lengths. Consumed by his gaze, I held my next breath. The wind whistled around us, drizzling rain, slicking everything in a gloss. He opened his mouth, his fingers pressing gently against me. "Do you love him?"

The hairs on the back of my neck raised. Droplets of rain caught on my lip and eyelashes, and I blinked them away. "That… That does not matter. He is my soulmate."

"You are certain?"

"Nothing else can explain how I felt when I woke up."

"But do you love him?"

I sighed, releaszing he would never let me go. Without Sebastian or anything else, maybe I would have ended up with Draven in a different life. I supposed I loved him, but in a different way. He was attractive, and I'd not given it a chance, but I couldn't think about it now. Not at the end. I let out a long exhale, hearing the beating of wings flapping against the wind from behind us. Probably those vampire visitors from earlier. I would not let it interrupt our goodbye.

"I love Sebastian," I said, so he would let me go.

His hands dropped to his side, and he nodded slowly. Wings slowed, and the crunch of shoes hitting the ground slammed into my ears. I turned slowly to Erianna and saw Sebastian in my peripheral vision. My eyes widened, my heart racing into a gallop. Erianna's lips stretched as she whistled air between her teeth, her expression matching my mortifying realization that Sebastian had to have heard that.

If he did, he didn't let on. "Hi."

I forced a smile. "Sebastian." I looked at him, and then at Zach, whose smirk told me at least he'd heard. "Zach. I didn't realize you were out flying."

Zach shoved his hands in his pockets. "Sebastian needed to do some soul searching."

Sebastian shot him a glare, and my cheeks heated.

Erianna took Draven's hand and pulled him away. "We can make arrangements."

I reached out for Draven. "Wait."

Erianna shook her head. "You'll have time to say goodbye later." She glanced from me to Sebastian and back. "You two should talk first. You know, actually communicate."

Zach blew out a long breath, following Erianna and Draven. "That'll be a first."

As he passed me, I gave Zach an extra hateful glance, then wiped the rain from my face. Drizzle turned to thick droplets, and strands of hair stuck to my cheeks and neck. My stomach whooshed as a large, black wing stole the light from the sun, shielding me from the rain. His heat lured me closer, his scent pinching my eyes shut as his arm brushed against mine.

Suddenly, nothing else mattered.

His arm slipped around my waist, curling me into his arms. "Come, Princess," he whispered in my ear. "Let's go talk."

TWENTY

Niall

Women surrounded me, mortals waiting to be fed on. But they weren't what I was searching for. They were a taste of the hidden, merely objects to stare at on the way to falling further into obsession.

Gwen sat with her boyfriend. He leaned forward, shoulders slumped as he tried to engage deeper into conversation over a glass of blood, but she wasn't focused on him. Instead, her gaze flitted around the room, her mind elsewhere. A smirk danced over my mouth.

I had intrigued her, and I wanted to bet her eyes hadn't truly looked at Astor since. Or I hoped. Rage clawed at my chest, waiting to be unleashed on the pair of them. I didn't want to care, yet she was so far embedded in my thoughts, there was little room for anything else.

Pinching my eyes shut, I pressed my thumb against my lips, an echo of feeling her against them. She'd only kissed me once, before I'd flown from this castle to forget her, but she haunted me in every woman I saw since. Whenever lavender bloomed, or a hint of vanilla reached me, she was brought back to life through the memory of her scent.

Averting my gaze, I stepped out of the room before they could see me watching. My stomach dipped, and I shook my head, refocusing my thoughts. I had a new desire now. The crown, and the princess who'd give it to me. Gwen wasn't going to screw me again, not like before.

Half a century passed me before I cared what anyone thought of me. Until I met her. I had been in the castle for mere weeks after Kalon finally brought me here to meet Sargon. His disapproval of his brother's adoption of me had finally dissolved, and I was welcomed to live just outside the royal ranks. Not a noble, or one of them. I was an outsider, but I made a name for myself quickly. Everyone learned to bow to me without a title or induce my wrath. Political schemes earned me a place in the war meetings, and my ability to read people pushed me close to the top. Especially when the Blood Brothers rose from nothing. Adrian—my ancient friend—helped me build the club.

I felt people out, especially the nobles. Some called it manipulation. I called it survival. I invested my father's wealth into those I saw becoming somebody and reaped the benefits. I had hundreds of friendships formed under a pretense of who I was to them.

Then there was Gwen.

I met her in the ballroom. Smiling across the room, eyes burning into mine, she consumed me from the beginning. Her doe-eyes blinked slowly when she walked over to me that day. I couldn't look away from how her hips swayed, her confidence in each step, and her siren gaze. At first, it was purely physical. That quickly changed. Her wit, understanding, and lust for life lured me like a moth to a flame. She saw through me, mostly because we hid in the same darkness.

I'd never been on the receiving end of being manipulated before, and I never would be again. The feeling of being with her chipped away at my resolve and heart. We'd never even fucked, yet Gwen had stolen the parts of me I'd kept buried since I'd turned.

I hated her for it, and yet she remained the very thing I desired more than anything else. Even the crown. Not that I'd admit it to anyone, especially her.

Losing myself was the worst consequence of Gwen. I strayed so far that it took me a long time to find my way back to myself.

"Adrian!" I shouted as my old friend approached me, then placed his arm around me, patting me twice on the shoulder before stepping a pace back.

"Niall, I heard you were back. I just got here a couple of hours ago. Looks like I missed the ceremony. We have a new princess, I'm told."

The corner of my lip lifted. "Yes, and she is a beauty."

He ran his hand through his blond hair, his smile dimpling his cheeks. He and I had always gotten on the best out of everyone else here. He may have been the only person I had who I actually enjoyed. But, like me, he had a taste for the reckless. "Still wearing suits, I see."

He brushed down the front of his immaculate blazer, then adjusted the collar of his shirt. "Some of us have taste."

I let out a low chuckle, peering around him at the hordes of late-rising vampires making their way to the feeding room. "Hungry?"

He wetted his lips. "Always. Know of any quieter spots?"

I grinned, rubbing my hands together. Before I'd left, he and I were the real princes of this court. Self-made men who bowed to no one, respected by everyone. Even the king had taken a liking to Adrian over the years. We had our secret club, invite only, for the more affluent people in the castle. There, we had 'quiet spots', just rooms made to hold the most attractive, best tasting mortals for the pleasure of our club members. Everyone knew about the 'Blood Brothers'. At one point, everyone desired to become a member. Until Gwen fucked it all up.

"Not yet, but I met a girl, Alana, in the feeding room. She would be perfect."

He shoved his hands in his pockets, wrinkling his ironed pants. "I hope they've not all sunk their teeth into her already. You know how I feel about used goods."

"She tastes good, takes care of herself somehow. Comes on command."

He blew out a long exhale, his lips spreading into a grin. "Let's get her out of there then." He glared after the nobles falling into the feeding room, and his nostrils flared.

"There's this other woman, too, from Asland. Sebastian Vangard was feeding on her the other day."

Adrian clicked his tongue, rolling his eyes up to the high ceiling. "Fucking Vangard. Does he still think he's better than everyone else?"

I raised my brows, sucking the inside of my lip between my teeth. "Yeah, and he's 'Your Highness' now."

He slid his pale blue eyes to the windows, his eyelashes fluttering against a twitch. "You've got to be kidding?"

"It's all right, he won't be a prince for long."

Adrian's eyes widened, a cruel smile curling up one side of his face. "I sense we need to have a catch up over some negative O."

***

I glided my tongue over the last of Alana's blood, then slumped her against the sofa as she finally lost consciousness. Adrian dropped the Aslandian girl Sebastian had fed on before on the ornate rug. Her tanned skin appeared paler under the dappled blue light seeping into the large living quarters. He pulled out a crimson stained silk handkerchief, and dabbed the corners of his mouth, careful not to get a drop of blood on his white shirt. He threw his blazer on the back of a chair, then rolled up his sleeves.

"Now we've eaten, do you want a drink?" He gestured to the mirrored tray of whiskey and scotch on the wooden bar.

"Scotch."

He stood, and walked to the stools, reaching up to grab two glasses hanging above the wood countertop. He brought them, and the bottle of dark brown liquid with him, placing them on the table between us. "Tell me everything I've missed."

"Ah, a hundred and seventy years old." I waved the bottle, smirking. "This scotch is almost as ancient as your ass."

He pressed his shoe against the side of her head, tilting the Aslandian girl's face upward. "Do you think they realize how unfortunate they are? They always act as if they're better than us, and yet, this one must be in her mid-twenties and she's already a blood bitch."

"That's why they come here, friend," I replied as he removed the underside of his shoe from her cheek. "Trying to obtain immortality."

He scoffed and poured himself a drink. "Idiots." He kicked his legs up on the table, crossing them. "Tell me more about our princess."

"Seraphina." Her name felt like butter on my tongue. "She's a true immortal. Not a vampire."

He leaned forward slowly, moving his feet back to the ground. "You're certain? How is that possible?"

"I wasn't sure at first what she was, but it's the only thing that makes sense. It happened when she passed over and saw the gods. There are whispers, too, all around the castle, that Sargon is jealous of his daughter. A servant saw them fighting in the courtyard."

He shook his head. "And she married Vangard?"

My smirk fell into a frown. I fucking hated that name. "Like I said, he'll be gone soon."

"I'm telling you, I won't bow to that idiot. There are not enough gods in the heavens to make me."

"Patience, friend. Good things come to those who wait."

His shoulders relaxed, and he poured himself a second drink. We'd hated Sebastian since he snubbed us in front of the entire court a couple of years ago, tearing our invitation with a smirk on his face. The desire to be in the club slowly waned after that, as he ruined our reputation. But, then, all it took was for Gwen to come along and break down any respect anyone had left for us. That was another thing. "Gwendolyn is here."

The glass shattered in his hand, sending ringing through my skull. Blinking slowly, I glanced at the shards of glass covering the girl's hair and part of the rug, pointing up with trickles of vampire blood in the fibers. "Her."

"She's with her mom, and she has Kalon's protection," I reminded him as he jumped to his feet.

"I want her dead."

"So do I."

He brushed specks of glass from his shirt and growled under his breath. "You don't have the stomach to kill her. She had you wrapped around her finger last time, so don't mind me if I don't believe you."

"A year has passed."

"A year is nothing when you love someone."

Heat rose through my stomach and chest, burning adrenaline into my arms. "Don't mistake infatuation for love. I do not and never did love her. She hurt me just as much as she broke you."

"She took everything from me! My reputation, my business, my wealth, because you let her close enough."

"I thought we solved our issues before I left?"

He shrugged. "I don't hold it against you." He let out a breathy sigh. "You slipped up. Women will do that to you. I've been in love once. I know how much it can cloud a powerful man's head. Even ones like us." He looked over at the window, lost in a memory of someone who no longer existed. Rain pattered against the window, thunder shaking the pane as the sky grew darker. Obsidian clouds blotted the horizon, flashing purple streaks across the heavens. "What's your plan?"

"Regarding Gwen?"

"No." He faced me, caution lacing his stare. "Stay away from her. I'll deal with her in time, but I want you nowhere near the whore."

"Adrian," I warned.

He sat back down, drinking straight from the bottle before wiping his lips. "I'm only saying for your own good. Gwendolyn is a seductress; she'll lure you in again. I know you're strong, and I'd trust you with anyone else, but I can't see you hurt again. She broke everything you built. Don't forget that."

I leaned back into the cushions. "I don't want to be around her anyway. My desires have shifted."

He arched a brow. "Do tell."

"Seraphina is the rightful blood heir to the throne. With Sargon gone, it would go to her."

"If Kalon lets her live that long."

I shrugged. "I know his movements. I'll thwart his plans from within."

"And why would you do that?" he asked with a tilt of his head.

"Because I plan on making her my bride."

He laughed, choking on a swig of scotch. "You're kidding, right? She's married."

"Yes, but Sebastian is disposable. Once dead, I'll let her grieve. Divorce may not be allowed in Sanmorte, but you *can* remarry if your spouse dies."

"You intend to widow her." He raised his pale brows. "I assume you have thought of a way to do this."

"Yes, but…" I ran my hand through my hair, pulling the strands over to one side of my neck. "He's her soulmate."

"Oh, damn. How do you know?" He kicked away a shard of glass.

"I've met several couples who are. They acted just the same. I could sense the connection between them. You know how it is. Soulmates usually realize after they become immortal and as soon as she awoke, she looked at him differently than before."

"Well then, it seems we have our work cut out."

"We?"

"You wouldn't be telling me all this if you didn't want my help. I know you, Niall. Besides, having a prince as my ally wouldn't be the worst thing."

A grin spread over my face. "I think it's time to bring back the Blood Brothers Club."

"Just in time for the King of Asland to come."

I poured a glass, then lifted it. He clinked the bottle against it, and we both drank. "To new allies."

"And old enemies."

TWENTY-ONE

Sebastian

"You seem troubled, love," I said as I placed her in front of our bedroom door.

Her red eyebrows pinched together, her doe-like gaze refusing to meet mine. "Did you hear what I said outside, when you and, uh, Zach landed?"

Of course, I did. I'd thought of nothing since.

Breathing in her warm vanilla scent, I closed the distance between us, then tucked a lock of hair behind her ear. Her next breath caught in her throat as my fingers touched her skin, and she closed her eyes. My stomach dropped, the chaos in my soul silenced by those three words. Words I wanted to hear again. "Yes."

"You didn't say anything before."

I exhaled gently, my breath hitting her forehead. "Everyone was there, love. You were upset, and I wanted us to be alone." I swept my lips closer, losing myself in her smell, her breaths, her sound of her quickening heart. I wrapped my hand around the back of her neck, a soft growl erupting up my torso. "Did you mean it?"

"D-Draven," she stumbled, "he, um, he wasn't going to leave. He wanted to know if I love you."

Do you? I wanted to ask, but my question remained strangled in my throat. *Say something.* The silence was suffocating.

She choked out a sob. "I told him I love you."

My heart leaped. Her guided gaze met mine, her lips gently parting. I didn't move a muscle; I wasn't sure why. I didn't do those three words—never had—but as I stood there, I'd never felt trust like that, despite everything we had lied to each other about. It was like I *knew* her. As my soulmate, I supposed I did.

She loves me?

"Sebastian?" Her throat bobbed, her fingers curling around my hand before pulling away. "Well?"

I stood stunned, listening to the clock's second hand ticking down.

After a minute, she sighed. "I just told him that," she finally admitted. "So he would let me go. I need him to leave the castle. He's in danger here."

She pushed the door open, and I tucked my wings behind my back, swallowing the truth that slid like lead into my stomach. She didn't love me. Of course, she didn't. Perhaps we weren't soulmates, and I'd mixed something up. Even Zach was wrong at times. I held my breath as I followed her into our bedroom, an attempt to suffocate the pang of pain slicing through me.

Shoving my hands in my pockets, I stood by the windows. "Good," I finally said, but it wasn't. "Now Draven can let you go."

The sky grumbled, gathering ink blot clouds over the trees and mountains, shrouding the sun. Rain beat against the glass, pounding through the awkward quiet. The last of the orange rays kissed the horizon, disappearing completely behind a darkness prevailing in a fog of matte black.

Heaving out a breath, I moved my eyes back to Olivia. She was just as beautiful in death as she was in life. Her emerald gaze burned into me, her arms splaying out to her sides as she sat on the bed, knocking one of the tiny cushions onto the floor. I almost smiled. "Love?"

"Don't call me that!" she snapped, sending an icy chill washing through me. Her stare seared into mine, her face twisting into a scowl. "Stop calling me 'love' all the time."

Hesitating in my response, I tipped my head to the side. What happened to our touches just moments ago? She'd never hated me calling her that before. Clearly, I was mistaken.

Tears glossed her eyes. She lifted her chin, clenching her jaw before a single one could fall. "Just stop."

"Okay." I took a careful step closer. "You seem upset."

"Nice observation skills, genius."

I jolted an inch, halting mid walk. "Did I do something wrong?"

Throwing her hands up, she stood from the bed. "No. You did nothing wrong."

"Lo—Olivia." I stopped myself. "What's bothering you?"

"Suddenly, you care?" Her fists balled. "Just… it's nothing."

"You've always been terrible at hiding your emotions."

She clenched her jaw, and a tear trickled down her cheek. "You know, apparently we're soulmates."

"I heard the same. It's crazy, right?"

She gave me an incredulous look, her glare knife-like. "Yes, it is because there is no way we are!" She stormed out before I could say anything, then slammed the door behind her.

What the fuck just happened?

Several minutes later, Erianna came flying through the door, speeding up to me until we were mere inches apart. "Olivia's crying. She's gone downstairs."

I put my hands in the air, taking a step back. "Yeah. She just lost her shit out of nowhere. Probably the heightened emotions. I know she's not a vampire, but there must be similarities in becoming immortal."

Erianna rolled her eyes. "Seriously? Men can be so fucking oblivious sometimes."

"What is with all the hate today?" I pressed my back against the wall.

"She was waiting for you to tell her you love her, too. Idiot."

"No." My eyebrows pinched downward. "She told me she just said that so Draven would leave."

"She said that immediately, did she? Or was there silence?"

"Well, yeah, I mean. But, look, I was processing."

She loosed a sigh and paced away from me. "Seriously? She told you she loved you, and you stayed silent."

I arched a brow. "You were eavesdropping."

Her cheeks flushed. "No. Well, I came to relay a message from the king, and it was hard not to hear."

"Some things never change."

She inched closer to the dagger on her thigh. "Don't play with me."

"I'm not. This is all ridiculous. She just told me there is no way we could be soulmates."

"She was saving what little pride she had left." Finally, she sat on the sofa by the unlit fire, drumming her fingers on the arm. "So, do you?"

"Do I what?"

She shot me a look. "You know what."

"I—" My stomach dropped, and I walked to the small cabinet where I'd stored the whiskey. I was going to need a drink for this conversation. Slowly, I poured a glass, knowing better than to ask Erianna if she wanted one. I don't think I'd ever seen her drink.

She clicked her tongue as I sat across from her. "Sebastian Vangard stuck for words. I never thought I'd see the day."

"Zach said we're soulmates."

"Yes?" she said, as if it were obvious.

"You think we are?"

She sighed as she pressed her fingers against her temples, muttering under her breath. "I do, but what matters is do *you* think you are?"

I swallowed a gulp, the alcohol burning in my throat as I tasted the subtle hints of honey and nutmeg. Then, placing the glass on the mantle, I leaned against the fireplace. "It doesn't matter. Look, Olivia would tell me if she loved me."

She scoffed a laugh, pulling her braids over one shoulder. "Ah, yes, because it's so easy to communicate matters of the heart, as you are clearly demonstrating right now."

"It's complicated."

"These things usually are. Gods, do I have to spell it out for you, Seb? She loves you."

Butterflies swarmed in my stomach, my heart swelling at the words. Closing my eyes, I basked in the feeling, but doubt trickled in. "You can't know that. She deserves better. Why would she love me?"

"If I have to hear this one more time, I swear, I'm going to throw you out that window."

The storm picked up speed, hammering against the windows and walls like an enemy trying to barge in. "Where is she?" I asked.

"Gone to see Draven. He's leaving tomorrow. In fact, you'll be helping get him out of here."

I exhaled a shaky breath and poured myself a second drink. "I'll talk to her later, then. I don't want to interrupt their time. It'll be hard for him to let her go. He loves her, too."

"He does, doesn't he?" She lowered her head. "He's a good man. I'll miss him."

"Wow."

"Don't," she warned.

I put my hands up again, then drank my drink. "I won't force you to talk about your feelings." Under my breath, I mumbled. "Unlike some people."

"Heard that."

"I know." I swallowed the second glass, already reaching for the third. The gentle buzz clouded my mind, a welcome relief from the unending swirl of thoughts matching the clouds outside. *Love. Soulmates.* The words were soon swallowed by the intoxication humming through me.

TWENTY-TWO

Olivia

I tossed and turned all night as Sebastian slept soundly beside me until the morning sun peeked through the windows. He was asleep when I'd returned to the room after running out of it hours before.

His light snores crawled agitation over my skin. I moved onto my side, puffing out my cheeks. The awful truth kept sinking back in, no matter how much I tried to fight away the thoughts.

He doesn't love me.

Slowly, I lifted my fingers, massaging my temples to calm my racing mind. Why did those words sting so much, especially when he'd made it clear time and time again that he didn't want this marriage and only went through with it because he had no choice? But there were moments when we touched, kissed—when we had sex—that I felt something from him. Even with his barriers up against my ability, I could have sworn I felt affection slip through. Yet, when he heard those three words fall from my lips, he said nothing. I saved face, pretending I didn't mean it, but I don't know if he bought it. Either way, I'd driven him into an alcohol-fueled coma.

Sleep would not save me from my anxiety. My brain was far too active to get any shuteye. My eyelids closed against the soft hue of morning arrowing through the gap in the drapes. I savored the last seconds of comfort and curled in the blankets, rubbing my feet against the soft cotton. Then I stood.

I cast my eyes over my shoulder, and my heart swelled. He reached out across the space of the bed in his sleep. His eyebrows pulled down as a grunt left his mouth. I waited until I was sure he was in a deep sleep before creeping across the floor.

I didn't realize how I felt about him until I said the words out loud. As soon as I spoke them, everything clicked into place. The story of us flitted into my mind, and I tried to read between the lines so I could understand when I'd fallen for him. Maybe it was how he just accepted me, from the beginning. Even when he was an asshole, I'd found him amusing. Although, I'd covered it up. He was kind and always made me laugh. There was a sense of home when I lay in his arms, and for a moment, all I wanted was to feel his hold on me.

To hear those three words whispered back.

Resentment built in my soul, which he didn't deserve. He wasn't required to feel the same way I did. Yet, the pain of my unrequited love burned deeper than I thought possible.

Astor abandoned me, too, and I wondered if I was truly that unlovable? The sunrise soaked me in warmth as the orange blur slipped over the misted mountains in the distance.

I sat on the sofa, curling my legs against my chest. I reminisced about fading memories of Astor and me, realizing I'd created a fantasy of him in my head. Now, I couldn't believe I didn't see it.

I'd believed in our love story so much that I convinced myself that I somehow deserved every painful thing he did. When I caught myself thinking how stupid that was, I instead trusted he would change. It was a vicious circle I was trapped in, like a fly in the middle of a spider's web.

I didn't know how it felt to be accepted and cherished until I met Sebastian and Erianna. They never made me feel unworthy, and they treated me with respect. The illusion of Astor shattered when I'd learned of what he'd become, and how he'd done it.

The stark horror that he was capable of handing over his friends at the guild, and to put his mom and me through suffocating grief was enough to harden my heart against him. To realize the version of him I had adored was just that—the version I wanted to see. It wasn't true, and now I wondered if I'd done the same with Sebastian, but differently? Perhaps I'd found more meaning in his touches than was there. Maybe I'd mistaken the tender moments for something more. I longed for him, and now I felt like an idiot.

Shaking my head as if to scatter the thoughts of him, I stood. A slight click echoed through my bones as I stretched my arms. Every part of me ached, which was ironic considering I was immortal now, and every movement felt lighter than air. But I felt like I was wading through water as I dressed and walked down to the breakfast room, rounding the corners until I found my destination.

Fortunately, my ability to eat food had remained, thanks to the gods. My stomach rumbled despite my nausea, and the only thing keeping me going was the thought of a plate of waffles covered with syrup.

Gold drapes were slathered over the walls of the feeding room. Even the chandeliers had been dusted and polished, scattering shimmers of light. The privacy tents were gone, with only splatters of blood clinging to stone as a reminder they'd ever been there.

The long tables had been replaced with new ones. I hurried to the windows, smelling the faints stink of smoke as the wood was set ablaze of the old, crimson stained furniture stained with venom and cum.

Alongside the burning evidence in the courtyard were the last of the dead mortals, joining the pillar of smoke into a cloud hovering around the castle. Slowly blinking, I stepped back, twisting myself to see the room. It was as if I'd stepped into one of the books I'd read as a kid, with lavish ballrooms and decadent décor. My father had done a beautiful job of covering the darkness and debauchery with pretty, sparkly decorations.

I whipped my head to the double doors as Gwen and Velda entered, followed promptly by a sheepish Penelope. Thankfully, Astor was nowhere to be seen.

Gwen twisted her waves over one shoulder, her gaze pinning me from across the room. Then, with a soft sway to her hips, she strode over, the scent of lavender clinging to her body. "Congratulations on your marriage," Gwen said with a bright smile. "Although, I will admit, I am a little envious. You get to fuck Sebastian every night." She tapped her finger against her chin, peering up to her right. "At least I got to taste him one last time, I suppose."

I clenched, then unclenched my fingers, holding back against the magic sizzling underneath. "I don't think so."

"It's true, and right before your wedding, too."

Her admission sent goosebumps over my skin, and I steadied my uneven breaths. "You're lying."

Velda came up behind her, pulling out a case of clove cigarettes. "Good morning, *Your Highness.*" Her thin, painted lips pressed tight as she placed a cigarette between them. Then, lighting it, she sent a cloud of smoke my way. I waved my hand in the air, coughing, almost tumbling back.

I scanned her dress, stretching against her figure in a layer of thin, red nylon. Her eyes flashed with anger when she caught me looking. "It seems you and your husband just can't keep your eyes to yourself."

Heat prickled into my neck, flushing my cheeks. "Nothing about you is alluring enough to capture either of our attention, but I wouldn't expect a narcissist like you to believe that."

She clicked her tongue, taking in another drag of smoke. She turned her focus onto her daughter, running thin fingers through her hair. "Sweetheart, what were you saying to our princess?"

She grinned, showing off her pearly white teeth. "I was just about to go into heavy detail about how good her husband tastes. He was more than happy to spill his cum down my throat in the dungeons."

A picture of him kissing her, his dick deep in her mouth, formed in my mind. My appetite quickly faded, and swirling hurt forced vengeance into my voice. "If you're telling the truth, then I guess we're even," I snapped, and her smile fell into a frown.

I cocked my head, the muscle above my jaw twitching as I took in her wide, blue eyes. "Astor came to my room only days ago," I said, practically smiling. "He begged me to take him back, even kissing me." I paced forward until she was inches from me. "But don't worry. I didn't kiss him back. I wasn't that desperate. I am, however, wondering if you're obsessed with me. First Astor, now Sebastian. Do you enjoy having my seconds?"

She gritted her teeth. "I had Sebastian long before you arrived."

"Yet he married me, and even Astor wanted to put a ring on my finger before the ceremony. So clearly, you're not wife material. Just something to fuck," I bit out, normally despising tearing down another woman. But Gwen made it impossible to feel a shred of sympathy.

Velda coughed on an inhale, wheezing as Gwen turned on her heel, her face redder than the roses blooming in the arches.

I forced my way past her, knocking into her shoulder. "Oh," I said before weaving through the confused crowd of vampires as they searched for their food. "There are no mortals here. My father sent them down to the dungeons, so it looks like you'll need to take another trip down there."

Carefully, I tucked away the anger and sadness as I strode away, lifting my chin because I refused to let her see I cared about her confession. Truth was, I had no right to him or to his loyalty. I knew he didn't want this when I chose him as my betrothed, and I'd pretended I picked him just to save his life. But that wasn't the only reason.

I *wanted* him, and I hated it. Even more now.

Azia approached me from across the room before I could grab any breakfast. "Your Highness." He sunk into a deep bow, then raised his dark eyes to meet mine. "Your father sent me for your lesson."

"Lesson?"

"Yes. I will assume by the puzzled look on your face you were not made aware."

"No. I was not." I paused, staring at the colorful tattoos covering his arms, neck, up to his bald head. "What lessons?"

"My king would like to enhance your powers, so you may become more of an asset to the crown."

"I see." I did remember my father saying he wanted to teach me more about being a princess, but I hadn't known he meant he'd be doing it through someone else. "I don't know. There's so much going on right now, I don't think I have time."

His forehead wrinkled. "You will make time. I can teach you how to control your powers, use divination, and mold the surrounding energy. With practice, you will have more power than anyone. Being immortal with magic is a miracle indeed."

The burden placed upon my shoulders by the gods grew heavier with each movement. Nevertheless, I owed it to them and myself to try.

"I guess…" I trailed off as I spotted Kalon gliding across the room. His snake-eyes slid to me, the green in them more prominent from the forest color of his robes. Within half a breath, he was standing in front of me.

"You didn't bow," I snarled, remembering his plot to keep me in limbo on the other side.

"I am a prince, you a princess. As I've said before, we are not required to bow to one another." The corner of his thin lips lifted. "I'll forgive your naivety. You are so new at this, after all." His head tilted to the side, disheveling his red curls. "Azia," he addressed the sorcerer, with a quick glance.

I saw Azia nod in my peripheral vision, then focused on Kalon. "I know what you tried to do to me."

"And what is that?" he asked.

"To make me stay in the afterlife with your little herbs." His eyes widened, and I smiled. "Shame it didn't work. I admit, it was a good plan. Just not good enough."

His bony fingers entwined as he looked me up and down. "I would never try to do such a thing, and to my only niece," he enunciated in a tone far too hurt to be genuine. "Even if I did—which I would never—there's no proof of this so-called plan you've imagined."

My nostrils flared, but I swallowed the anger, refusing to surrender my control to his provocation. Sticking only to the facts, I kept my expression empty. "I already know what you're capable of. You want me dead and you're vile enough to see it through."

He tutted under his breath, sighing with exasperation. "I truly do not know what you're talking about."

I noticed a man, pausing and listening, in my peripheral vision. Kalon wouldn't admit it, not in public anyway. I shrugged and gave him a small, knowing smile, promising payback. Kalon was diligent, but everyone had their weaknesses. I just had to find his.

"I'm not afraid of you," I said with a scowl. "The gods chose me to make a true immortal. You are cursed with vampirism, although it suits someone like you well. I, however, am no slave to blood lust or losing control. I even got to keep my magic." A shock wave went through him as I touched his arm. A small, but important reminder of my power over him, and how the last time I sent my power through him, he was on his knees, clawing at his skin.

Centuries of experience with pain meant he didn't even wince. "I am terribly sad you think so little of me," he said hollowly, acutely aware of the small crowd we'd amassed. "Let's hope Azia can manage these delusions of yours. It would be impossible to have such an unstable princess on the throne." He pressed his hand against Azia's arm, barely repressing his snide smile. "I truly hope you can help my niece."

He smoothed the top of his robes with his palms, then turned to the vampire's side-eyeing us from the tables. With a tight-lipped look of sadness, he made his way out of the room, toward the staircase. I was confident he had a mortal or two stashed away in rooms somewhere for his personal feeding and wouldn't dream of joining the non-royals in the dungeons.

Rage seethed through me, and I let it out in a tense breath. Everyone was watching.

"Ignore him," Azia whispered so gently. "Good things come to those who wait. Now, shall we go to our lesson and get you out of here for a couple of hours?"

"Yes," I answered, desperate for a reprieve from the people's accusing stares.

TWENTY-THREE

Olivia

Azia led me out onto the grounds. The cold sank into my bones, chilling me to the core. Fortunately, the cold didn't bother me as much as before, but it still wasn't pleasant. I followed him around the weathered fountain and glanced inside at the icy prison of dead bugs.

Dead leaves crunched under my shoes as we made our way through rotting flower beds. Withered bluebells were captured by frost, covering the plants like tiny white body bags. A powerful, musky scent hit the back of my throat on my next inhale. Having heightened senses was proving to be both a blessing and a curse.

Gliding over the snow-carpeted ground had never been so easy. Clumsiness was left behind with my mortality. Branches hung over us like contorted bones as we strode over the path between two tree lines. A pond emerged from tall grass, and I noticed glimpses of orange and gray as fish swam under a thin layer of ice covering the water's surface. Climbing my gaze up, I saw the small cottage strangled with ivy, slipping through the cracks like a python choking the life from the red-bricked building. We reached the ethereal blue door, and I breathed in the wood burning as it poured from the chimney.

The inside was much nicer, with floor to ceiling bookshelves, and sage green walls. The chamomile and frankincense notes from the candle flickering on the windowsill calmed me. Knitted, brown throws covered the sofas, inviting a feeling of home.

Azia threw his jacket over the back of an armchair and rolled his shoulders back. "Please, make yourself comfortable."

"Thank you." I walked over to a large, brown globe, appearing as if it were parchment under the layer of gloss.

Twirling it on its axis with my index finger, I took in the details of the nineteen kingdoms. Dotted between them were small islands, not ruled by monarchs. I recalled the folklore of some of the forgotten islands. One in particular stuck out—Polgoria. Whispers of creatures that dragged ships into the depths and ate men's souls traveled between kingdoms. Most fleets avoided the cruel seas between Polgoria, and those who braved them often never made it home.

I paused my nail over the largest kingdom—Asland. If we were going to war with them, we were royally screwed. Their population far outnumbered outs. Then there was its neighboring land, Kabet. Like Asland, it was a hot country, sharing their same religion. Most worshipped gods far older than ours, from a realm beyond anything we could comprehend. They preached of reincarnation, intertwining the beliefs that the stars from the time a person was born predicted their future.

Aslandians and Kibetans were known for their hallucinogenic teas, ones my mom had enjoyed occasionally with protectors from the guild in our garden. She thought I was asleep, but I never could rest while watching them sitting in a circle on our lawn, laughing and talking until the early hours. It was a hard pill to swallow, knowing most of them were dead now.

I spun to the other side of the globe, stopping on the only home I ever knew—Baldoria. My heart skipped a beat as I dragged my finger around the edges of the kingdom. I may have been born in Sanmorte, but it wasn't where my heart was.

"I'm sure you miss Baldoria." Azia's voice startled me. I'd almost forgotten he was sitting there, or even where I was. "There's nothing quite like home."

"Where are you from?" I asked, presuming he wasn't born here. Most sorcerers were kidnapped from their homelands, just like I had been.

"Istinia. I was known as a warlock there. I left when I was a teenager, like yourself. Sargon recruited me to work at the castle, and I got my freedom from being trapped in a coven, working the rest of my life in a job I didn't want."

I found it difficult to comprehend anyone coming here of their own free will. "Sanmorte is hardly a kingdom of liberation."

"I have rank here and can do what I please." He gestured around his home, and I glanced over the relics he'd collected on his travels around the kingdom. My eyes landed on a skull, painted with swirls of black. It reminded me of the decorations for Vitarem—the holiday for the dead—when I'd been in the City of Nightmares.

I looked back at the globe, finding Istinia, which bordered another kingdom, Salvius. Between them were mountains and what appeared to be a magical archway. There was a strange power in holding the details of a place under one's thumb. "Do you ever miss it?"

"I used to, but the feeling faded with time. I'm happy here."

"Surrounded by vampires."

He nodded, but didn't elaborate. "While I'm happy to discuss my roots with you, I would rather talk about you. You are immortal now, gifted with the golden elixir from the gods. Many would do anything for such an honor."

I sat on the sofa across from him and tucked one leg behind the other. A spiral of dust danced in the light from the lamp on the side table, and I watched it, dissociating for a moment. "I'm very lucky," I said, feeling nothing behind the statement.

He leaned in, propping his elbows on his knees, and clasped his hands together in the middle. "I'm sensing you're not happy about it."

I grasped the cushion next to me, pulling it onto my lap. "I should be pleased."

"The word *should* is a strong indicator of how you really feel. You wish to have remained mortal?"

I slumped forward. "I don't know. The gods were incredible to meet, and I've never felt so at peace. I spent my whole life praying to them, hoping they could somehow hear me, but now I know they could not."

"You're saying our prayers cannot reach them?"

I shook my head. "They're in another realm cut off from ours."

His eyes narrowed, and he peered to his right, pausing for a minute. I cast my eyes to the globe, then at the dusty liquor bottles on the shelf behind it. "You drink?" I asked.

He glanced back at me, curling his lips between his teeth. "Rarely, but I like to have them there. For special occasions," he added. "How do you feel about the gods being unable to hear your prayers?"

"Lied to," I admitted out loud for the first time. "They have no power over anything here, so I'm alone. They gave me all of this, and I am grateful, but I can't fulfill the purpose they gave me."

"His Majesty filled me in on your immediate plans when you returned," he said after a moment. "You would like to rule Sanmorte."

"It's not about what I want." I swallowed hard, an attempt to remove the lump forming in my throat. "The gods want me to be queen, which should mean something. When they anointed Sargon as king, he obeyed, but now their orders don't suit him he won't step aside."

He arched a thin eyebrow, wrinkling his forehead. "What you want matters, too. You don't need to obey anyone. Not even the gods."

"That's blasphemy."

He shrugged. "Humor me, Olivia."

"I go by Seraphina now."

"Not to your friends."

I dug my fingers further into the cushion, looking down at my feet. "You seem to know everything."

"It pays to be observant when you're a mortal surrounded by vampires."

I dove into my heart, searching through my feelings. Did I want to become the queen? Distrust crept into me as I looked into his curious eyes. "You're just going to go back and relay everything I said to Sargon."

He shook his head. "Everything that is said in our lessons will remain between us."

"If these are lessons," I pried, "then why are you asking me everything except questions about my magic?"

His lips stretched into a kind smile. "Knowing who you are and what you want is a part of these lessons. Learning to master magic is different for everyone. It is infused into our personalities—our souls—and it's easier for me to teach when I know how each person will best learn."

I bit the inside of my cheek, averting my gaze to the gold drapes covering the windows. "This feels more like therapy."

He laughed softly and opened his arms. "We're just talking, and I am no therapist. So, as I was saying before, do you want to become queen?"

My chest tightened. How could I trust this man when he was close to my father? I couldn't take him at his word. I barely knew him. "Yes," I said, although I was unsure if that was the truth or a lie. Perhaps it was somewhere in between.

He raised his eyebrows, suspicion crowning his broad features. "If that's true, then you must have some desire to be a part of the people here. After all, that's what being a leader is. Loving the people. I sense you dislike the sangaree and aniccipere."

The muscles in my neck and shoulders tensed as the image of the demonic creatures swam into my mind. I remembered seeing the decaying corpse of a mortal on the streets in the City of Nightmares, at the hands of the soul sucking aniccipere.

"I want to help the vampires—I mean, I know they're both vampires, but I only really refer to the sangaree as such," I admitted. Mostly because they weren't born from darkness. Just cursed by it.

"Not the aniccipere?"

"They are bred from demons."

"They are your people," he said slowly, evaluating me with his eyes. "Mortal blood runs in their veins, too. If you want to be the ruler of this kingdom, then you must accept that you will lead all of them. They all have souls, and I believe everyone can be redeemed."

"Even the aniccipere?"

"Yes."

Silence hung around us for a few minutes, but it wasn't as awkward as I expected.

He stood, and I went to follow him, but he gestured for me to stay seated. "Do you want tea?"

My stomach rumbled before I could answer. "What kind do you have?"

"All of them." He smiled, showing his teeth. "What do you like?"

I curled a lock of red hair around my finger, tightening the strands against my skin. "Peppermint," I admitted, hoping to ease my stomach.

"I'll be right back."

He ambled to the small kitchen, and I watched as he filled the teapot, placing it on the stovetop. I gazed at it, transfixed, as it leaked droplets. My mom hated my little 'drifting off' moments, but she never understood. Staring at inanimate objects helped me think, like I could go more into my mind and picture things better.

Azia returned with two teacups on saucers and placed them on the oak coffee table between us. "So, you wish to help the cursed?" he asked, continuing from where we left off.

I took a sip of the tea, soaking in the tingle of peppermint coating my tongue. The warmth heated me from the inside. This felt like the most normal thing I'd done since coming here. I analyzed his question, finding grounding in the feeling of the hot teacup cupped in my hands. "Yes, I suppose I do. It's not their fault they're this way. Salenia made them this way."

I thought back to Sebastian, and even through my unfair resentment, I felt a twinge of pity. He wanted none of this. All he wanted was his mortality back, something I could never give him. Especially not while he was a prince and married to me.

I launched into the depths of my mind. "Laveniuess preached to embrace the darkness so we can find light. I resonate with that, and I guess it's naive, but I want to help them find the light. Things here are out of hand. How can anyone choose to be good when there are no limits or consequences to their decisions?"

"Everyone has free will," he argued, "but yes, environment affects many things, too. I do not think you naive, wanting to bring good to Sanmorte. I find it noble of you."

My resolve dissolved a little as I warmed to him, finding ease in his presence. I still wouldn't trust him with everything, but I trusted he was genuine. I could sense it in his expression and body language.

"I think it's unfair. Every vampire has to go to the underworld when they die. Even the good ones. I didn't want to believe it, but the gods confirmed it. How can I preach kindness and redemption when they already know they're damned?"

He sipped his tea, then placed it back on the table. "You show them that doing the right thing, whatever that may be, feels better than hurting another person. They still have empathy—well, most of them anyway. Humanity does not just go away when you're immortal. Besides, I think everything will change now that you're here. Nothing is forever, not even the underworld."

My stomach dipped. "Is that possible?"

"Nothing is impossible. Except getting out of these lessons." He gave me a wink and smiled. "Now that I know you better, would you like to discuss your powers?"

I hesitated, but my magic thrummed inside me, urging me to release it. "Yes."

"You are an empath," he stated, and lowered his internal barriers. "Your magic helps that ability, as it is a part of you. You can influence others, correct?"

"Can't we all?"

"Yes, but we are not all empaths. That is a very mortal trait."

"Yet I am immortal."

"You are different." He lowered his gaze to my teacup, and we both watched the illusory dance of the steam pillar up. "What am I feeling right now?"

"You want me to read your emotions?"

He only nodded.

I took a deep breath, pressing my fingers deeper into the pillow. Reaching out was easier than breathing. Tentatively, I touched his emotions, enjoying the peace radiating from him. "You're calm."

Challenge glinted in his eyes. "Dig deeper."

I closed my eyes, concentrating solely on him. Plunging into the depths of his soul felt horribly intrusive, but I reminded myself he wanted me to do this. My cheeks tingled as I sensed the harsh twinge of rage under the control. Everything in me begged to retreat as the emotions affected my own, but I forced myself to keep going. The smell of peppermint and parchment filled my nostrils as I focused.

There was grief in him, but only a touch. Then, as I drowned in the heaviness of his feelings, I found it, buried deep—loneliness.

I pulled out before it could consume me. I opened my mouth, but couldn't say it. It was too personal, and I worried I went too deep.

"It's okay," he said, as if he could sense my fear. "I am not embarrassed. Tell me what you sensed."

"You're lonely."

He clapped his hands together. "Great work. Most stop at the calm."

"You've dealt with empaths before," I stated.

"Mmhmm," he hummed and finished his tea. "It's a good start."

"Start?"

"These things take time. You still pulled back once you touched that part of my emotional center. Did it affect you?"

I nodded slowly. "I can't always draw the line between mine and others' emotions."

He gave me a knowing look. "Then we will work on that in our next lesson."

I glanced at the clock, the ticking clicking deep into my ear canals. "We've been here two hours already?" I asked in disbelief. "That flew by."

"That is a good sign," he said. "Tomorrow, at the same time?"

"Yes." I stood and placed my hand over my stomach. Those waffles with syrup were still calling me. "See you tomorrow," I said, then added, "Thank you," and left, feeling a little lighter than when I had come in. I hurried up the path back to the castle, my head ringing with the screeching coming from the courtyard.

Breaking into a run, I swept over to the entrance, spotting Erianna holding her dagger at Kalon as a body lay at her feet. Slowly, I ran to her, ready to defend whatever she was trying to do. I stopped at her side, my gaze sliding down to the corpse drained of blood.

My heart palpitated as disbelief and shock whittled into me. “No,” was all I could whimper as I refused to believe that the body belonged to my best friend. “Draven.” I whispered his name. Dizziness consumed me as the world fell into slow motion. My vision blurred and Erianna screamed something at Kalon, but I wasn’t listening. All I could hear was the deafening absence of a heartbeat.

TWENTY-FOUR

Sebastian

Darkness shrouded me as I awoke. Groggily, I moved over to the other side of the bed, flicking the lamp on Olivia's side. I rolled my shoulders back, then stretched my wings, gliding them slowly outward over the sheets until they covered the entire bed.

A deep ache plummeted into the depths of my heart before I could catch my next breath. I sat upright, clipping one wing against the bed spot. *Something is wrong.* Placing my hand over my chest, I inhaled deeply, slowing my racing heart. Was this a panic attack? I hadn't had one since I was a mortal.

The feeling went as quick as it came, and I stood, checking the time. How the fuck was it earlier than when I'd gone to bed…unless, had I slept all night and day? The perks of being a vampire meant no hangover. Still, I'd never drunk so much liquor in my life.

Pain tore through me again, doubling me over. Grief tugged at my core, enough to match how I felt watching my mom die years ago. Unexpectedly, tears welled in my eyes. I hugged my waist as nausea stole my immortal reflexes. I knocked against the nightstand, sending an empty glass of scotch onto the floor, shattering shards everywhere. Before I could wonder if I was dying or not—however impossible that was—the emotion floated away. This grief wasn't mine.

I headed for the door, noticing Olivia's nightgown crumpled on the floor. I raced down the corridor, then the stairs. She had come back, and I'd been asleep, drunk, and hadn't gotten a chance to talk to her about our argument. About anything.

Urgency sent adrenaline through my veins, propelling me faster. I took flight instead of running, swooping over the steps, gusting air under my wings until I reached the foyer.

No one was here, but the sound of the party echoed from behind the doors of the throne room. Olivia's bloodshot eyes found me across the room as I entered, and my shoulders tensed. Her fingers dug into her palms as she clenched them so tight, her knuckles had turned white.

"Sebastian," Sargon shouted jovially when he spotted me walking through the crowd. He gestured for me to join them, moving his gaze to my disheveled hair and wrinkled clothes. His expression hardened.

I reached them, focusing only on Olivia. She didn't want to be here. I could just feel it, somehow.

Sargon patted me on the back, then gripped my shoulder tighter than needed. "This is Prince Sebastian," he said to a tall man with a thin band of gold over a sheet of white covering his head, stopping halfway down his back. His tunic was embroidered with gold stitching which almost glowed against the white. His thick, black eyebrows raised half an inch as he looked me up and down. "Sebastian, this is Ibrahim, the *King* of Asland."

I sank into a bow at my waist, uttering the words "Your Majesty" before rising. "It's a pleasure to make your acquaintance."

His thick, guttural accent reminded me of the woman I'd fed on days ago. "You are late," he stated, then turned his attention to Sargon. He moved gracefully, for a mortal, and raised his hand to the king. "I would like to see my daughter now."

Sargon glanced at Olivia. "Seraphina," he snapped, his tone clipped, "will you accompany us?"

She nodded, her throat bobbing as she held back tears, blinking several times. She stood, almost toppling over as she almost missed her step.

Grabbing her by the waist, I caught her in my arms before anyone could notice something was wrong. "What's wrong?" I whispered, hoping chatter and music masked our words.

"I'm fine."

"You're stumbling." I held her tighter, bringing my lips to her ear. "Immortals don't stumble unless something's really wrong."

"I-I'm okay," she stuttered.

"You're not," I whispered back. "My king," I called to Sargon as he paced away with the King of Asland. "I require a moment with Oli—Seraphina," I corrected myself. "There's an urgent matter. We will find you shortly."

His jaw clenched, but he didn't want to lose his temper in front of his guest. "What could be more important than accompanying our guest to see his daughter?"

Olivia squeezed my hand, removing it from her waist. I inhaled deeply, breathing in her vanilla perfume mixed with her own scent.

"Don't," she pleaded, and spoke to her father. "Nothing is more important."

I arched a brow as they walked away. "I know you're angry…"

"This has nothing to do with you," she said under her breath, and followed the kings through the party.

Her mind was elsewhere, her eyes unfocused as she took slow steps, almost knocking into a woman. I noticed the disheveled hair curling out from her braid, and plucked out a twig from the strands. She glanced at me, glassy-eyed. I took her hand in mine, but she didn't squeeze back.

I searched her expression, knowing it all too well. After my family died, I'd worn it myself. The emptiness in her face wrenched my heart, and I squeezed her fingers harder. She halted, holding her breath under the flickering flame of an iron torch.

"Stay with me," I whispered. "I'm here, love. I'm here," I assured. Gently, I slid my hand up to her back, guiding her as Sargon walked with the mortal king. "Tell me if you want to get out of here, and I'll fly us out now." I knew Sargon could hear every word on their wordless walk, but I didn't give a fuck. "Tell me what you need."

Hollowed words fell from her parted lips. "Stop, please," she pleaded, her voice cracking. After several, painstaking minutes, we reached the doors of Penelope's bedroom.

Kalon creaked open the door, bowing as Ibrahim and Sargon walked inside. Olivia and I followed. I noticed Penelope had been moved into a nicer room in time for the king's visit.

We sat together on the sofas in front of the fireplace. The fire crackled and hissed as it withered to embers between charcoaled logs.

Ibrahim adjusted the gold band around his head and placed his hands in his lap. Penelope played with a lock of hair that had escaped her bun, clearing her throat every now and then.

The King of Asland stared down at Penelope, his dark brown eyes narrowing. "Oh, daughter." He sat in stunned silence as he examined the creature resembling his daughter. Yet, she was different now. Every blemish and scar gone. It was always a shock to see the mortality gone from a person you loved. He tilted his head, as if unsure if it was even her. "What have you done?"

She closed her eyes, hiding the glaze of darkness which accompanied every vampire. It was hard for people to place, like knowing something was off, but not being able to identify what it was. Watching her become undone by her father would have been far more satisfying, if it wasn't for the heartache I felt sitting next to Olivia, barely present, stole any other feeling from me. She was all I could think about.

Penelope stumbled the words out clumsily. "I didn't… it… so I was killed." She glanced at Kalon, who gave her an almost imperceptible shake of his head. "Well, I died," she continued, "purposely. I wanted to become a vampire."

Kalon nodded, out of the king's view.

Ibrahim hung his head. "You are a disappointment to us all. Your mother is beside herself, and your siblings are humiliated." He slammed his fist down on the sofa's arm. Unclenching his fist, he seemed to regain some composure. "Regardless, I will not have you disgrace this family." He looked from her to Sargon. "How do you plan to remedy this?"

Kalon leaned forward as Sargon opened his mouth, interrupting before he could speak. "Your Majesty," he said tentatively, "the last thing we wish is to embarrass Asland. We have great respect for you and your kingdom. This was an unfortunate incident, and we will do everything to make this right."

The king gritted his teeth. "I do not want flattery, I want action. How am I supposed to explain my daughter becoming a vampire? There are already whispers in my castle!" His face flushed red.

I eyed Sargon's crown, an object Ibrahim couldn't stop staring at in the moments of silence. He valued Sargon's status, even if he hated our kind. I shifted forward, deciding to speak up.

"What if she were to become a royal?" The room silenced, but I continued. "We're required to become immortal before attaining any title in court." I ignored Sargon's glare and looked into Ibrahim's eyes. Curiosity threaded through his expression as he tilted his head, his fingers uncurling from his palms.

"Continue." He waved his hand in a circular movement.

"You could pose it as a political decision. This can be explained and put rumors to rest. You can say you decided Penelope would go through the Shadow Kissed Ritual and become the immortal Princess of Sanmorte."

"My people know I would never converse with your kind."

Kalon's lips curled. I could see the restrained power behind his eyes, his fangs elongating, desiring to tear into Ibrahim. "With all due respect," he spat behind clenched teeth, "we were held in high regard for centuries."

Ibrahim waved his hand dismissively. "Your time has passed."

I chimed in before things turned ugly. "Royalty is respected anywhere," I pointed out. "Even with vampires. She would only need to marry into the bloodline."

He scoffed. "Are you offering your hand?"

I brushed a gentle touch against Olivia's hand. "I have my wife already, and I am not a blood prince, but Kalon…"

Kalon interrupted, "I am already spoken for. However, my son, Niall, is available."

Niall had no real authority. He had no crown or was recognized as royalty. He was the adopted son, but Kalon glanced at me with a look to tell me to keep that part a secret. "Yes, Niall," I said. "He is a noble prince," I said. "He will make a fine husband for your beautiful daughter." The last part wasn't a lie. They were two egomaniacs who deserved each other.

Ibrahim paused, stroking his black, groomed beard reaching around his chin, up to his sideburns. I parted my lips, but Sargon put a hand up, silencing me before I could speak. After a long minute, Ibrahim nodded. "It is the only plan I can see that will work," he admitted solemnly. "Bring this Prince Niall to me and begin your preparations for the wedding. She will marry in Asland, for my people to see. This Niall and all of you will attend."

Kalon spoke. "It would be an honor to visit Asland again. We are most grateful for your mercy and understanding."

Ibrahim humphed, then looked at his daughter. "You will return home in one month so we have enough time to make the preparations. In the meantime, I must decide how we explain your becoming a vampire without confirming the suspicion that vampires can be made."

She bowed her head. "Yes, Your Majesty."

I butted in as Kalon started to talk. "You can say only those of royal blood or marrying a royal can be turned, in a special ritual not available to any other mortal?"

Sargon nodded, his eyes lighting up. "Yes. We cannot let the truth be known."

Ibrahim agreed. "People whisper rumors, but we must keep them as nothing more than folklore." He turned to Penelope. "You will come home as an engaged woman with your husband. Do nothing else to humiliate your family further."

She nodded, and a couple of unruly curls which had escaped dropped around her forehead as she cast her eyes downward.

I looked at the King of Asland, noticing he'd adopted the term immortal instead of vampire. It sounded more regal. "Is there anything we can do in the meantime?"

"Yes," he replied. "None of what we discussed today must leave this room."

Sargon spoke this time, his fingers adjusting the rubied crown on his red waves. "Everything said here today is top secret. I trust every person in this room."

"Hmm." Ibrahim stood. He gave me a curt bow of his head, then strode to the door.

The door swung shut behind him and Kalon wrinkled his nose. "It seems the Aslandian king likes you," he said snidely. "Excuse me, I must tell my son about his new arrangement."

I moved an inch closer to Olivia, the cushions dipping beneath us. "Liv," I whispered, and she flinched. I touched the back of my head, pressing a thumb against the skin.

Sargon growled as soon as the king would be out of earshot. "Niall is not a prince. I suppose this means he will now get a crown."

Kalon's nostrils flared. "Unfortunately."

Sargon looked at Olivia. "I must find your mother," he said and stood. "Do not screw this up, Seraphina," he warned, and my fist balled. He sped out the door, and Kalon followed without saying goodbye.

"Get me out of here," Olivia whispered once they were gone. Penelope gestured to the door, tears welling in her eyes.

I placed an arm around Olivia, walking her out the doors. She probably could have run faster than I could fly, but she wanted to be held. I could tell by the way she clung to me. My heart raced as I took off, flying us up to our bedroom, landing as softly as I could on the carpet.

"I'm sorry," I started before we opened the door. "About yesterday." I could still taste the liquor on my breath and took a step back. "I know you said you didn't mean what you said, but I need you to know how I feel, because if there's a chance there's any truth at all to what you said, then you should know I do. I…"

She burst into tears before I could finish. My eyes widened. "What's wrong?"

Her sobs increased, and she reached out—for *me*—stealing my next breath. I grabbed her, pulling her into me, cradling her head as she sobbed into my chest. I squeezed her tighter, resting my lips against the top of her head, inhaling the smell of her shampoo. "It's okay, just tell me what's wrong," I hushed as her muscles heaved, her cries muffling her intelligible words. "I can't hear you, love."

"D-D-Draven," she stuttered, putting all her weight on me. "H-he's…d-d…" She gripped into my t-shirt, tugging it down as her knees buckled.

Fuck.

"It's okay," I said, holding her tighter as an icy shiver curled down my spine. She didn't need to finish the word. Her reaction said everything. He was dead.

She slumped over and I held her up, pressing a kiss against her forehead as her pain mixed with my emotions, blurring them. I enveloped her with my wings, wanting to shield her from the rest of the castle. Hell, the rest of the world. She'd had so much loss, and I was terrified she wouldn't be able to come back from this one.

Whoever killed Draven was going to pay. Even if it meant I had to tear out the hearts of every fucking vampire here until I found the bastard who shattered my girl's heart. I placed her on the bed, then tucked my wings behind my back. She snuggled into the blanket, and I re-wrapped my arms around her. "We're going to make whoever did this pay."

She sobbed out '*Kalon*' before losing herself again, holding onto me. My heart softened, and I stroked her hair. I wanted to take it all away, to take her pain as my own, and that was the worst part about loving someone—seeing them broken and not being able to do a thing about it.

An hour passed before she fell asleep. I held her tighter, clenching my jaw. I would make Kalon pay for every tear she shed for Draven.

***

The morning fell into afternoon, and we hadn't moved. I pulled her closer as she turned on her side, eyes still closed. She looked so peaceful. I didn't want to wake her.

A knock sounded on the door, and I tensed.

Everyone needed to leave her alone. I swore to the gods if Sargon was outside that door, requiring her to fulfill her duties as he'd done last night—when she was *grieving*—I was going to kill him. King or not. He made her sit in the same room as her best friend's murderer.

Tap tap tap.

Grinding my teeth, I sat upright, sliding Olivia onto a pillow, which she hugged in her sleep. I crept over to the door, creaking it open a slither.

"Erianna, Zach." I sighed in relief, opening the door wide. Pressing a finger over my lips. '*Outside*,' I mouthed. I clicked the door behind us and walked with them into an empty room farther down the corridor, passing two stoic guards on the way.

Erianna took a seat on a four-legged blue sofa underneath a gigantic painting of Sargon with a frame worth more than my entire house back in the city. Zach sat on a chair in the corner, sitting Anna on his lap. I evaluated Anna. Her hair was a couple of inches longer, her smile a little wider than normal.

"You look well, love."

"Thanks, Seb." Her cheeks reddened. "I'm so glad Zach's back and not hurt." She glanced at Erianna, her forehead wrinkling, a bead of sweat gathering between her brows. "I wish I could say the same for both of you."

I shot her a look. "Both of us?"

"You were forced to become a prince and get married. Now you have no chance of mortality. I know how much it meant to you."

"Oh." My stomach dipped. Since Olivia died, then awoke immortal, I'd forgotten all about my desires for mortality. "You know, the bonds of marriage aren't as suffocating as I thought they'd be."

Zach smirked. "Ah, finally admitting how you feel, then?"

Erianna cursed under her breath, and I took the seat next to her. She white-knuckled the arm of the sofa, glaring ahead at the empty table over the other side of the room. "I'm sure you've heard, Draven's dead."

"Shit, I'm a terrible friend. I'm sorry. I know you two were getting close."

She shrugged. "Maybe a little." But the gloss of her eyes told a different story. "Sargon wants me reprimanded." She tapped the dagger sheathed on her thigh. "I may have stabbed Kalon with it."

Zach pursed his lips, and Anna let out a pitiful sigh. I couldn't bear this anymore. Kalon deserved everything he got, and I was going to make him hurt for this. Kill him, even. Fuck Sargon and his punishments.

"Erianna." I took her hand in mine. "I will not let them do anything to you."

"You may not have a choice," she said. "It's fine."

I squeezed her fingers gently. "It's not. Kalon has gotten away with far too much, for far too long. He needs to be stopped. Before he kills one of you next—or Olivia." My heart shattered at the thought of them dead, and that's when I knew, the reality of it would kill me. I wouldn't lose anyone else—not to them or any vampire—again. "I'm going to bring him down."

I waited for the lecture from Erianna, as expected, where she'd tell me not to be hasty, and I'd get myself killed or something along those lines.

She squeezed my hand back. "Then we will kill him."

Anna gasped. "No, you'll get yourselves killed. Like you almost did last time." She wrapped an arm around Zach, stroking his silver hair with her delicate fingers. "I won't allow it."

I gave her a soft smile, my heart opening inch by inch. "I love your protectiveness over us, but we need to do this. Zach does not need to partake."

"You know he will." She glanced up at him, a tear rolling down her cheek. "He always does." She stood, hands on her waist. "I'm not going through that again, thinking you were all going to die. We should leave, go back to the city."

I chose my words carefully, not wanting to set her off. "Anna, I am a prince now. I can't just leave, and Erianna—she doesn't have her wings, and life will only be harder back in the city."

She stood, gazing down at Zach. "Then we go. Please, my love."

He hesitated on the edge of words, his expression filling with more compassion than I'd ever seen. Confliction darted his eyes from her to us, then back again.

I found my voice, my chest aching. "You should go with her."

He rubbed his hand on his knees, over and over. "I promised to protect you all. You're my family."

Anna sniffed, then wiped her eyes with the back of her sleeve, pressing her tears into the fabric. "I'm also your family."

"My love, please understand—"

"Don't!" She headed to the door, slamming it behind her. He shook his head, running out after her.

After a few seconds, Erianna let out a heavy sigh, rolling her shoulders forward. "He'll end up going with her."

"It's for the best."

"I know."

She swallowed thickly; the sound of saliva forced down her throat slammed into my ears. I purposely looked away as her tears formed, and she blinked them away. She hiccupped a sob, then sat up straight. "I'm fine."

Wrapping my arm around hers, I pulled her into a side hug. She rested her head on my shoulder and closed her eyes. "If you're not, that's okay, too."

She half-smiled through the pain, and I rubbed her forearm. "You know I don't cry," she said as a tear trickled onto her nose.

I nodded, feeling her wingless back. "Don't worry. I won't tell anyone."

She gave a short laugh under her breath, then sighed, falling silent. The clock ticking reminded me of how little time had passed since our arrival, and yet so much had happened. I was wishing away the days, to when things might get easier.

Erianna unraveled herself from me, and wiped her nose. "Go to Olivia. She might be awake and needs you more than I do."

"I will, but please know that while she may be my wife," I said, the word still sounding strange in my mouth, "you are my family, too. I will *always* be here for you. No matter what."

TWENTY-FIVE

Olivia

Leaning into the fluffy pillows, I turned onto my stomach, burying my head into a tear-stained blanket. Three days had passed since Draven died. I glared at every sunset and sunrise since, furious at the world continuing as if the worst thing hadn't just happened.

My stomach rumbled, aching a hole under my rib cage. But I couldn't bring myself to eat a thing. It was like grieving Astor all over again, only more painful. Sometimes darkness leaked through the sheet of shock keeping me going, and in those moments, I wanted to unleash my powers onto the castle. Daydreams of turning Kalon into ash, and crumbling Gwen, Velda and everyone else I hated, pulled me further away from my morality.

In between the endless nights and frequent wakings, Sebastian held me. I let him in, despite what Gwen told me, and the unrequited feelings. He brought me comfort, and I couldn't push that away. Not when I needed it the most. All the fights and worries I had before suddenly seemed so minute in the overwhelmingness of Draven's death.

Sebastian had gone to see my father and the King of Asland, Ibrahim. He took over both our duties, excusing my absence to sickness. Except, we all knew physically I couldn't be.

My mom had come knocking twice now, but I refused to unlock the door. The only reason I even met with the King of Asland after Draven died was because my father threatened to execute Erianna for plunging her dagger into Kalon if I didn't. I still don't know how I made it through that meeting without tearing Kalon's frigid heart from his chest.

Naturally, he claimed killing Draven was in self-defense. As if Draven would try to poison Kalon knowing he was a vampire and couldn't die from it. It was the most ridiculous excuse I'd ever heard. Still, Sargon believed it without hesitation and didn't even listen a word I said. Which I did understand. I had threatened his life and his place on the throne.

Tap tap tap.

I lifted the cover from over my head, glaring at the thick, wood door as the handle rattled. Sebastian had the only key, so it couldn't be him, and I was far too comfortable to move from the bed. I didn't want to see anyone anyway.

Azia's low voice resonated through the cracks in the door. "Your Highness, may I speak with you?"

I turned slowly. He didn't have immortal hearing, but I knew he could sense my magic. There was no pretending I wasn't here. Begrudgingly, I stood, pulled a dressing gown over my clothes, then opened the door.

His brown eyes regarded me softly, and his shoulders relaxed. "I am sorry about what happened to your friend. Please accept my deepest condolences."

After hearing it so much in the last year, I hated that word. "Thanks," I mumbled, stepping aside so he could walk in. I locked the door behind him, in case my mom came back.

Ever since she turned, she'd grown colder and more distant. Our relationship was hanging by a thread, and she spent most of her time with her abusive husband or talking with dignitaries. For someone who supposedly hated this life and everything Sanmorte stood for, she sure seemed content.

Azia sat on the sofa and moved his eyes to my unmade bed. The sheets hadn't been changed in days, as I kept refusing any servants to come in and clean. The pillows were still salty from my tears, Sebastian's cologne clinging to the sheets.

He cleared his throat and looked me in the eye. "Have you eaten today?"

I sat back on the bed, pulling a pillow onto my lap, nestling back into the covers. "Yes."

He glanced at the full plate Sebastian had brought me earlier and raised a brow. "It's okay if you're not hungry. You're grieving."

"Are you sure you're not a therapist?"

He chuckled softly. "I'm not, nor would I want to be. But I do need to talk to my students, especially when they most need someone to listen. What can I do?"

"Nothing," I said, because it was true. "How many students do you have?" I asked, desperately wanting to think about anything else.

He counted on his hand, then gave me a sly smile. "Just you. Only work with one person at a time. Usually, it's when His Majesty recruits a new sorcerer or sorceress into our care."

"What happens to them?"

He shrugged. "Many end up working in the cities for him, using their powers to detect the truth in those he wants to extract it from, amongst other things. He keeps them close, so he can call on them when he needs something done here." He paused, the corner of his lip lifting. "Some go on to be princesses."

I half-smiled, the first light emotion I'd felt in days. Pressing my lips tight until I felt the blood rushing from them, I considered my next question carefully. It had run through my mind many times since Draven was murdered. "We bring so many people back from death. Vampires and, well, me."

He nodded, a pitiful sigh on his breath.

Still, I continued, "Is there a way for me to bring Draven back? Erianna said it was too late to turn him, as he didn't have vampire blood or venom in his system, but…"

"Unfortunately, not," he said softly, cutting me off. "Did he have any interest in becoming a vampire before he died?"

I looked down at my hands, red hair spilling around my face. "No, he hated the thought."

"I see." He entwined his ringed fingers together, placing his hands on his knees. "How did you feel when you were forced to become a vampire, before you knew you would be something else entirely?"

My stomach knotted, a sinking feeling sending waves of nausea through me. "I resented everyone involved."

"Do you think your friend would resent you if there was a trend to bring him back?"

"Yes," I breathed, "but, I mean, *is* there a sense to bring him back as a mortal again?"

He shook his head. "He is at peace now, and in my experience, disturbing the spirits who have already passed on never ends well. It is too late."

It didn't matter how tall he built those walls; I could still sense his lie. There was a way, I just didn't know what it meant for Draven. He was too young to already be gone. He didn't even get to die with his friends and family in his home. Instead, his body was lying outside, discarded as if he were some mortal who'd been fed on and killed.

Sargon wouldn't even let me bury him. He was to be burned with the rest, once the King of Asland and his entourage were gone. For now, all bodies were stored in the dungeons, rotting next to the living mortals as a reminder of their inevitable fates.

A shudder stole my next breath, dancing a shiver down my spine. "I want to retrieve Draven's body, but my father won't allow it."

"Perhaps I can speak with him," Azia offered, then stood. "Please, take all the time you need to grieve. Just know, when you're ready, I'll be waiting to continue giving you lessons." He glanced at the windows and added, "There is no rush."

"Wait," I called to him before he could leave. "I do have a question. Were you at the castle when I was a baby?"

He ran his hand over his smooth head and looked back at me. "Yes."

"Can you tell me about what happened? I've heard stories, and my father sees himself as the victim and so does my mom. I can't get the full truth from either of them, and everyone else just knows rumors or won't speak the full truth." I hugged the pillow tighter to my chest. "Why is he so close to his brother? He takes his word above everyone else!" I seethed, anger prickling the magic to my fingertips like liquid fire.

Azia slowly descended onto the sofa, gazing into the empty fireplace. "The king says he loved your mom, and that she was his everything. They were well matched at the beginning. Ravena was a headstrong leader who challenged him, and he was the emotional, impulsive king who shared her fighting spirit. They would spar, he would teach her to fight." He let out a breathy sigh. "It wasn't long until that love became poisoned with jealousy. Bit by bit, he took away her freedom."

"Why?"

He shook his head. "Because he was so afraid of losing her that he tried to control everything, and in doing so, pushed her away. He believed she was having affairs behind his back, accusing her of planning to leave him. This all happened when she fell pregnant with you."

I curled my fingers into the covers. "I don't understand. Why would he think that?"

He glanced at the door, holding his breath for a few seconds before exhaling into a whisper. "He lacked the one thing she had in spades. Self-worth. While he may have inherited the crown, Kalon was always their father's favorite. Sargon spent most of his life believing he wasn't good enough, but instead of dealing with that, he buried it. That insecurity reared its ugly head once he found Ravena. I think he truly couldn't believe she loved him for who he was and wanted proof that it was because of his wealth, power, or any other reason to push her away."

My mind whirled, thoughts flitting like flies as I tried to piece together the dynamic of my parents. "That makes no sense. If he didn't feel worthy of love or whatever, why push away the person who did love him?"

He gave me a soft, incredulous look as if the answer was so obvious. "That's what people do when they don't love themselves. They both reject and crave it. Or, like the king, they want absolute proof that the person loves them, whether through testing or hurting. They can never be sure, and it's what pushed Ravena away. He got the opposite of what he wanted." He pressed his fingertips against his shoulders, massaging out a knot. "He looks for happiness in everyone else but needs to learn to love himself, not search for it outwardly."

I scoffed. "He seems to love himself plenty."

He gave me a knowing smile. "He would make it seem that way, yes. But deep down, he doesn't feel adequate. I've spent enough time with him to know, and that's why he was so wounded when you said what you did." He put a finger in the air to pause me before

I could argue. "It's not up to you to fix him or tread around him because of his issues, so don't worry about that. However, I will say this. You threatened to kill him, and I cannot agree with that."

I shuffled uncomfortably. "The gods wanted me to."

"Do *you* want to?"

I thought about Draven, and all the guild members back home who were so ruthlessly slaughtered. Murder had become a regular part of my life, and I didn't like it. "No, I don't want to kill anyone."

He smiled. "Good."

"You don't believe in killing, and yet you live in a kingdom filled with murderers."

He shrugged. "If I cannot help the worst of the most damned souls, then I am not a true lightworker. I also have my personal freedoms here, as I said before."

I arched a brow. "You want to help, too?"

"Naturally. I refuse to believe we should rid ourselves of thousands of people just because they were cursed by a goddess, and then send them to the underworld to suffer for an eternity. I do not like when the scales are tipped unfairly, and like you, I see it as my purpose to find a way to make it better. There are many vampires who do not kill for fun, and feed only when necessary."

"That's why you're helping me," I realized. "It's not just because Sargon wants you to."

Pressing his hands against the cushions of the sofa, he groaned as he stood, cracking his neck as he did.

"You okay?"

"Yes. It was just a bad night's sleep," he answered, then rubbed his forehead. "Please rest, I will see you when you're ready."

I watched him leave, closing the door gently behind him. He didn't say anything to my statement, but it had to be true. He believed in me, because we want the same thing.

I lay back on the blankets, closing my eyes for a minute. Kalon was always respected, so that made sense given his superiority complex. That's why my father always took his word over everyone else's. He was constantly seeking his brothers' approval, thinking if Kalon could approve of him, he was worthy.

For the first time, I didn't hate my father. I *pitied* him. He was far more broken than I knew. It didn't excuse a thing he did, but it did help release the rage I'd held inside for so long. Now I could direct it all where it needed to go. To Kalon. To the bastard brother of the king who truly deserved the damnation which awaited him.

The Underworld was built for a reason, and I planned on ensuring Kalon got to see it very soon.

***

The next morning, I awoke in Sebastian's arms again, after dreams of distorted childhood memories of Draven and I were pieced together in some hazy sequence. The second I opened my eyes, I wished I hadn't. I wanted to travel back, between the pages of old chapters of my life, and live there. Instead, I was here, trapped in a time when Draven was dead.

Anger was the only thing more potent than the grief I felt. My magic thrummed around my center, begging to be released. Visceral rage shot energy into me, pulling me out from the depths of depression I'd fallen captive to.

I pushed Sebastian's arms off me, remembering what Gwen had told me about their little rendezvous in the dungeons before his execution. I'd forgotten, with Draven's death wiping my mind of anything but that. Now, anger was all I could feel, see, and taste.

Sebastian rolled over as I climbed out of bed, then opened his eyes. "Morning, love."

"Don't *morning* me."

His eyes widened. The sheets clung to his bare chest, his arms tensing, bulging his muscles. "What did I do?"

I gritted my teeth, the anger spilling out of me like venom. It was all I could feel now, as it swirled unexpectedly. "Did you enjoy fucking Gwen?"

He blinked twice, his lips jaw slacking. "I… Okay." He leaned forward, pressing his fingers against his forehead. "I didn't fuck her, but yes, we did some things," he admitted, and the monster in my chest growled, clawing from the inside to be unleashed.

Reason fell away to rage, and even though I knew he wasn't with me when it happened, and we had no commitment then, I still couldn't shake the hatred, the disappointment.

"Great. Well, enjoy fucking her because you sure as hell won't be fucking me."

He side-eyed me. "I didn't know fucking you was on the table."

I balled my fists. "Seriously? I can't..."

"You're going through a lot," he said carefully. "Now is not the time to talk about this."

I placed a hand on my hip, wrinkling my night dress. "But I want to talk now."

"Fine." He stretched out his wings, sweeping a couple of pillows onto the ground, and lay back. "Gwen came to me in the dungeons right before I was supposed to be executed. She wanted to…" He paused, slowing his tone. "Go down on me. I needed to feel something. I was about to die, so I let her. Had I known your feelings for me then—"

"Feelings?" I cut him off, heat rising in my cheeks. "I don't have feelings."

He pressed his lips tight, a whisper of a smile on his mouth. "Then why do you care about what happened with Gwen?"

I froze, my heart picking up speed, a tell I hated he could hear. "It's just, well, she's here and Astor left me for her. So, that's why I'm mad."

"So, if it was anyone else, you wouldn't care?"

Jealousy tugged at my heart, and I wished I could say no. I wanted to say no. "What does it matter? You don't care anyway."

"Are you serious?" His jaw clenched, and he sat back up, tucking his wings behind his back. "Do you really think I would spend my nights holding anyone if I didn't give a fuck about them?

That I would sacrifice myself to protect them? I gave you up in the dungeons to save you. I never thought I would be given anything as a reward! I accepted my fate, and I didn't know why then, but I liked you. I didn't want to, yet here I am, your husband, unwilling to let you go. I tried telling you how I felt a few days ago, because when I heard you say you loved me, my heart stopped," he said, wild-eyed. "I could feel your heartache over Draven, and all I wanted to do was destroy anyone who ever made you feel pain. Tell me why that is?"

I stuttered for words, my breath hitching. Bravery was never really my thing; I usually shrank into the shadows or kept quiet, but today I felt it. The spark of courage as I asked the words I really wanted to know. "Do you believe I'm your soulmate?"

"Yes," he admitted, and stared deep into my eyes. "More than that, I *want* you to be."

I swallowed hard, trying to remove the lump in my throat. Butterflies erupted in the pit of my stomach, dizzying me. The anger, even the grief, was smothered for a moment when I looked into Sebastian's eyes. They were the color of night, with flecks of silver like stars, reminding me of when he'd flown us to the Lake of Laveniuess that night and I'd seen the beauty in him for the first time. Maybe I knew it then, that undeniable pull I kept denying, refusing to think of it as anything more than just physical attraction.

"I want you to be, too," I said, and his eyes lit up.

"Then come here," he said, pulling me to him.

His kiss was gentle at first, aching against me with urgency. Feather light touches from his lips sent tingles through my torso, and down between my legs. His fingers were in my hair before I could take a breath, his lips crashing against mine. A groan grumbled from his chest, and I wrapped my arms around his neck, forgetting everything as I lost myself to him. I wanted a break from the pain I felt—to find anything to hold onto. Suddenly, I just wanted to be close to him, in every way. Even if it didn't make sense.

"I want to do something," I said slowly, and pressed my hand against his chest, lying him against the bed, climbing on top of him.

"Anything, my love."

The words tugged at my heart, and I kissed his lips, then his neck, moving down with each kiss until I reached his stomach.

I unbuttoned his pants, then yanked them to his knees, smirking as the bulge in his underwear hardened. Licking my lips, I looked him straight in his eyes, desire building in the pit of my stomach. He was mine, and I was his, and anyone before now didn't matter. I wanted to feel every part of him, to be consumed in his love until I couldn't feel anything else, a welcome distraction. Slowly, I stripped him from the bottom down.

Lowering my mouth to his dick, I pressed my lips against the tip, enjoying the way it twitched against me. I placed a hand around his length, stroking slowly as I opened my mouth. His lips parted as I ran my tongue over the head of his cock, applying gentle suction, swirling around until I felt the satisfying thrust of his hips. Only allowing half of him into my mouth, I guided my tongue down, teasing him.

His fingers gripped the blankets. "Fuck," he gasped as I took it all in and hardened in my mouth.

Licking the base of his length while deep in my mouth, he touched the back of my throat as it enveloped him in the warm wetness. I moved back up slowly, moaning softly with each suck.

Adding pressure with my fingers, I took the bottom of his length in my hand, stroking as I moaned a vibration around his dick. His wings flew outward, followed by rhythmic, deep grunts, his ass rocking against the bed, fingers gripping into mine.

"Oh my gods," he said between heavy breaths, and I took him deeper, feeling arousal slick wetness between my legs. I moved one hand down to my panties, sliding under them, touching my clit with the tips of two fingers.

He moved to pull me off, presumably so we could fuck, but I wanted to finish him. I removed my fingers from my panties, then gripped his hips hard, holding him in place. Refusing to swallow to keep it as wet as possible, he thrusted deep into the back of my throat.

My nipples hardened as his cock throbbed, his erection so hard I could feel tiny pulses against my lips. I moved softer, not wanting him to come yet. His jagged breaths picked up, his body convulsing, his racing heart thrumming in my ears. I ran my tongue up the underside of his dick as I brought my mouth up slower, then down again a little faster.

I placed my hand on his balls, squeezing gently, running whispers of touch over the most sensitive areas. Gliding my finger down, I touched the sensitive stretch of skin behind them, and his legs jerked as I held him in place. I gagged as I deep-throated him, not wanting to stop.

Doubling my efforts, I slide up and down, feeling his dick at its stiffest. Pausing again, edging him closer, I pulled back, breathing hot air onto the shiny, throbbing tip. I looked at him, tasting the pre-cum fresh on my lips, licking it off as he watched. Then I moved back down, swirling slow circles around the tip.

He twisted his fingers in my hair, and I let out a moan of approval. I could feel his emotions through our soulmate bond, as if I was experiencing the feeling with him. I cupped his balls, gliding my tongue up the shaft, my panties soaking through with my wetness as I felt his orgasm build.

My heart pounded, my arms shaking as I curled my nails into his thigh, shutting my watering eyes. He reached down, grabbing my tits under my shirt, teasing my hard nipples between his fingers until I groaned loudly, clamping my thighs together.

He let out a low grunt and thrusted up. "Oh, baby, I'm going to come."

I felt the pulses again, like shock waves shooting up the shaft. This time, I didn't stop. I sucked faster, redoubling my efforts, showing him I wanted him to finish in my mouth. He fisted my hair, guiding me faster, moaning rumbles resonating in my ears. His dick hit the back of my throat, and he lost all control.

I could feel the orgasm spread throughout his entire body as he came down my throat, his cum pulsing warm gulps. I swallowed, continuing to suck more gently than before, coaxing the last of his orgasm from his body, feeling his legs quaking. Sitting back, ass clenched against the bed, I licked my lips while staring at his wild gaze. Shakily, he turned onto his side, his skin puckered into goosebumps.

He was weak, unable to move, his eyes closing. "I have never," he said breathily, "felt like that before." After a few heavy breaths, he crawled over to me, nudging a kiss against my neck. "Turn over. It's my turn."

He stripped me of my clothes, his eyes tracing over the curves of my breasts, gliding his gaze down to my stomach. "You are everything," he said breathily, and I closed my eyes. Without breathing, he ran kisses down to my navel, then grabbed the under curve of my ass cheeks. "Spread your legs, my love."

Every word sank deeper into my consciousness, stealing away anything else. His fingers grazed a path to the top of my thigh. I rocked against him, wanting nothing more than to feel him inside me.

"You're so wet, love."

I smiled. "Feeling you come in my mouth, it… did something." I traveled back to that moment, falling deeper into lust as I felt the power of having him become undone beneath me.

His length hardened, pressing against my hip. I guessed vampires had more stamina than I realized.

A low growl escaped him as my restraint snapped. His fingers grazed my throbbing clit. My thighs quaked as he used my lubrication to gently circle the area. He slipped a finger down, gliding two fingers around the sides of my opening, and I moaned behind closed lips.

"Come here," I teased, "and fuck me."

"With pleasure." He brought his lips to my ear, whispering a breath against the lobe. "I love you," he said, with a vulnerability I hadn't seen before in those starry night blues.

"I love you, too."

He stared at me, wild-eyed, then curled his fingers around the back of my neck, crashing our lips together. Deepening the kiss, his tongue swirled with mine. His scent, his warmth, was everything. I traced my fingers along the curves of his abs, feeling the love in our connection deeper than ever.

He released my mouth, kissing down. The curve of his chin dipped against my chest, and he took one nipple between his lips, softly rubbing the other between his fingertips. Tingles shot down to my groin, as he flicked his tongue, then circled it slowly. My eyes rolled into the back of my head as I lifted my hips, sensitive to every touch.

I pulled him on top of me. His lips parted as he looked into my eyes. "Do you know how beautiful you are right now?"

I pressed my lips tight and blushed. He pushed his cock between my thighs, teasing me with just the tip. Beads of sweat collected on my forehead as heat rose, desire moving through every part of my body. Fucking while immortal was unlike anything before.

I pushed my hips upward, forcing him deeper inside. I couldn't tell where I began and he ended as we entangled ourselves in the sheets, the bed splintering beneath me with each thrust. My pussy tightened around his dick. He entwined his fingers with mine, clamping his eyes shut as he thrusted faster. The bones of his hips dipped against mine, and I wrapped my legs around them, holding him until there was no space left between us. He dropped his head against my collarbone, grazing his teeth against it.

I love you. I fucking love you.

The statements passed through our bond, intertwining with my own thoughts as he thrusted harder. The wall shook as I dug my nails into his back. I closed my eyes as I tipped into my orgasm.

Moaning into his shoulder, I was undone. My thighs quivered as he came inside me, his body convulsing against mine.

The tallest of mountains couldn't reach me up here. I held my breath as my mind numbed. Wave after wave of pleasure ran from stomach to my toes, tingling my whole body, plucking my skin into goosebumps. He groaned into me, stilling for a moment, then rocked slower.

Instead of rolling over, he ran his finger down my neck, brushing his lips against mine. His kiss lingered as he pulled out. Softly, he curled his arm around me as I felt his cum spilling out between my legs. He pulled me against him tightly from behind and pulled a blanket over us. His fingers ran through my hair until I slipped into my dreams, wanting nothing more than to spend an eternity by his side. And an eternity is what we had.

TWENTY-SIX

Niall

The thunder didn't end the night I was turned.

Closing my eyes, I recalled the memory as I sat on an armchair by three, narrow windows.

Fog had cloaked me in the ship's wreckage as the waves dragged half-eaten corpses into the depths. The broken mast creaked as a gust of wind circled over the beach we'd washed up on, the cold chilling deep into my bones.

The stench of seaweed and death clogged my senses, sending retches up my throat. My screams were useless, dry gasps by the time night fell. Hours before, we'd lost the bearings on our compass, unable to tell north from south. The sea stretched out into an endless horizon, no land in sight. We were utterly lost, and that's when the voices started. Unintelligible whispers danced from the ocean herself, and when I peered over the side, I saw them. Wide, orb-like eyes watched us from just below the surface, the colors as dark as the depths from where they'd come.

I'd heard stories of the demons of the seas, but held no truth to them until they clawed their way up the bow of the ship, their talons tearing into the wood, breaking off pieces onto the water's surface.

Only two of us out of a crew of twenty survived. John hadn't made it through the day, and as I looked down at my gutted stomach, I knew it wasn't long before I joined him.

Then a crimson-haired man robed in green swept through the mist, stretching out a pale hand as he reached me with immortal speed. I was convinced I was hallucinating from blood loss, until his fangs elongated, and he fed me his blood.

Before I could take my next breath, he sank his teeth into my throat, and I descended into darkness, reborn there. When I awoke, I was different, given an eternity of death and destruction. Back home, I had a girl waiting for me with the promise of a ring. I let her live and die believing I had gone down with the ship. It was a kindness because she would have never loved what I turned into. A slave to my urges, and eventually, with decades of living in darkness, I learned to enjoy it, to embrace every part of me I'd buried.

I both hated and loved Kalon for turning me that night. He'd robbed me of a mortal death, damning my soul to the underworld, but given me immortality and a life of experiences in exchange. Ultimately, I figured I wouldn't have to worry about what awaited me if I never died.

"Niall." Kalon's words cut through the room, pulling me from my memory before I was ready to let it go. I didn't turn, but I peeled back my eyelids to stare at the night. "We have much to discuss."

I glanced at him, then lifted the glass of liquor I'd left on the table, wetting it on my lips. "If it's more plans regarding Seraphina…"

"This isn't about her!" he snapped, as the mere mention of her name exposed the anger he held deep inside. "I know you've always wanted to fit in here."

"I do fine on my own," I said, finishing the rest of the drink, breathing in the last of the spiced scent. "Adrian is back. He and I are restarting the Blood Brothers."

Kalon stepped into my view, casting a shadow from the dim light of the lamps. "Is that wise after last time?"

"I will never let a woman get close enough to destroy anything I build again."

"What if you don't need a club to have status? What if," he said with an arched, thin brow, "you were recognized as a legitimate heir to the throne?"

If I had still been drinking, I would have choked. I leaned forward, tilting my head to examine his expression. Did he know my plans? I hadn't been subtle the night I foiled his own. Carefully, I sat back, inhaling slowly. "What do you mean?"

"The King of Asland wishes for his daughter to become a princess here. Unfortunately, that means she will need to marry a prince."

My stomach knotted, a rare symptom of emotion when I'd become so accustomed to feeling so little. "I assume I'm the prince."

"You will be."

"I would have to marry Penelope?"

"Yes."

I gripped the arms of the chair, rising to my feet. "No."

"What do you mean, no?"

"It means the opposite of yes."

"I am offering you a title."

My fingers flexed, my teeth grinding. For me to inherit the throne, Sargon, Kalon, Seraphina, and Sebastian would all have to die. Even then, my rule would be scrutinized as not legitimate because of the way I would be crowned—as an adopted son. If I married Penelope, having Seraphina as my wife would never be an option. Only through her could I rule, with her by my side.

Sanmorte deserved a strong, decisive king. Not the shit show currently parading around this castle. The south of Sanmorte was hell, with rogue vampires living in ghost towns, stealing mortals without planning, bringing unwanted attention to our kingdom.

There was talk of Hamza's followers making their way north, fueled by their rage against our princess for Hamza's death. They wanted to remove her, and when they made it here, and found a way through these walls, Sargon would hesitate as he always did, and Kalon would let them tear her to pieces. Even as a true immortal, she was not immune to death. No one could survive being torn to shreds or decapitation.

If I wore the crown, I would execute all of them. Cut the root before more poison could grow and wipe out all who dared go against the hierarchy. The south needed building up, with cities like the City of Nightmares, where vampires could become a feared, organized people once more.

"Niall!"

I blew a puff of air through my nostrils. "Why can't you marry her? You seem cozy with her already."

"Velda would kill her, and regardless of that, I do not wish to be married to Penelope. She is a good fuck, but she is too young, without the wit of intelligence to carry out a conversation."

"So I must marry the woman who sleeps with my father?"

He shrugged, turning to look at the moon, hands clasped behind his back. "It will be the least of the messed-up things either of us has done. You will take her as your bride if you wish to remain here. I will not let Sanmorte fall under a war with Asland. If there were no other option, I would have taken her as my wife, but I have you."

I balled my fists, adrenaline surging as he imposed on my will. "I will not be made to do anything I don't want to."

"It's too late. We've all agreed on the engagement, and unless you plan on renouncing that and allowing our kingdom to descend into chaos, you have no choice."

"I'll fucking kill her, then she won't be any of our problem. Accidents happen all the time."

"Not here." His fingers flexed. "Not in our castle, not to the royal family. Penelope is betrothed to you, and her death would be cause enough to wipe us out."

"We should have been prepared for this! If Sargon didn't keep us in the dark ages, brought in the right weaponry, and made deals with Baldoria, then we wouldn't be in this position. Vampires were once the most feared of all. Baldoria doesn't even know we can be made. They suspect, but the truth is hidden from them. Only the royal families know, so how will the King of Asland explain to his people that his daughter is a vampire without revealing their secret?"

The vein in his temple pulsed, his forehead wrinkling when he turned. Pointing a long finger at me, he snarled. "Do not think I haven't thought of all this. As if I have not acted behind my brother's back to build forces where I can. The king can tell his people whatever he wants because it does not matter to me if the world knows or not. That was my brother's choice, not mine. We should be feared, and when I take his throne, all his degradation of Sanmorte will be undone." He paused, then paced a few steps away, blocking the view of the door. "Once we have risen back to our former glory, and only then, you can destroy your princess and be free as a prince if you wish, but you will sacrifice yourself now, for us."

"What of Velda? She will have a lot to say, I'm sure. She despises me."

He shook his head. "She will do what is best for us, too."

"Because she believes one day you will make her queen?"

He hesitated, mulling over my question, one I had been itching to ask for years. She had remained loyal, through all of his lovers, plots and schemes which could have gotten them killed. There had to be an ulterior motive.

"Yes," he confirmed, and I scoffed. I knew it.

"Do you intend to keep your promise to her?"

"I do."

I wrinkled my nose. Gwen would be a permanent resident at this castle if her mom became queen. She'd be a princess, and I'd never get rid of her. She would continue to haunt me, and I could not allow it.

"I will agree to the arrangement," I decided, but I wasn't doing it for him. I would discard her before we could utter the words I do; I just didn't know how. Seraphina would be the only woman I would marry, the blood heir of the throne, and a pure immortal—the crowning jewel of prizes. "When is the wedding?"

"One month from now. In Asland."

I rolled my eyes up, the corner of my lip twitching. "I hate that place."

"As do I," he agreed, whistling out a breath. "Now go downstairs and dance with your betrothed for the king to see."

A month wasn't long to form a plan that would work, so I had to devote my time to it. The Blood Brothers would help plan a scheme once we got the club up and running again. Then there was the grisly business of taking Sebastian out to deal with. I had planned to kill him during the harvest season. The older mortals from blood dens across Sanmorte are brought to the castle to be slaughtered in the masses to make room for newer crops. The blood lust did something to us all around that time, and with so many vampires out of control, it would be easier to pin Sebastian's death on one of them. Aggression was heightened during feeding.

Never mind, I would need to speed things along. I watched Kalon leave, shutting the door with enough force to shake the wood. Quickly, I changed into a fresh pair of pants. I wouldn't wear a suit. No one would make me dress up, especially not for a mortal.

***

The sounds of the Aslandian mortal's heartbeats thrum in my ears. All mortal slaves had been taken down to the dungeons. Out of sight, out of mind. Our visitors had to know what we did here, but Sargon had tried to remove every piece of evidence, but there were still signs. The harmonious pumping of their blood mixed with the music playing from the string quartet. And if we weren't on the brink of the wall, I'd happily sink my teeth into the King of Asland's entourage until they weren't dancing anymore.

Before heading to the ballroom, I'd diverted to the dungeons to feed. The thrill was stolen when I was surrounded by all the mortals in one place, whimpering, as they withdrew from our venom. Without them so easily accessible, we were forced to only feed when we needed to, rather than indulge. That meant less venom for them, and I heard the withdrawals were agony, depending on how long they'd been fed on.

Thump, thump, thump. Their hearts raced faster, and I ran my tongue over my fangs behind closed lips.

Penelope peered at me with her honey-brown eyes, her tanned skin glowing from rose-scented lotion. I leaned in, smelling the rosewater on her neck and chest. She placed her hand on my chest, glancing in Kalon's direction, who was far too busy talking to both kings to concern himself with us. Occasionally, I'd catch them watching, so I did my best to put on a show. "Did no one teach you how to dance?" I asked, as she missed another step.

"Not to this terrible music."

I rolled my eyes. "All I've heard is complaints and comparisons. If you don't like it here, why make yourself a permanent resident and mess up all our lives?"

She took another misstep, and I corrected her. She let out a breathy sigh. Her tiara—held in place by her golden ringlets knotted into a high bun—glinted under the catches of light from the chandelier. Seraphina walked in with Sebastian, meeting a praised smile from Sargon. Kalon's eyes followed them across the room. She was paler than usual, even for an immortal, and the bloodshot tinge in her eyes dulled the olive green. Sebastian twirled her around, holding her close as they stepped in perfect sync to the music. Unlike my dance partner, Seraphina was perfect.

I let out a low growl as Penelope swung herself around on one foot, facing me with a pointed stare. "I don't like the way you look at her." She glanced at Seraphina, the muscle in her jaw twitching.

"She's the princess, I can't help it," I admitted, not really caring what she thought of me, or knew.

"I'm a princess, too."

Not the one I want. Placing my hand around her chin, I pulled her gaze back to mine, away from the only women who mattered in this castle. "Jealous?"

"Of her?" She scoffed. "Why would I be? She doesn't have anything I don't."

"Who are you trying to convince?" I asked. "Me or you?"

"You."

I released my grip, then pressed my thumb against the trickle of blood dried on my bottom lip. I must have missed a spot. Alana tasted good when I'd fed on her in the dungeon, like liquid ecstasy, even if the experience was ruined by the environment. Bloodlust lingered in my veins, shooting arousal down at my hardening dick at the thought of feeding on her again. "I'm hungry."

"You just fed." She rolled her brown eyes and let out a mocking laugh. "You can't control yourself. It's pathetic."

"You're making a scene, darling!" I shot her a warning glare; Seraphina moved her gaze to us. And I wasn't about to let this bitch make a fool out of me.

"I am? You're the one who won't stop staring at her." She lowered her voice to a whisper, her words lost under the low chatter of the room. "If she's going to be a problem, I'll remove her. For good."

Her threat cut through the lust, sweeping rage into my tensing muscles. "Say that again," I warned, gripping her shoulder, digging my nails in until I could smell blood, "and I'll tie you up, duct tape that vile mouth, and fuck her in front of you." Silence befell a couple of nobles in eavesdropping distance, and I sucked in a deep breath, holding back my growl. The quiver of Penelope's bottom lip satisfied the monster inside. "Do we understand each other? Princess or not, I won't have you make a fool out of me."

Her fingers touched mine, forcing my hand from her arm. "Perfectly."

"Good." I peeked at Seraphina, who stared back, slowly blinking at us. She returned her gaze up at Sebastian as if he was everything. I hated him.

I knew that smell from anywhere. Lavender and vanilla. Closing my eyes for a moment, I let the scent drift into my nose, intoxicating me more than I thought possible.

Gwen glided past us, pausing by Penelope, looking at me with those fuck me eyes. "Congratulations on your engagement, Niall." An amused smirk lifted from her painted lips. "It must kill you to be made to do this against your will."

Penelope's eyebrows shot up her small forehead as she placed a hand on her hip. "Excuse me?"

"Forgive me if I'm wrong. I just never took Niall as the marrying type." She touched her clavicle, then pulled her blonde waves over one shoulder.

I stared at her neck, wondering how it would feel to trace kisses down the side. "You should know no one can make me do anything I don't want to," I snapped, noticing Astor was no longer with her.

She smirked. "Then I must have been really special."

Don't react. It's what she wants.

For once, I was glad for Penelope as she stepped up to Gwen. "We're dancing. You need to go. That's an order."

Gwen let out a hiss between her pearly whites. "Bitch, princess or not, I will never obey an order from *you*." She tapped her long nails against her waist. Fuck the way she spoke only made me want her more.

She's a nobody, a liar and a whore. Stop thinking about her. Yet, I couldn't move my eyes from hers. She wetted her lips with her tongue and moved a pace away from Penelope.

"Go away," I ordered with a sharp inhale.

"I'm leaving anyway," she said with a glint of mischief in those glacier eyes. "I'm going to take a long, hot soak in the tub. Me and Astor are in a fight, so I'll be alone tonight. Honestly, I've been dying to have some me time." She gave me a wink and turned her back to us.

She was toying with me. This was a year ago all over again. Purposely, I pulled my focus to Seraphina, but even with her I felt the longing to turn my head back, so I could watch Gwen's hips sway as she walked.

Penelope's guttural tone cut through the music. "I've always despised her. We at least have that in common."

"Yes." I swung Penelope around again, wondering how many dances it would take to appease the kings. I was already hungry, and now I was fucking horny, too.

TWENTY-SEVEN

Olivia

My mom pulled her long nails through her raven-hair which fell like silk down her chest. She pressed her burgundy painted lips tight, leaning over the armchair in her and my father's bedroom.

I stared at the flames engulfing the logs in the fireplace, watching as the wood turned into ash, transfixed by the sparks of color in each ember. The fire sent a hiss through the logs, and I tore my gaze away, angling my head at her. I rested back in the armchair and drummed my fingers against my knee. "You wanted to see me," I said, breaking the icy silence.

We'd barely spoken since I came back from the dead, and not since Draven died.

Sebastian's scent lingered on my body, bringing me back to the events of last night. My chest tightened as I carried the heavy guilt with me. I'd felt happy yesterday, even if it was brief. All the while, Draven was gone, and I shouldn't even be able to smile right now. Yet, there was something so captivating in our soulmate bond, that it suffocated everything else. Being with my husband pulled me further away from every other emotion.

Last night and this morning, as I lay in his arms, lost in our little bubble of kisses and snuggling, I'd felt love more profound than I thought possible. It was as if I was tumbling into oblivion, unaware of anything but him. I wondered if I could lose myself so much to it, that I wouldn't be able to find my way back?

My mom's dark eyes evaluated me, and I tried my best to remain as stoic as possible. "I'm tired," she admitted, and my eyebrows raised. "I'm sick of pretending everything is fine when it's not." She moved her eyes down to the fire. "This is not how I imagined you turning twenty."

She remembered it was my birthday. Not that she'd ever forgotten before, but since becoming a vampire, I barely recognized the woman who'd brought me up and was uncertain of what she would remember at this point.

"What's done is done," I replied, running a hand over my black lace sleeve.

She put a finger in the air to stop me. The pain cracking through her inched over to me, drowning the surrounding energy until the heartache was too much. I inhaled sharply, but she stopped me from speaking again.

"I have stayed here with your father to stop him from doing anything... impulsive." Her heart picked up speed, hammering against her chest like something trying to get out. "I have obeyed him, been as loving as I can so his focus would not be on you as much. Do you know how taxing it is to be the wife of the paranoid king?" Her jaw clenched, the muscle in the corner of her eye twitching. "My comrades from the guild came to rescue us time and time again, despite my warnings. Every time I've had to watch Sargon rip out their hearts. Now Draven, a boy I watched grow into a young man, is dead. You're married to a heartless vampire and forced to be a princess to this awful kingdom." She clamped her hand over her mouth, pinching her tear-welled eyes shut, and drops slid out onto her lashes. "I didn't want any of this for you."

My chest tightened as she hunched over, inhaling deeply to regain some composure over her emotions, like she always did. "Mom." I leaned forward, extending my arm, but she shook her head.

"Don't take my emotions from me," she chided. "You know how I feel about it, Oli—sorry, *Seraphina*."

I rolled my eyes up, feeling bad for making her call me that before. "Olivia is fine."

"Good." She puffed out her cheeks, bringing her hands down to her knees, squeezing gently. "We need to get out of here, before anyone else is killed. The guild won't stop looking for me. Draven is already gone, and you've already threatened Sargon. What were you thinking?" She shot me a glare. "I've never seen him so hurt."

"Why do you care?"

"I don't," she snapped, "but when he's hurt, he's dangerous. I wouldn't put it past him to kill you if it came to it. I don't judge you for choosing to stay when I made a good plan that would have gotten you and Draven out of here. But I hope you learned from that mistake and heed my warnings this time."

Anger bubbled, singeing my veins with heated loathing. "Are you insinuating I'm to blame for Draven's death?"

"No, honey. Don't blame yourself. You didn't know this would happen when you refused to run."

"Seriously?" I stood, flexing my fingers, glaring her down with pure, unadulterated hatred. "I would have left my friends to their deaths had I run, besides it was unlikely we would have gotten out alive. Sargon would have sent half the kingdom after us, and we were just two mortals then." I pointed a finger, and her eyes widened. "Your plan wasn't as foolproof as *you* think. You always thought you knew what was best for me, so much that you never let me make a choice for myself. Like now, you're forcing me to go without even asking if it's what I want."

"Honey…"

"Do not honey me! Draven is dead because of Kalon. He is the one who sent his followers after us in Baldoria. *He* is the reason you are here, why Draven was kidnapped, too. He tried to have me killed, and when he couldn't, he stole Draven from us just to hurt me." An unstoppable rage built inside me, blazing deep. Every breath was clipped as I tried—and failed—to contain it. Magic sizzled at my fingertips, buzzing against my skin.

My mom's eyes widened, her stare fixated on my flexing palms. "Honey, control yourself. I'm not saying it's your fault. This is also down to Sebastian. He should have never brought you here."

The anger bubbled up my throat, setting every nerve ending hot. "If my so-called heartless husband hadn't kidnapped me, I'd have died at the hands of the Nightshade. Sebastian kept me safe, along with Erianna, Zach and Anna." I took a deep breath, calming my thoughts as they flitted around my head like restless flies. Slowly, my chest rose then fell, until my powers slipped deeper back into myself. "If I escaped with Draven," I continued, guiding my tone, "then I would have left them behind to be executed. I owe them my life." I spun back to the memories of them protecting me.

At first, Sebastian had ulterior motives, but that changed. Erianna never did, she just wanted to help Sebastian, and then quickly, me. He hadn't sold me out in the dungeons like I thought. He'd saved my life, and I understood why now. Even then, when I was mortal, there was no denying what was between us. Although we both were masters at hiding from it.

She shook her head. "You owe them nothing."

I furrowed my brows, feeling the rage creep up to the surface again. "I care for them, and as for Sebastian, I love him. He's my soulmate, and I will never leave him." I licked my lips as I watched her jaw slacked. I continued breathily. "I'm devastated my best friend is dead. Believe me, I will ensure that Kalon pays for his sins with blood. But leave here? Never. My fate is sealed, and the gods want me on this throne." My stomach knotted as I realized there was nothing left for me back in Baldoria even if I could return.

The guild I knew were gone, my mom was here, and Sebastian and my friends could never survive there. Whether I liked it or not, Sanmorte was my new home. Adrenaline puckered my skin into goosebumps.

"Azia is teaching me how to control my magic." I paused, choosing my next words carefully. "You are still my mom, and I will always love you. The whole reason I came to the castle was to find you, and I would do it all over again if I had to. I know you've lost and risked a lot, but that's no excuse for making me feel like shit about my decisions. I won't be made to feel like some naive girl who knows nothing anymore. You're not the only one who has changed through all of this.

"I know I still have a lot to learn, and sometimes I make mistakes. I'm not stupid, I know everyone sees me as overly emotional. You always did. But I don't care anymore. I'm embracing that part of me, and you know why? Because I care—deeply—and that is a strength, not a weakness. When I rule Sanmorte, I will devote myself to helping others." I pointed at the portrait of my father hanging next to their bed. "That is what he is meant to be doing. Kings and queens should never have a crown if they only do it for power. That is how kingdoms fall, and empires fade. It is why the gods gave me true immortality. They wanted me to keep the mortal parts of myself. Vaneria dove into my head." I placed my hand on my chest. "She saw my heart and knew what I could do. That is all that matters."

"That crown," she said, pointing at the same portrait, "will kill you. You have inherited all your father's enemies, along with your own. You are my only child, and I will never be okay with you putting yourself in harm's way."

"I can protect myself."

She huffed. "I know you don't want me telling you anything, but you don't know this world like I do. The gods may be on your side, but they are not here. This is Sargon's world and he will never give up his throne. Not even to you. So whatever you're thinking of doing, don't."

I chewed the inside of my lip, refusing to meet her stare. "I'm not going to do anything," I said, but kept the *'yet,'* silent.

"Olivia…"

"What?" I bit out. "Let me make my own decisions."

"At least let me in." She said, folding her hands. "If you insist on taking on a role you do not need to, then let me help."

I mulled it over, but anger cloaked reason for now. "I need to go. The King of Asland is leaving, which means they'll start burning the mortals soon. I won't let him be treated like some nobody, thrown onto a fire."

"We will say goodbye," she agreed. "In a way he deserves."

My heart plummeted as a sinking feeling ran into my stomach. "Yes." I blinked several times, refusing the tears to come. I was afraid if I started crying, I'd never stop. "I'll meet you downstairs in an hour."

I lingered by the door, and she grabbed my arm before I could leave. "Be careful with Sebastian. I know you say you love him, but he's been involved in some dark things." She lowered her voice to a whisper. "I have spies who work solely for me. They told me he was seen walking down to the dungeons. They say Hamza and two guards were found dead. He deserved what he got, but if you knew how they found his body, even you'd see. Only a psychopath could tear someone apart like that."

My heart pounded. "I know what he's done. Erianna already told me."

Her forehead wrinkled. "And you are okay with that?"

"I melted Hamza before he was arrested, and I did the same to Kalon. Honestly, I would have done the same thing if given the chance." I realized I hadn't even spoken to him about it.

Swallowing my regret, I opened the door. Casting my eyes back over my shoulder, I seethed as she rolled her eyes. She would never take me seriously, so I closed the door.

Rounding the corners, sweeping past flickering candles, I searched for Sebastian.

Everything was crystal clear as I ran. I could see every slice of light in each glass vase on the tables pushed against the walls, on the fibers in the paint of the portraits hanging. The dust particles swirling in the air, caught under the hue of lamps.

Astor came into view, and I stopped before I slammed into him.

"Liv!" he called before I could speed away. "Wait."

"Careful!" I scorned.

He didn't bow. "Your *Highness.*"

"I am not in the mood to deal with you right now," I warned.

"Thanks for telling Gwen about our kiss."

I shrugged. "Just a little payback. Also, it was your kiss. I didn't kiss you back."

He clicked his tongue, shooting a glare from me to the ceiling, then back. "I tried to save you, and you're such a bitch to me. I never mentioned who you were to any of them when they kidnapped your mom. Do you know how much shit I got in when they found out who you were?"

"Don't care," I said, tight-lipped, and stepped around him. "Also," I added before leaving, "Gwen has no reason to be angry with you. She sucked Sebastian's dick right before he was supposed to be executed."

I could feel the humiliation and seething anger radiating from his aura, latching onto my emotions, sparking my own rage. "She said he was just saying that to hurt us. That it wasn't true."

I shook my head. "Believe what you want. Why would *I* lie about that? He's my husband. It was a bitter pill to swallow for me, too, except he wasn't committed to me when it happened. You're both cheating liars who deserve each other, and I'm glad karma is catching up to you. Have a nice life, Astor."

"You're going to regret marrying Sebastian," he called after me as I attempted to break away. "Just remember, you sealed your own destiny. I offered you a way out, and you refused. Now you'll reap what you sowed."

I turned. "Is that a threat? Because that's grounds for treason, and I've been looking for a reason to lock you up since you sold out the guild and got everyone killed. Draven ended up here because of you, and now he's dead." A lump formed in my throat. "So don't test me, because I will fuck you up. I hurt Kalon, destroyed Hamza—and they were much stronger than you."

His muscles flexed in his arms, and the man I stared at was a shallow ghost of the boy I once loved. He shoved his hands in his pockets, shaking his head at the ground. "You always underestimated me, Liv."

"Apparently, I did. I never thought you could be such an asshole," I snapped. "Goodbye."

TWENTY-EIGHT

Olivia

I gazed over the grounds as the drawbridge lowered and the king and his entourage left. Once they were a dot in the distance, the bodies were brought out. Sebastian flew down from behind me, pulling me into him. "I've been searching for you," he said, his grip tightening.

"Me too." I sucked in a deep breath, regretting it instantly.

The stench of rotting flesh suffocated the air, and I was only grateful we were outside. I couldn't imagine how the other mortals trapped down there next to the dead coped with being stuck in there during the King of Asland's visit.

Draven's body was brought out. I recognized his brown leather jacket. A sob caught in my throat, and I looked around to double check Sargon wasn't around. He'd stopped me from going down to retrieve his body, putting several guards at the dungeons. Mostly so Asland's people wouldn't accidentally make their way down there and see the genuine horrors of Sanmorte.

My heart skipped a beat as they threw him onto the mound of contorted bodies. "Sebastian," I choked, and he let go of me.

He stared down at two of the guards. They reluctantly bowed, slowly rising to meet his glare. He was still their prince, even if they didn't like him. "We'll be taking that one." He pointed at Draven's body."

One shook his head. "We have orders to burn them all."

"Then stop me," Sebastian challenged, his eyes sparking with rage. He picked up Draven's body, holding him against his chest, not even flinching at the putrid stench.

My mom walked out from behind us. "Oh, Draven," she whispered, and closed her eyes.

Sebastian brought him to us, hesitance strong in his expression, as he halted a few paces away. "Ravena," he focused on my mom. "Take his body. We will bury him away from this place."

"We can do that?" I asked.

She glanced at the double doors, her teeth clenching. "I'm the queen. I'd love to see them try and stop us."

I couldn't bring myself to look at my fallen friend. Instead, I moved my gaze to the mountains silhouetting the horizon. I saw Sebastian hand Draven to Ravena with care, then race to my side.

"Let's get out of here." Sebastian's wings exploded from his back, blocking the sunlight, absorbing the rays into the matte black. His eyes glistened as he took me in his arms, cradling me to his chest. I breathed to the steady thumping in his chest, closing my eyes as a whoosh of air pounded into my ears.

Flapping against the wind, he lifted us above the tower and castle spikes and into the layer of fog surrounding the ancient, weathered walls. With each beat of his wings, we emerged out of the constraints of the castle and towards the freedom of the forest. A heavy weight lifted from my shoulders at the thought of Draven buried away from the court and the monsters who killed him. I could still smell the cloying, rotting scent lingering on his shirt from Draven, and held my breath.

The evergreen forest inked out into the distance in a spectacular green, blotting through the powdered blanket of snow. We descended into the trees, my mom holding Draven not far behind, her red wings beating against the pockets of air.

Glancing back, I watched as the castle turned into a dot, and we lowered through the thick canopy at the edge of the forest, close to the mountains. He landed us softly against the mossy mattress crusted in ice, and I leaned against a time-chiseled tree.

The temperature dropped a couple of degrees, bringing bitter gales from the mountains into the forest. A spiderweb glistened between branches above me, the poor creature frozen in the spot, a fly just out of its reach. I nudged the trunk as I pushed myself to walk to where my mom was laying Draven. Dead leaves and feathery moss broke off delicately from the interlocking branches. I stumbled back, almost hit a hollowed-out log.

Fog left my mouth with each breath as I approached him, and a sinking feeling forced me to my knees. Ice pricked my legs, stinging them, a welcome distraction from the aching in my heart. Until this point, I'd kept dissociating, staring off into nothing, thinking of nothing, but the reality of his death was in front of me. Draven's body was empty of energy, not one feeling to hold onto, and as I reached out with my gift, I touched nothing but emptiness.

Whispers of wind whistled in my ears as I stared at his body, suddenly realizing we should have told Erianna we were coming here, even if the decision was last minute. She'd have wanted to say goodbye. Sebastian could have probably carried us both.

A slither sounded between snow and twigs, emerging from the underbrush. I glanced to my side as a snake hissed out an inky black tongue, sliding toward Draven's body. Grabbing it by the head, no longer filled with mortal fears of snake bites, I threw the creature between the trees. Nothing would touch my friend again.

Draven's face was as pale as the white blanket beneath him, his eyes closed. I couldn't bear to see those eyes without the light dancing in them. This felt like a dream, and the world fell into slow motion. Numbness swept through my body in waves, a heaviness settling deep in my chest. I looked over every part of him with swollen eyes. Tears fell thick and fast, shudders of sobs wrenching my shoulders forward.

Raising a trembling hand, I touched his forehead. "Maybe there's a way to bring him back."

Sebastian's lips parted, his sigh louder than it needed to be. "I'm sorry, love, but there's nothing we can do for him now."

My mom gave me an imperceptible nod as she blinked back tears.

I breathed fast, deeper, but nothing helped. I dug my nails into my palms until the beds bled, leaving half-crescent marks of crimson.

My mom's cracked voice broke the silence. "He's at peace, sweetheart."

I let out a resounding howl behind my lips, holding onto my stomach as bile bit up my throat, my head throbbing. Another growl of a scream vibrated through my core, a sound I didn't even know I could make, as I grabbed Draven's stiff hand. I wanted to bring him back, for him to spar with me like he used to. I hadn't let it in properly until now.

Grief came in waves, and this one was the biggest, drowning any resolve I had into the depths of a pain I'd never felt before. Draven was always there through every part of my life, a light in my darkest moments, and now that was forever extinguished.

The laughs we shared echoed in my brain, chilling me to the core as I became lost in memories of someone who no longer existed. I couldn't survive it. Breath barely escaped as I clutched my stomach harder. Chills spread through my torso, shivering me until my teeth were chattering.

I shook my head, as if to scatter the memories, searching through the sheet of shock desensitizing me from shattering into a thousand pieces. "Kalon," I choked on his name. "He has to die."

Sebastian crouched at my side, his hand on my arm, bringing a hint of comfort to the pain searing in my chest. "He will."

His promise brought me to my feet, anger fueling everything as I turned to my mom. "Burn his body. Don't leave him to the bugs."

"We have nothing to do that with, honey," she admitted. "I will bury him. It's okay, it's his body. His soul is safe."

I couldn't stand to look at him a moment longer, not even to say goodbye. Sebastian grabbed my hand, and I held back a desperate scream, refusing to believe any of this was real. "Take me back. Now."

My mom nodded at him, and Sebastian's wings extended. I pinched my eyes shut as he took me in his arms, lifting us out of the forest and back to the castle. Thoughts of torturing Kalon carouseled in my mind, my only reprieve. I let out the sob quaking softly behind my closed lips and rested my head on his chest. I wasn't ready to say goodbye to Draven yet, not until I destroyed the one who stole his life from him. My magic thrummed with ancient power, as if in agreement.

TWENTY-NINE

Sebastian

Kalon's face split into a mocking grin as Olivia failed to contain her hatred in front of her father. If I didn't think they'd kill her for it, I'd help her carve out his heart here and now, but she couldn't be implicated in his death.

We'd called the meeting with them both after returning and discussing our plan with Erianna, Zach and Ravena. Now it was time to put on the act of our life. "Your Majesty." I sank into a deep bow at the waist to Sargon, then slowly rose, looking around the office where the latest meeting was being held. "Thank you for seeing us."

A map of Sanmorte laid out in parchment was held in place by paperweights. Next to it, a larger map of Asland showed all the territories. On them, little painted figures representing armies and weapons for both countries. They were preparing, in case the betrothal between Niall and Penelope didn't work out.

Sargon walked to the frosted windows overlooking the falling night. The snow keeping the world from falling completely into darkness, reflecting the moon and coating everything in a luminescent gray. "If this is about Kalon, he will not be punished for killing Draven. He was defending himself, not that it matters. Your friend was a mortal. We do not lock anyone up, especially a family member, for killing one of them. He would still be alive if you had turned him as I suggested."

Olivia's fists balled, and I lightly touched her shoulder, sharing in her rage, but knowing I needed to keep her calm. I had to protect her, even if it was from herself. Fighting needed to be sly in the political world. "Neither of us would wish to bring any embarrassment to the royal family."

Sargon's green eyes narrowed, and he looked at his daughter, who eventually gave a quick nod. "Then why are you here?"

"To make things right." I clasped my fingers with Olivia, letting her know it's okay, opening myself up so she could feel my emotions. *Trust me.* "We know it was not Kalon's fault for defending himself against Draven. Clearly he felt threatened enough by Draven's great mortal strengths if he felt the need to rip out his heart. So for that, we cannot blame him. If I were in such danger, I would have done the same thing."

Kalon sneered, and I kept the snide smirk from lifting my lips. Olivia rubbed her thumb over my finger, and my heart stuttered. I continued, "There has been a lot of bad blood, and things have been said that we both regret."

Sargon turned his attention from the drifting snowflakes outside, back to us. "You mean she said."

I side-eyed her, and her chest rose with a deep inhale. She pulled her free hand through her loose curls, pushing the unruly strands away from her face. "Yes, I said some things. Like I said before, it was a mistake. I meant it. You're not only my father but my king, and I've had time to reflect." She let go of my hand, stepping closer to him.

There was no denying she was his daughter. I was surprised he didn't recognize it when we first came to the castle, even with the dyed hair. They looked at each other with the same olive-green eyes, sharing their hesitant expressions. Her cheeks dimpled the same way his did when they smiled. Even their walk was the same.

She cleared her throat, her trembling fingers steadying as she placed her hand against his chest. I watched Kalon's lip twitch, his thin eyebrows deepening into a frown. "Father," she whispered his name so lovingly, I had to wonder if it was really an act. "We were ripped away from each other before I could even know you. I never told Mom this, but I resent her for it. Things have been distant between us, and I want us to be closer. I blame her for all of this," she said, holding back tears as they gathered in the corners, her voice quaking with a sob. "If she hadn't taken me away, I would have grown up here. You would have taught me how to be a princess. I've made so many mistakes because I don't know this kingdom, and now—" She stumbled over her words. "Draven is dead because he was brought here. If we never went to Baldoria, then I wouldn't have met him. He'd still be alive."

His lips parted, eyes widening as he slid his gaze over her features. She said all he wanted was to be loved, but he wouldn't believe it. Now I saw why she was blaming her mom; a common enemy, someone to place the responsibility of his failings on. I smiled, adoring how smart she was. Sargon squinted slightly, his hollowed features softening. "I didn't know."

"It's fine," she said, and wiped her nose on the back of her sleeve. "I'm just so angry at her, and I've been confused by everything the gods said. Especially considering they aren't even here, they don't know what's happening in our world. How can they know what's best for Sanmorte? They were setting me up for failure and I feel like an idiot."

He lifted her chin as she cast her gaze down to her feet. "You are no idiot, Seraphina. You are still so young—only nineteen."

"Twenty," she corrected. "Today was my birthday."

My eyebrows shot up my forehead. *She kept that quiet.*

He winced. "Your mom said nothing. We should have celebrated."

She hunched forward, refusing to meet his eyes. "I don't deserve it," she said tearfully. "I've messed everything up and all I ever wanted was to meet you, and it's all ruined. It's…" Tears fell down her cheeks, patterning her face with trails of wet against the glow of the candles and lamp. "I don't know what to do, Dad."

His eyes twinkled, lashes fluttering as he placed an arm around her back, pulling her tightly to his chest. Kalon's face contorted, and I shot him a sardonic smile. *Game on.*

"Dad," she said again, and he rested his head against hers, squeezing her tighter. "Will you help me? Azia is coaching me, but there are things only a king can teach. Like how to be a princess." She glanced at the maps from his arms. "I can help, however needed. This is my destiny, and I have magic. I'm still a sorceress."

His two weaknesses: wanting to be loved and his adoration for power. *Well done, sweetheart,* I said in my head, hoping she felt the admiration through our bond.

Kalon stepped forward. "I can help teach you, *niece*. My brother has many duties as it is." He kept the contempt from his voice, but I spoke up.

"We appreciate the offer, Your Highness," I mocked, keeping my tone light, "but there are things only he can teach, like working the delicate politics here. But thank you," I added, and his chest heaved.

Sargon chimed in, pulling Olivia at arm's length. "He's right, brother. I need to be the one to show my daughter how everything works."

I noticed a demon board, a wooden board used to send back demons to the underworld when they broke through, usually when mortals played with dark objects or those same boards. "Why do you have that? Demons rarely come here. There are not many mortals for them to mate with."

Kalon touched the board, sliding his hand to the symbols branding each emperor demons of the underworld, serving the goddess Salenia. "One mortal gave birth this morning."

"They couldn't have slept with another mortal?" Occasionally, two mortals we fed on would fuck, too, or nobles would force them to so they could watch.

Kalon shook his head, his nose scrunching. "The offspring is an aniccipere."

"Ah." I stroked my chin, glowering at the board. "So, there's a demon in the castle?"

"Mayb—"

Sargon interrupted. "No one has had any sightings in the four months she's been pregnant."

Olivia chimed in. "Four months? Shouldn't it be nine?"

Sargon answered, "No. Aniccipere babies are born sooner. They reach adulthood faster, too. It's the only way for demons to unleash their forces into our world. Normally, when they come here, they can't stay for long. That's why we're not worried about it still being here. The board is just a precaution."

Olivia shuddered. "What will happen to the baby?"

Kalon grimaced. "We'll send it down to the south."

"Why?" she asked.

"That's where the aniccipere live. Occasionally, we will allow a few into the castle. Some live in the cities, but most stay down south. There are old towns that were never fixed up."

She swallowed hard, the sound bubbling in my ears. "Isn't that where you said Hamza's supporters were?"

Sargon only nodded.

Fear leaked into our bond, and she held her next breath. "The vampires who want to kill me for his death are aniccipere?"

Sargon glanced at the floor, then climbed his gaze back to his daughter. "We're managing it. No one's been able to get into the castle. So you don't need to be concerned." He placed a hand on her upper arm. "I won't let them get to you."

She rubbed her forehead, smoothing the wrinkles which formed from her frown. I sped to her side, wrapping an arm around her waist. "It's okay, love. If they try to get you, I'll kill them."

Sargon tilted his head. "Besides, you're not the one who killed him. We still don't know who's responsible."

Olivia casted her eyes over her shoulder, a look of knowing piercing through. *Fuck.*

Kalon spoke this time, his voice resonating around the room. "It doesn't matter. They know she was the reason he was locked away. They won't just be after her, they'll be after all of us. They never did like a royal hierarchy." He gritted his teeth, grating the noise through me, crawling a shiver down my spine. "I have no issues sending them down to meet their fathers."

She walked to the demon board, passing her fingertip over each of the sigils, each engraved with an animal representing the demons. "I'd heard stories of possessions and incubi sleeping with people in Baldoria, when I was younger, but I never thought they were true."

Sargon nodded. "We kidnapped any babies born as aniccipere before it could be proved."

Kalon glared. "We have spies in every kingdom. So it's important we know what's going on."

I scoffed. "We know," I stated, my tone laced with threat.

Sargon still didn't know Kalon was behind the vampires sent to kill Olivia. He spun it as they went to kidnap Ravena for Sargon, and Kalon would just deny any part to play with Olivia, anyway. We had no proof, but doubts were the best seeds to plant, severing ties slowly. Their bond was one we would snap, then let the brothers destroy each other once it all crashed and burned.

It was a long time coming, with Kalon's resentment of Sargon, and Sargon's jealousy. Love was the only barrier, and with the king having a doting daughter and people he trusted, that love for his brother could finally be redirected.

Kalon glowered in my direction, but I didn't so much as flinch. I wanted him to squirm, unable to control what was coming, only knowing something was happening, unable to see what. His eyes glinted madness, his eyebrows drawing flat, bulging the top of his nose.

Sargon stepped back, pulling the board away from Olivia. "No need to worry, daughter. Go get your rest. Tomorrow you can have your lesson with Azia, and I will show you the inner workings of this court in the evening."

I took her hand, knotting it with my own. "Come on, love. Let's get to bed." I bowed to Sargon, and to put on the genuine show, also bowed to Kalon, even though I didn't have to. Not with the same title as prince.

Olivia curtseyed, and we hurried out of the room. Once we were out of earshot, she spun to face me, her hands clasped in front of her, smiling wider than I'd seen in weeks. "It worked. He believes us."

"You were quite the actress," I whispered a kiss against her lips. "This was clever."

She nudged her nose against mine. "I learned from the best." She paused, twiddling her thumbs. "I need to tell you something. I know you killed Hamza."

Ice prickled through my core, rooting me to the spot. My heart galloped in my chest, a tell she felt instantly. Before I could choke out the lie, out of fear of her seeing the monster I'd become. Because I didn't just kill him, I'd have admitted that in a heartbeat. But because I also killed two innocent guards to cover my tracks.

She splayed her fingers over my chest, calming me. "It's okay, Sebastian. I know about the guards, too. I love the very best and worst of you."

I breathed a sigh of relief, realizing she was pulling the worry from my head through her gift. "He needed to die after what he did to you."

She closed her eyes, rubbing her thumb over my shirt. "Thank you for protecting me. Please don't keep anything from me again. You can always tell me."

My gaze burned into hers, her soul reaching to meet mine through our touch. "I know. The same goes to you. I didn't know today was your birthday."

She pressed her lips tight. "I didn't feel like celebrating."

"I'm still getting you a cake. I'll head to the kitchens now."

She chuckled. "I can't imagine you *baking*."

"I'm not that bad of a cook you know," I said with a wink. "Almost one of my many skills." She grinned, and I was just happy to see her with some light in her eyes. "Sweetheart." I tugged her closer. "Happy birthday. I understand you don't want to celebrate, especially after burying Draven. I'm sorry this day was tainted with sadness for you." I rested my forehead against hers. "When you're feeling up to it, I'd like to take you somewhere with Erianna. We can take a break from this place, if only for a little while."

"What about Hamza's followers?" She shuddered, and I closed my eyes. The idea of them reaching her brought out something primal in me.

"I won't let anyone hurt you."

She let out a long exhale. "My powers are growing stronger too. Azia is helping me a lot. He says he's not a therapist, but he acts like one. I like him."

"Good." I brushed my lips against her temple. "I know you can protect yourself, but I will always put your first. I don't care who I have to kill."

She placed her hand on my chest, splaying her fingers over my racing heart. "I'll kill for you too."

My stomach knotted. I had never felt so much love from anyone before, except maybe my mom. The memory of her washed into my mind, like a faded picture.

"Sebastian?" Her gaze bore into my own. "What's wrong? You forget, I can feel the same pain you do."

I didn't realize I'd lowered my barriers. Mostly, I kept them up because I didn't want to overwhelm her with my emotions. She already took on the grief of the world, that I couldn't add to that. "I'm okay," I said and tucked a finger under her chin, forcing a smile. "I promise."

THIRTY

Niall

The grounds were quiet at midnight. The trees moved in the breeze as I strode around the edge of the castle, enjoying the wind whistling in my ears and crickets chirping in the distance. The pond emerged from the shadows, the lights from Azia's windows glistening gold against the black water. Shards of ice floated as they slowly melted.

I kneeled at its edge, gliding my fingers through the still water. Fireflies lit up from the tall grass, penetrating the darkness. We were the evilest creatures to walk this world, inclined to the deepest caverns of sin we held as mortals. Yet, darkness didn't exist in immortality. My eyes could pick up on every flicker of color, and even in the most palpable of nights, I could see the ugly in each thing, finally learning to appreciate all things. I gazed at the flutter of the bugs' wings, undisturbed as they feasted on the dead bodies of other bugs. Spiders crawled over blades of grass, the hairs on their legs shining under the pale moonlight.

I could have stayed there forever, stuck in a memory of a mortal life I grew more distant from by the day. Ever since the night Kalon changed me, I vowed to never look back. But every now and then, I found myself coming here. The only place by the castle that reminded me of the home I grew up in.

It was a modest cottage, but my mother did her best to give my brothers and me a good life. At night, we'd sneak out to the pond out the back, much like this one. I would catch fireflies, giving them new homes in glass jars, then cry when they died. My mother put it down to my young age, but even then, I was captivated by collecting things.

Gwen was my firefly, luring me back to old habits. My father was different. His expectations were high, and when I didn't live up to them, he would beat me worse than my brothers. I only went home once after I died—to return the favor.

I couldn't even remember how any of their voices sounded as the memories of them dissolved over time. The world I grew up in had lived and died, and I remained young while everyone I used to love succumbed to old age. I wondered, from time to time, what happened to my brothers and mom.

Snapping myself from useless thoughts, I glanced back at the castle. I'd lost so many within those walls, old friends who became like family. Some had fallen prey to the rage of the aniccipere, who were segregated to the south. Others had been executed under Sargon's laws, by killing another vampire, or treason. He was always paranoid, and if I didn't have Kalon's protection I would have fallen to the same grisly fate. Since then, I'd distanced my heart from any soul, feeling the sting of grief so much that it had become numb.

Azia's door opened, and I lifted my gaze to meet his. "Who's there?"

The instinct to hunt was strong tonight as the thought pricked my adrenaline. The blood of the sorcerer was an elation better than any drug. Not even my father could save me from Sargon's wrath if I touched his precious sorcerer.

Grinding in my jaw, I raced away before my desire overcame my better reasoning. If I wanted to rule Sanmorte, I had to control my impulses. Once I was on the throne, I would restore the kingdom to its former glory. Wiping out the soul vampires would be first, rebuilding the south from ghost towns and rotting buildings into cities where vampires could thrive.

I'd integrate the modern world with ours, build armies of immortals that would tremble even Asland. No more living in the shadows, keeping the secret of how we can make other vampires from the world. No, mortals would come to us, wanting to feel our venom in their veins. Seraphina would be lured to the dark side; they always did submit once they tasted true power. With her at my side, we could build something unlike anyone had ever seen.

Sargon had us cower away, as if we weren't the strongest. It made me sick. First, I had to kill Sebastian. His heart would be a trophy, a warning to all who would dare challenge me.

The feeling of being watched hung over me. I knew it well, but usually I was the one hiding in the darkness. Whipping my head around, I saw the soul vampire staring at me from behind some trees, its beady eyes focusing before it fled in a blur. I took off to chase it, when Gwen's boyfriend came into my view. *You.*

I grinned, fangs glinting. If I couldn't kill the sorcerer, I could at least destroy this leach. "What are you doing out here with an aniccipere?"

His eyes widened. "Oh, I didn't know there was one."

My eyebrows pulled down, wrinkling my nose. "I'm not as stupid as the others you might be able to convince. Why else would you be out here alone?"

"Maybe for the same reason you are."

I half-laughed. If I took off his head right now, no one would be able to trace his death back to me.

I let out a hiss, moving faster than he could block. Sinking my fangs into his neck, I drank, even though vampire blood did nothing for me. He weakened quickly, and I wouldn't stop until his head was detached from his shoulders. Then, biting my way through veins and bone, I slammed my hand over his mouth, muffling gurgled screams. Blood leaked down my chin, sliding between my fingers and over my arms.

"Stop!" Gwen's voice sounded behind us.

Letting out a growl into his flesh, I pulled out. Then, with a smirk, I wiped the blood from my mouth.

"Astor," she panted, running to his side as I dropped him onto the grass with a thud. His heart slowed as he lay unconscious. She glared up at me. "You bastard."

"He'll live." I shrugged, and she ran at me. I wrapped my hand around the back of her neck, nestling her into my arms. "Don't be a fool, sweetheart. We both know you can't take me."

Her knee slammed into my dick, a sharp pain, stealing my breath. I folded, holding my stomach as the nausea leaked up to my throat. "That," she said breathlessly, "is just a warning."

I paced closer, lifting her chin with a tight grasp, my gaze burning into hers. "The next time you do that, I will rip out his heart."

She spat on my cheek. "Fuck you."

I laughed, wiping the saliva with my hand. "Gladly," I whispered, tugging her closer. "Admit it, you miss the thrill. You can't really like being with him."

She swallowed thickly. "You know nothing about me."

"You and I are far more alike than you want to admit."

"You're delusional." She paced closer, her lips inches from mine. "If you must know, I'm happy with him. Astor accepts me for who I am. He owns who he is, the bad and the good."

"If you're so happy, why are you still standing here with your hand on my chest?" I asked, moving closer. She moved her hand off me, and I noticed her heart pick up speed. "We both know you'll tire of him."

"Why must you always be so cruel? You used to have dignity."

My fingers curled into fists. "I will kill anyone who gets in my way. He was out here with a soul vampire, and there have been rumors of him holding private meetings. It's better to kill a problem at its root before it blossoms."

She shook her head, bobbing her blonde curls. "You're mistaken. Astor has honor. He's not like you."

"I'd hope not." I grabbed her wrist, tugging her close. "He's a pathetic rat. Look at him. You think he can protect you?"

She ran a thumb over her lips. "It's a good thing I don't need protecting."

"We both know that's not true."

Her pupils dilated under the powdered, white light from the stars and moon. "I'm taking him inside. Don't offer to help, I don't need it."

I grinned. "Oh, I know you don't. It's just one of the things I enjoy about you."

She raised an arched brow. "Touch him again, and I'll tear your throat out." She showed me her pointed, painted nails, and tilted her head.

"That's a tempting offer. I'd love to see you try." Challenge burned in her eyes. Astor slowly came around, choking out blood as he healed. "Looks like he can walk himself back inside. Goodnight, Gwen."

***

The following day, Penelope sauntered into my room. I let out an irritated sigh. "Go away. I'm busy."

She ran her hands through her ringlets. "That's no way to speak to your wife."

I rolled my eyes up. "You're not my wife."

"Yet," she added, smiling brightly. "We should share a bed," she offered, her voice sinking into a whisper. "You can move into my room now we're to be wed." She looked around my chambers. "It's much bigger than this one."

"I would rather hand myself over to the soul vamps."

She rolled her expressive, brown eyes. "Is this just because I slept with Kalon? He's not even your real dad."

I put down the book I'd been reading. "Maybe I'm just not that into you."

She huffed out a breath. "Is this about that bitch princess? You need to get over it. She's married and you're about to be."

Her voice ran through me like nails scraping against a chalkboard. She placed her hand on her hip, her eyes wide with condescension. She hadn't even reached her mid-twenties yet and she spoke to me of maturity? "What can I say to end this conversation?"

"What are you reading?" she asked, changing the subject. "A war book?"

I moved it across the table. Learning the art of war, the strategies of the winning side and mistakes from the ones who lost, was always a hobby of mine. Now, it was more than that. As a ruler, I had to know how to counter attacks. The world was cruel, and to survive it, I had to be worse than the darkest of them. "If you won't leave, I will." Pushing my hands into my pockets, I sped out of the room before she could say another word.

I headed to Adrian's room, which was only a rush down the end of the corridor. Slamming three resounding knocks onto the wood, I looked over at the portraits on the walls. I'd been here when most had been painted.

The door swung open, and Adrian stood, suited as always, holding a glass of scotch. "Good, you're here. We have new recruits."

I stepped inside. "The ones we discussed?"

"Yes." He hesitated. "Why do you want a mortal in our club again?"

"He's valuable. Just trust me," I said, not wanting to admit the truth. That he was the servant who attended to Gwen's room, lit her fires, ran her baths. "Did he agree?"

"Of course." He lounged into an armchair. "Are we going to turn him?"

"Not yet. We can ask Sargon for his permission if he proves himself worthy."

"I still don't understand."

I put my hand up to stop him. "Servants hear everything. Words fall from the lips of nobles so easily around mortals. They don't even see them."

He offered me a drink. "Smart. So, you ready to introduce them? I got back our old space to hold the meetings. Of course, we'll need to initiate them first."

A sadistic smile stretched my lips. That was always my favorite part. "Let's go."

THIRTY-ONE

Olivia

Azia ran a hand over his tattooed head, looking at me from across his desk which stretched out ten feet wide, covered in maps, and the various tools for reading them. The rain thudded against his cottage window, thunder grumbling the gray skies as morning slipped into afternoon.

"How are you feeling?"

"I get nightmares," I admitted, placing my hands in my lap as I adjusted my posture against the hard chair. "I keep replaying the moment I found Draven, and every time we saw each other before then."

"You're wondering if there is anything you could have done?"

I nodded, and he cleared his throat. "There isn't," he said. "Everything happens for a reason."

I glanced at the fireplace crackling next to us, emitting heat over my bare legs under my knee-length, green dress. "I don't want to hear that right now."

He picked up his steaming cup of nettle tea, breathing in the vapors before taking a sip. "Let's move forward with our lesson then. I'm surprised to see you back so soon."

"I need this." My stomach dipped as thoughts of Draven flooded my mind, but vengeance buried them somewhere deep within my psyche.

Kalon had to pay for all of it, and my father, who'd come around over the last few days, was trying to spend more time with me. My heart tugged with guilt, but I quickly reminded myself of all the pain he'd caused. I was using him, and I'd never done anything like this before. But things couldn't continue the way they had.

If I had to sacrifice my father to help thousands of mortals out of slavery, to bring justice for Draven, then it was a small price to pay. But first, I needed to control my powers, to become something so frightening that the vampires would respect me. With Sebastian at my side, and Erianna, my mom, and Zach—four of the strongest immortals I knew—we could rule this kingdom as the gods intended.

It would just take time, and I understood now that I'd been too hasty before. Sargon did have a point. They would not accept me as their queen if I took away all their pleasures, so we had to do everything slowly, insert ourselves and leave no doubt behind when it came to the king and his brothers' deaths. I couldn't be accused of regicide.

The invigorating scent of lavender and jasmine calmed me as a candle flickered from the mantel, mixing with the smoke and burning pine wood from the fire. A crackle sounded between two logs as a flame licked against the sap.

"I wish I could live here," I admitted, rolling my shoulders back as I took in the relaxing atmosphere. "I hate the castle."

He smiled. "You can make your room your own, too. You must feel at ease where you rest your head at night. I recommend taking candles of your favorite smells and lighting them in the evening. I sometimes use incense and different colors in each room depending on the mood I'm trying to achieve. For example, I like to use shades of purple in my office area." He gestured to the lilacs in a vase, and various ornaments. "Helps creativity. I also keep an amethyst close by."

I looked at the tall crystal quartz glistening from the stone, moving up into a point, noticing the blues and reddish tones within the purple. "You believe in crystals?"

"I like to give everything a try, and if it works for me, then I'll keep doing it." He leaned forward, squeaking the legs of his chair under his weight. "We will be splitting our lessons in half, in the future," he said, changing the topic. "Your father wants me to teach you about the history of Sanmorte, your bloodline, politics, and the origins of your magic. In the other half of our lessons, I would like to continue working on harnessing your empath gifts with your magic and controlling your emotions. All are imperative to growing into who you want to be, and to rule a kingdom. Heavy is the head that wears the crown, so the saying goes. If you are to be their princess and heir, your head must rule your heart."

I nodded, tucking the inside of my lips between my lips. "Where do we begin?"

He pushed a map of Sanmorte across the desk. I trailed my gaze over the entire kingdom, gliding my fingertip down from where the castle was in the north-east. Surrounded by mountains and forests running all the way down the coastline of east, where a large tower stood overlooking an ocean. Close to it, moving westerly, was the Black Mountain Retreat where Sebastian had taken me before our first visit to the castle. It was the first time we'd shared a bed, while tucked into a luxurious room in the most elite hotel in Sanmorte.

"I've been here." I pointed at the collection of buildings, then glided my finger to just left of the center of the kingdom. "The City of Nightmares. I've been here, too."

"It used to be called something else, but everyone knows it by its nickname. They even changed it on the maps." He let out a heavy breath, shaking his head slightly. "It was originally named Cinnatua. The walled city was originally a beautiful place, I've seen old drawings. Now it's a playground for the lawless."

I swallowed thickly, tracing my eyes over the rest of the map. "Lake of Laveniuess." I pointed at the beautiful lake north to the city, bowled in mountains. "Sebastian took me there, too. He thought it would help enhance my powers."

He nodded. "The waters are infused with the power of Laveniuess, still holding residual energy from the god's birthplace in this world."

The rest of the map was filled with ghost towns, abandoned cemeteries, and wide-open space. Especially the south. I pointed at one, which appeared to be a desolate city south to the City of Nightmares. "Is that where the aniccipere are?"

"Yes," he confirmed. "It was left behind from when the mortals used to run Sanmorte, before vampires ran them out of their kingdom centuries ago. Some new buildings have been built, but most are crumbling foundations. This whole territory—" He circled a finger around the buildings, over to the shipwreck in the bottom southeast, to the cemetery and open space in the west. "—is run by the aniccipere."

A shiver tingled down my back. That was a lot of land they had. My stomach churned as I recalled their beady, devouring eyes and needle-like teeth. "They're after me. Apparently, a lot of them were Hamza's followers."

"Yes." He took his hand off the map and sipped his tea. "They hate the whole idea of a monarchy. Hamza played both sides for a long time. He stayed close to the king and prince Kalon, making friends at court. He also built followers in the south, sending them supplies, riches, going down there and making speeches all in the name of peace." He tutted under his breath. "Really, he was ensuring the aniccipere's loyalty to him, in case anything went wrong here. He could use them. Unfortunately, they believed he hated the monarchy, too, but I don't believe that was true."

I understood. "He just wanted power, wherever he could get it."

"Yes." He finished his tea and placed the empty cup back on the saucer. "Also ensuring his own survival. It is why the king was reluctant to execute him, even after his crimes against you."

I sucked in a deep breath. "I'll guess we'll never know who really killed him."

He arched an eyebrow. "I'm sure at least one person in this room knows." Suspicion crowned his earthy irises. "Regardless of who did it, I am grateful he is gone."

My eyebrows raised. It was the first time I'd really heard him express his feelings about anything political. "Do you think the soul vampires will be able to get into the castle?"

His expression darkened. "Yes, but it's unlikely. There are few here who would want to help them. They've been outcasts of society for a long time. Your father also has guards monitoring the situation in the south. You're safe here."

I remembered when we'd flown out to the forest to bury Draven. I had my mom and Sebastian with me, but we'd strayed so far from the castle. Suddenly, this fortress didn't feel so suffocating.

He continued. "We will delve into the history of the mortal kingdom before Sanmorte in another lesson. But, for now— " He placed a paperweight against a curling corner of the parchment. "—lets go over your bloodline."

"Sebastian told me the basics when I found out about my real identity." I pressed a finger against the dimple in my chin. "He said the gods instilled a king to rule over the vampires. One who they dubbed the Chosen One, and had brought order to vampires before."

"Yes. His name was Edlor. The gods felt responsible for their sister unleashing such an awful curse onto the world and making the underworld. It created an unbalance, and this was their way of tipping the scales back. Eldor was promised an afterlife, with the ability for him and his children to become mortal again when they chose to retire the throne. The crown passed down to his son and his sorceress wife. They had two sons, one of them is your father."

"So Edlor is my great grandfather?"

"Yes."

"What would happen if the bloodline wasn't continued?" I asked. "Like, what if I can't have children? I am an immortal."

He leaned back in his chair, the orange from the fire shining on his bald head. "The gods were able to have children. It is how we are here. If they could have children, I don't see any reason you shouldn't be able to."

A lump formed in my throat, and I swallowed thickly. "What if I don't want to?"

"You can choose a successor. It hasn't needed to happen yet, as most monarchs rule for centuries unlike the mortal monarchs. Still, if you really do not wish to continue your bloodline, then that is an option."

I looked back at the map, feeling the responsibility weighing on my shoulders. Curiosity spiked as I moved my gaze from each part of the kingdom. These were questions I'd always wanted to know, when I was little, and we learned of a secluded kingdom of vampires. Immortals existed, and yet there was so little information about them. History books were hidden—and for good reason. The guild and royal family in Baldoria didn't want more of us than there already were seeking out the vampires, like Astor had done.

"What do you know about the underworld?"

"Not much," he admitted and opened the drawer to his desk. Then, after a moment of rustling through papers, he pulled out a paper covered in symbols like the ones I'd seen on the demon board in my father's office. "We know there are emperor demons. They control lesser demons and are Salenia's creation. Their only job is to stop any souls from escaping."

"Why does she care? She only built that prison for Vener and his lover."

He shrugged. "She's also trapped there for an eternity, and either she doesn't like that she can't leave, so wants to keep everyone else trapped there, too, or maybe she reflected and felt responsible for the curse and wanted to keep the evil trapped away from the other realms and her siblings."

"Not all vampires are evil," I argued, thinking about Sebastian, my mom, Zach and Erianna. "She can't just do that."

"She's a goddess with powers unlike any we've experienced. But, unfortunately, she locked herself inside her own magic when she made the underworld. There are cracks, those who have found ways through the weaker areas of her magic and aren't bound by it. That's how demons come into our world for a short time."

A thought crossed my mind. "If souls can't escape, then there would be no demons. So that means some must have escaped, through those cracks you mentioned."

Hope rose in me. That meant there was a way to ensure my family wouldn't end up damned there forever. I stored the information away in my head.

"I wish I could know for sure." I glanced at the demonic symbols and thought back to the demon board. My father said they were used to contact demons, and maybe if I could get ahold of it, I could speak to one.

"Don't go playing with demons," Azia said, sensing where my thoughts drifted. "We can't know everything, and sometimes that has to be enough."

For you, I thought and gazed at the fire, transfixed by the flames. I wondered what the underworld was like and how it looked. If the aniccipere were only half-demon, then I shuddered to think what an actual demon was like.

"I won't," I half truthed, because while I didn't want to speak to a demon, the idea still lingered. If only to see if there was a way for the people I loved to not end up in that dark prison for eternity.

Draven's soul was at peace, at least. Knowing that brought me comfort. I was so glad I'd never changed him into an immortal before his death. I couldn't bear it if he had ended up in that awful place.

Azia stood, screeching the chair legs back slowly. "Shall we move on to the next part of your lesson?"

My magic prickled my fingers. "Yes. Let's do this thing."

He let out a soft chuckle, and I followed him to the living area, readying myself to feel his emotions again. I wasn't ready to go back to the castle, anyway, wanting to spend the rest of my day with Azia. The cottage was the closest I'd felt to anything homely since arriving, but the pull of being with Sebastian was just as strong.

Closing my eyes, I reached out, touching his emotions, and spent the next hour exhausting my gifts until there was nothing left.

THIRTY-TWO

Olivia

I walked into the private dining room, clutching the paper Sebastian had left on our bed. ***Meet me downstairs.***

I brushed a kiss against his lips, then pulled back before he could fully embrace me. He wrapped his arms around my waist. "Don't tease me," he warned.

"You left me a note, like you had when we first met. Are you trying to recreate the scene?" I asked, smirking.

"You hated me then," he stated. "Now you don't. I wanted us all to be together again, for one meal. Zach agreed to go to the city with Anna tomorrow, and I don't think they'll be back anytime soon."

"Is Erianna coming?"

He nodded. "I invited your mom too, but Sargon wants her to attend some meeting with him. She can feed any important information back to us."

"Good." My eyes widened. "I don't want her at our friend dinner, anyway. She's my mom."

He arched a brow. "*Friend dinner?* You know we're not eating them, right?"

I arched a brow, followed by a stilted laugh. "Real funny."

He pulled out my chair first, then took his own seat. Zach walked in with Anna on his arm. Her smile was wider than usual, her brown eyes glossy, sparkling as if she'd aged back a year. I was certain it was the idea of getting out of here. "Brother." Sebastian stood, giving him a half hug, patting me on the shoulder. He gave a bow to me, his expression as stoic as ever. "Princess."

I tilted my head. "Are we not on first-name terms anymore?"

Sebastian shot him an incredulous glare, and he sighed. "Olivia, you look lovely tonight."

I grinned. "How painful was that?"

"Excruciating," he replied, a hint of a smile on his thin lips.

Anna ran down his arm, touching his fingers as she brushed past him, and leaned down, pulling me into a tight hug. "It's good to see you again."

"You, too, Anna." She let go, and I smiled up at her kind face. "I'm glad you've decided to get out of here. The vampires here are savages."

She nodded. "We need some time to ourselves. He's always so busy."

I glanced at Sebastian, grinning. "Sebastian's always running off, attending meetings."

He shrugged, sitting back in his chair. "I like to know what's going on."

Zach smirked. "He takes his princely duties very seriously." He peered at Sebastian. "You look great in that crown. It's so…sparkly."

Sebastian laughed. "Don't be jealous, brother. Not all of us can look so good wearing anything."

Zach rolled his eyes, then grinned. Erianna opened the doors. She seemed happier today, and I made it a point not to stare at her back, which was covered by a long, sunset-orange dress. "It's good to see your egos still in check." She took her seat, and Zach and Anna sat beside her. She turned her attention to me. "Now you're married to him, Liv. You'll need to try to knock him down a notch or two. It used to be Zach's place."

He laughed. "Oh, come now, Erianna. You always helped."

"Someone had to."

A vampire server walked in, holding a platter of three goblets. "They're still warm, Your Highness," he said, placing one each down in front of Sebastian, then Zach and finally, Erianna. He snapped a glare at me. "Your food will be ready momentarily, Your Highness." He barely glancing at Anna. "Yours too." He hurried out the doors.

Anna leaned across, lighting the candles down the center of the table as Zach hissed air between his teeth. "Your *Highness*." He grinned at Sebastian. "I bet you don't tire of hearing that."

"It's nice to be finally recognized," he replied with a wink.

I was surprised at how quickly he'd leaned into his role, despite not wanting any of this and losing any chance at becoming mortal again. But when he looked across the table at me, his gaze widening, I realized it was love. Us. Affection floated in our bond, and I touched the side of my cheek.

Zach groaned. "I will never get used to that gooey look in your eyes."

Erianna drank her blood, then wiped her mouth with a napkin. "He's in love. I admit, I never thought I'd see the day."

My face heated, but Sebastian only focused on me. "What can I say?" He tilted his head. "I didn't think I'd find my soulmate, especially one so amazing."

Anna pouted. "Aww. That's so sweet."

Sebastian rolled his eyes. "Don't start," he joked and drained his drink. "Where's that server?"

I shuffled against the hard wooden chair. "Probably in no rush. I don't think he likes me." I glanced down at my place setting. "Most don't."

Erianna clicked her tongue. "Most of them are assholes, anyway."

I chuckled. "I think they just need a little help to see the light."

Zach snorted. "Good luck with that."

Sebastian lifted his chin. "If anyone can do it, it's her."

"You give me too much credit," I responded, but my heart swelled regardless of my doubts. He believed in me, so did the gods, and that's all I needed. "Azia's helping me a lot, though. I like him."

"Uh oh," Zach said, with a teasing grin. "You have competition, brother."

Sebastian rolled his eyes, and the doors reopened. The server placed a plate in front of him, his glowering, intrusive stare never leaving mine. I glared back into those deep, black pools and held back a shudder.

He sank into a reluctant bow, then stepped back. "Enjoy your meal, Your Highness." He walked to Anna and shoved a bowl of freshly cut orange slices on the table, not saying a word to her.

I stared down at my plate. A slab of what I assumed was pork from the smell, yet looked like beef, was coated in thick gravy, served with chopped carrots and roasted potatoes. Everything smelled delicious, and I pressed my fork into the tender meat, my stomach rumbling. I cut through it, and it was unlike anything I'd tried before. But then, I hadn't had meat since I'd become immortal. My senses were heightened, and I could feel the strings in the meat stretching and breaking under the knife. Slowly, I lifted it to my mouth, pressing it to my lips.

Sebastian stood, his chair screeching back, and raced to my side. "Don't eat that."

"What?"

Erianna stood, unsheathing her dagger. "Sebastian?"

"That's not animal meat." He leaned over my plate, sniffing. "It's mortal."

I dropped the fork back onto my plate, holding back a gag. I wrinkled my nose, my eyebrows pulling down as I slid my chair back, backing away from the plate. "They served me a mortal?" A shiver tingled my spine, and bile bit up my throat, burning my esophagus.

Sebastian's upper lip curled, fury pouring from him, leaking through my barrier. "Where's that server?" he growled and sped from the room. Erianna followed; Zach just shook his head, staring at the plate. Anna stopped eating her orange slices, holding her stomach.

***

A chill washed over me as I entered the dungeons. The vampire, Henry, who'd posed as my server, stood behind solid bars. His jaw clenched when I saw him. My father had sent him down here once he found out what he'd done. I noticed the unhealing wound under the rib cage, from Erianna's magically infused dagger. She must have cut him deep. I tilted my head, and he winced when he moved.

I stepped forward, unafraid of the blond-haired man, whose fangs elongated when I got close. "They say you acted alone, but we both know that's not true."

"I don't care what you believe," he said, and spat on the ground.

"Why did you do it?"

He tilted his head, a sadistic grin lifting his lips. "Did they tell you who the meat belonged to?"

My heart skipped a beat. "No."

He sped to the bars, his face inches from mine, his putrid breath hitting my nostrils. "How adorable. They're trying to protect you from the truth." He laughed, his gaze maddening. "We dug up your little friend, after the queen buried him." His fingers curled around the bars, his long nails scraping the metal. "We seasoned him the best we could, but the smell was awful. Did you at least take a bite?"

A wave of numbness as the realization of what he was saying pounded into me. *Draven.* They cooked my best friend.

He moved back, amusement threading through his expression. "He was rotten, but we still enjoyed parts of him."

"We?" I noticed. He didn't respond. I paced in a circle, then placed my hands on the bars, scowling. "Who else was involved?"

He approached the bars, opened his mouth, beckoning me closer. I didn't budge. "I can hear you from here. I'm not coming closer."

His face contorted, the gray of his irises reminding me of the sludge left behind after the snow melts. "You're going to die."

"I already did," I said dismissively, placing a hand on my hip. "I'm going to give you one chance to tell me who you were working with. If you don't, then we'll do it the hard way."

He spat through the bars, landing saliva on my chest.

Gritting my teeth, I wiped it off with my sleeve. "The hard way it is."

Raising my hands, I allowed the darkness, purring with magic, to rip through my core, directing its energy into the cell. A high-pitched ringing shrilled into the dungeons, and Henry pressed his palms against his ears, dropping to his knees. Then, with another wave of energy, heat seared from me and into his body as I raised the vibration of the particles in his blood. His screams were like music in my ears as he clawed at his skin, trying to tear the pain from his soul.

I cocked my head, feeling nothing as I watched him writhe in agony. It was a full minute before I slowed my mind enough to pull back my powers, relieving him.

Sweating, he glowered up at me from all fours, his breaths quickening. "You're a freak."

I crouched down, looking him in the eye. "I'm a sorceress, a true descendent of the gods. I was granted immortality, so I could reign over dicks like you. I can take you to the edge of death, liquify your skin, causing you the most unimaginable pain. Then I'll bring you back—repeatedly—until you spill the names of your conspirators."

"They told me you were weak."

I laughed, a high-pitched noise unlike one I'd made before. Sadism ran through my veins, pumping my heart faster. "I used to be. That girl is dead. This one is sick and fucking tired of vampires like you ruining my life. So, like I said before, we can do this the easy or the hard way."

He huffed out a breath, climbing back to his feet. "You're going to kill me either way."

"You're wrong."

He arched a thin, blond brow. "You'll show me mercy? After I cooked your friend?"

My top lip curled. "No. But I will keep you alive if you don't tell me. I will devote every minute of my waking life to ensure yours is miserable. The underworld will feel like a vacation compared to what I have planned for you."

"I do not fear you, or the underworld."

I sighed slowly, shaking my head. Rage clawed at my center, growling to be let loose, but I recalled my lessons with Azia. Giving myself a moment to calm my emotions, I thought of Sebastian, Erianna and even Zach. My heart slowed as I held my breath until my head cooled.

Then, opening my eyes, I directed my magic at him. My powers grappled over to him, like arms stretching through the bars. Willing my magic to raise the vibration at his groin, he grabbed his dick, scowling. Embers and sparks burned holes through his pants as I set him on fire. In a trance-like state, I allowed the flames to lick up his torso, controlling each movement, prolonging the torture. The putrid stink of burning flesh and singed hair filled the cell, as smoke pillared up, choking the air.

Howling erupted from his insipid mouth, and I pulled back my bottom lip, pressing it against my top teeth. Seconds ticked into minutes, and I stopped at the brink, leaving enough of him to heal.

I coughed into the back of my hand and waited for the screaming to stop. A year ago, I would have never believed I could enjoy torturing another person, even one so evil. Yet, here I was.

Tears ran down his ashy cheeks as his body regenerated. I placed my fingers around the steel, glaring between the gap. "Ready to talk? I can do this all day."

He spluttered, sliding himself to the back of the cell as if distance would do any good against my powers. "You can't torture me like this," he shouted. "You're a royal. It's illegal."

"Ah." I placed my index finger on my chin, looking up to my left. "Yes, because no one breaks the rules here, right?"

His nose twitched, his jaw clenching. "Fuck you."

I tutted, then raised my hands to cause more pain when he cried.

"Wait, wait. Stop," he said exasperatedly.

"Who were you working with?"

"I will never tell you." He slowly lifted his head, pausing. "You will never become queen," he said, and brought his hand to his chest. "I have been alive for half a century. You are sorely mistaken if you think I will let some little girl be my downfall. Your fate is already sealed, and you will suffer far worse than me. If this means I'll stop you from ascending the throne, then so be it."

Without warning, he dug his nails into his ribcage, tearing at bone and muscle, ripping himself apart through wretched howls.

I stared, wild-eyed. "Stop!" I ordered, but his fingers were already curled around his heart. Then, with a wrenching tug, his heart rolled from his grip, his eyes paling under the dove-gray light. Blood splattered everywhere, and I stilled.

They'd blame me for this. Another vampire, dead. I'd been seen coming down to the dungeons, and he was right. I wasn't supposed to kill another immortal. I was only a princess, not a queen yet. We were not supposed to be the judge or executioner, and in doing this he'd ensured my fate in his last moment in this world.

I'd only planned on torturing him. But, I underestimated his hatred for me. My blood ran cold as realization washed over me. If he despised me—so much that he would end his life rather than allow me to hurt him or give up the names of others who wanted to kill me—then there were others who felt the same. I shivered as I stared at his corpse. They were going to destroy me, and this only gave them more incentive to. I ran down back to the entrance of the dungeons, feeling a metaphorical noose tightening around my neck.

THIRTY-THREE

Niall

Adrian stood at my side as we stared over the band of Blood Brothers. Four lords, a mortal who serves Gwen, and five others with a knack for espionage. Two had traveled from the city just to be here, and one was Sargon's footman. Every one of them was hungry for power, ambitious and wanted more than this kingdom was willing to offer them.

These men had passed initiation; each recruit was given a secret to guard. At the end of the week, only the people in this room had kept their secret, as each was closely watched.

The second initiation was another test of loyalty. They thought they were already in, but Adrian wanted to put them through a second test, and I was more than happy to oblige. "Congratulations on getting in. Ten years ago, Adrian and I had formed the club which you know as the Blood Brothers. You are here because you have shown talent, potential, and loyalty. We require all three."

Adrian cleared his throat, taking over the second part of our speech. "You will have connections and power through your brothers here. Mastering others is true power. The secret to getting everything you've ever wanted is community, learning control and patience. Those in positions of power simply handed to them do not know what to do with it. They did not have to fight to get where they wanted to be and had no idea what to do with it. Immortality is a gift, it gives us time to achieve what mortals must rush." He looked at the servant. "You." He pointed his finger at the mortal servant, who quickly stood. "Your name's Edwin, correct?"

"Yes."

"Do you desire immortality?" Adrian asked.

He looked from Adrian to me and nodded. "I do, but the king will not approve of servants being turned."

Adrian gritted his teeth. "He has no say here. We will build a community that can even overturn a king and his whims. Do you wish to be a slave to others' decisions, or are you ready to take the reins of your destiny?"

I watched his smile slowly build. "I'm ready."

"Then we will grant you immortality—once you have proven yourself. You will be welcomed as a blood brother and granted riches beyond your wildest dreams."

His smile dropped, and I stepped forward, sensing his waning disappointment. "What is it you truly want?" I gestured around us. "Don't be afraid to speak your yearnings. We do not judge here."

His throat bobbed. "I-I guess, well, there was this woman back home. She-she ruined my life."

He wanted revenge, the easiest of the desires to manipulate. I placed my hand on his shoulder, nodding as I looked in his brown eyes. "What wrong did she do to you, brother?" I asked, assuming his wife had cheated, or something along those lines. It was always the same.

He relaxed under my touch. "It's my sister."

My eyebrows raised, and I motioned for him to continue.

"She, well, when I was a boy, she would touch me. Make me do things I didn't want to. She lives with her husband now, but whenever she would see me, she'd mock me. My mom did nothing when I told her. They brushed it under the rug, acting as if I was telling lies." His face reddened, and he averted his gaze.

I grabbed his chin, bringing his stare to mine. "Never feel ashamed for someone else's actions. You will have your vengeance. This is your chance, brother, to tip the scales of power. We will all help you in your vengeance. A wrong done to one of us is done to all."

The others nodded along, and I glanced back at Adrian, who was smiling. "You are with us now, but we only ask for certain small things in return. You will be our eyes and ears, and once you've proven yourself, you will become a vampire. With it, you can return home and burn your entire house to the ground if you wish. Now—" Adrian pointed at the double doors leading into the room we'd prepared with long futons, the tastiest, most beautiful mortals ready to feed on privacy tents, and a fully stocked bar. "—we have a welcome party for you through those doors. Please, indulge. We only have the best for you."

They all stood, pouring through the doors. Once the music started, Adrian turned to me in a hushed whisper. "The mortals know what to do?"

"They'll report back any spilled secrets. Let's see how loose their tongues are with their guards down."

***

By the time I reached the throne room, I was already buzzing from the bottle of whiskey and Alana's blood. I took my seat on the steps, and Penelope tried to sit in my lap. I rolled her off.

She tucked a coil of golden hair behind her ear and pouted her lips. "We're getting married," she snapped. "Can you at least look like you want to? People are watching."

With a huff, I pulled her close, placing my hand on her waist. "That better?"

Her pupils dilated. "Much better."

My gaze slid over to the other side of the room, as Gwen walked in with Astor, his arm around her shoulders. The monster growled in my chest, envy searing my veins. They were back together, and she was clinging to him. Then she saw me.

My heart stopped as she pinned me from across the room with those sapphire eyes, a seductive smile against her thick lips. She grazed a kiss against Astor's neck, glancing in my direction as she stuck out her tongue, gliding up to the bottom of his ear. He closed his eyes against her touch, and she pulled back, lips puckered.

She glanced at me again, this time walking her fingers up the front of his shirt. He saw me watching, his face paling under the yellow light. I squinted, shooting him a sadistic grin at the memory of how close I'd come to killing him.

"I'm going to the feeding room," I told Penelope, leaving her side before she could say another word. I needed to get out of here. Everywhere I went, Gwen was there, haunting me like a ghost of the thing always just out of my grasp.

My goal was not her. It was Seraphina and the crown. I repeated that as I walked into the foyer, heading to the feeding room, breathing in the scent of blood.

"Niall," a familiar voice called behind me, and I groaned, turning. Sebastian grinned, wearing an obsidian crown encrusted with diamonds as he approached me from across the foyer. "I heard the Blood Brothers are back. Save the invite, I'm still not interested in your little club."

I tilted my head, sending my waves farther down my shoulder. "I'll admit I was wrong. When we offered you to be a Blood Brother, I thought you were ambitious and clever."

He placed his hand on his chest, amusement in his smirk. "I'm flattered."

"We all make mistakes."

"Oh, come now, Niall." He gestured to the thrones. "We're about to be family. How is darling Penelope? I can't imagine ever having to fuck someone who whored themselves to my dad, but to each their own I guess."

"No, but then you wouldn't need to be concerned about that, with your father dead."

His smile fell into a frown, and he moved closer to me. "It was my idea, you know. To have you become a prince so you could marry Penelope." He paused. "You're welcome, by the way."

I stared at his chest, daydreaming of ripping out his ribcage and painting the walls with his blood. "It seems we've both found ourselves forced into marriage. The only difference between us is I won't mope around like a little bitch about it."

"Oh, hey." He glanced over my shoulder. "Gwen's heading this way. I heard she broke you, and you ran away." He showed his teeth, enjoying himself far too much.

When the time was right and I killed him, I would spend my time picking him apart piece by piece until there was nothing left.

He tapped a finger against his chin. "You gave up everything for her." He laughed. "And I heard you didn't even fuck her. But, don't worry, I've sampled her pussy. You're not missing much."

"Careful," I growled, "prince or not, I will rip your spine out through your mouth."

He tutted with a shrug. "That's anatomically impossible, but good try." He patted me on the arm. "You need to control that anger, Niall. You're about to become a royal—a lesser one, but still one regardless."

I refused to bite. The asshole always tried to get a rise out of me, and unlike most here, he knew what buttons to press. "Don't you have anything better to do than talk to me? Some brooding perhaps?"

He chuckled softly. "It's always a blast talking with you. See you at the next family meeting." With that, he sped away.

I glowered after him, watching as he left. Rage built in the pit of my stomach, dragging the monster within to the surface. He always did push his luck, but he was just a kid compared to the rest of us. Only three years since he was turned. Shame he wouldn't see his fourth.

I turned, stalking Gwen as her and Astor went their separate ways. I couldn't follow her, not wanting to succumb to temptation, but I couldn't help myself. I'd learned everything about her movements over the past few days. Edwin had delivered the details of her schedule, which is why I knew she would be alone tonight. Not only had I been informed of her movements, but also of Astor's. He'd been disappearing at random times of the day, for hours sometimes. We'd yet to catch where he went, but knowing he was up to something put me on edge.

There was more to him than met the eye. He'd latched onto Gwen, using her and Velda to grow in power. I discovered he sold out the Guild for Protection of Mortal Beings back in Baldoria, giving up his own brothers in arms location, allowing their slaughter to save his own neck. Ravena was here because of his selfishness, and he'd hurt Seraphina in the process. I didn't trust him for a second, and Gwen shouldn't have either. I didn't know what he'd done to gain that trust from her, but he didn't love her. Nor did she love him. And for the life of me, I couldn't figure out why they were still together.

I followed her, giving her enough space that it wouldn't be obvious. I didn't want to be lured in again, but I couldn't help myself. Everything about her spoke to me; no matter how much I tried to fight the urge to see her, she kept slipping into my head. She closed her door, and I crept up slowly, listening from outside. The whoosh of the taps turning on, splashing water into the bathtub drummed into my ears, and I pulled down the handle, my heart hammering in my chest.

THIRTY-FOUR

Niall

Stay away. That's what Adrian told me, and yet I found myself standing in the corner of her room, watching the candle flickering from her nightstand, transfixed by the dancing flame.

She would be in any minute now, as I heard the water empty from the tub. There was no escape. Not that there ever was. Soon that bathroom door would be open, and she would climb in for the night. I eyed the sheets, envy purring in my chest as I imagined them clinging to her body.

I shouldn't be here. My heart raced at the thought of finally being alone with her, even if it wasn't her choice. But there was something about Gwen. I couldn't stay away, like a moth flying close to fire.

I recalled how her gaze pinned me across the room earlier that day as my betrothed unknowingly clung to my arm, pulling me into another dance. All while Gwen occupied my every thought as I undressed her with my eyes.

The bathroom door opened, and I peered into the darkness. An orange hue soaked the room, and adrenaline seared through my veins at the thought of being caught. A faint smell of vanilla and lavender drifted over, intoxicating me.

Even her fucking *scent* had me addicted.

She was my personal sin. I was crossing a line, one I wouldn't be able to come back from. I shouldn't want this. But I burned for her.

I would leave before she noticed, I reasoned. Once she was asleep.

I watched her from the shadows, taking in the curves of her figure as she walked, a slight tilt to her wide hips. A slice of black silk barely covering anything hugged her body, stopping at the top of her thighs. When she turned, the fabric moved, rippling enough to reveal a hint of the undercurve of her round ass.

My dick throbbed at the thought of running my fingers over her ass, cupping her cheeks as she lifted them, ready for me.

"It's not nice to stalk." Her voice was liquid sex as she innocently leaned over the dresser, the nightgown sliding up her lower back. She hummed under her breath, acting as if she wasn't purposely showing the slit of fabric covering her pussy. "You can come out."

My breath caught in my throat as I stepped out from the darkness, my dick hard in my pants.

She ran her fingers through her blonde waves. "Why are you in my room, Niall?"

"I shouldn't be." The words fell from my lips before I could take them back, not that it mattered. I was enraptured by her presence. My gaze dropped to her lips as she turned. Her eyes slid to mine, widening, as if she was just as captivated by me.

She was everything.

"You should leave—" She inhaled sharply, purposely averting her gaze. "—before anyone finds out you're in here and gets the wrong idea."

I stayed rooted to the spot, sucked into the way she moved, like she knew exactly what she was doing when she ran her fingers over her clavicle, glancing over her shoulder at me with those bedroom eyes.

"You looked bored earlier," I concluded, shifting a couple of paces closer. "On the arm of your asshole boyfriend. I see you two made things up."

"He'll be here soon," she said, as if I didn't already know every part of her schedule. We had about fifteen minutes at the most before he came to take the orgasm that was mine. "And you are engaged."

I wetted my lips, unable to even form an image in my mind of Penelope. She didn't know that I was thinking of Gwen when I was dancing with her. Of how she would taste, of the way she might thrust into my mouth.

My gaze drifted down to her chest, my dick pulsing with heat when I saw the perfect line of her cleavage. The light from the candle soaked her, revealing her large, hard nipples under the silk. It would be rude not to stare.

"Niall," she said, a strain in her voice. "Astor is coming any minute now."

She stepped closer, an unnerved edge in her movement as if she could feel the tight magnetism between us. If either of us got too close, we would both burn.

There were only inches between us, the bed a shove behind her. I couldn't be doing this. She was right; I had to leave before I was devoured into something I couldn't come back from. But I couldn't pull away, sucked in by the knowing, lustful sparkle in those sapphire eyes.

"You haven't screamed," I noticed as I took a careful step, closing the distance between us. "Or moved."

She held her next breath. I could feel the want in the inch between our bodies, smelling her arousal.

Something in me snapped. I had to touch her—just once. To know how her skin felt against mine, to get just a taste of her so I could carry the touch in my mind when I fucked someone else.

A lump formed in my throat as she swallowed thickly, gulping as she finally let out the breath she'd been holding.

I brushed my thumb over her chin, tilting her head up, stroking up to her plump lips, dragging her bottom lip until I could feel the fleshy inside against my skin.

Fuck.

My other hand grazed her narrow waist. I wanted to undo her, to steal every piece of her. A carnal need sharpened her features as she paused to look into my eyes. I felt like she was already mine, yet she belonged to another.

She leaned into me, the curve of her breasts pressing against my chest. She breathed hot air against my neck, teasing words from her tender lips. "We can't do this." They were desperate, as if she was reminding herself, not me.

"Then tell me to go," I said. "Like every time before. You've destroyed me."

The silence was deafening. The orange glow shone on her petite shoulders, over her sun-kissed arms and down to her fingers which whispered a touch to my chest. "Yet, here you are. I never stopped thinking about you. Do you want me to admit I was wrong for leading you on before?"

"Only if you mean it."

She splayed her fingers over my shirt. "I don't regret it. I enjoyed our games, and I loved watching you succumb to me. Niall, the guy who could love no woman, begging for my kiss."

The door creaked, and I grabbed her, pulling her into the bathroom, slamming the door behind us. I held her close to my body, clamping my hand over her mouth.

I could hear him from the bathroom, both of us lost in the dark as he rustled what sounded like papers and called out from behind the closed door, "Babe, you in there?"

Reaching into the shower with one arm, I turned on the water, smirking as it drowned out her quickening breaths. "Tell your boyfriend you're taking a shower," I whispered into her ear, feeling her body stiffen against mine, "that you'll be out soon."

She nodded behind my hand, a breath escaping through my fingers, the last of her resolve melting into me. "I'll be out soon," she called back. "Just taking a shower."

"Things have changed this time," I said, my voice barely a whisper. "There will be no begging. Now, be quiet for me."

She gulped, her voice barely a whisper. "Lock the door."

My chest tightened as I ran my hands down the curve of her hip, sending feather touches to her thigh. "No."

Before she could protest, I pinned her against the wall, hearing her boyfriend moving something in the next room. My hand glided around her neck, fingers tightening on her throat as our lips clashed, my tongue entwining with hers. The fleshy pressure against mine pulsed my cock, and a low, guttural groan escaped my mouth before I could stop it.

A warmth in my stomach spread through me, setting every nerve on fire as I deepened the kiss, guiding her movements. Something primal awoke, and I danced my fingers between her legs, her thighs falling open for me.

She was dripping, her panties soaked. Her fingers clawed into my hair, fisting my long waves. Her mouth bit into my chest as she moaned, my body muffling the sound. I'd wanted this for years, yearned for her in my dreams every night. I wasn't going to have Astor fucking ruin this.

I fisted her hair, tugging on the curls, angling her head as I brushed my mouth to her neck. She tugged me closer, fitting us together. I rocked my hips, and her thighs clenched. Every red flag was lost as I felt her on me, obvious now that we belonged together. Entangled as one.

I nudged her panties to the side, feeling the slick of her desire sliding against me. Her body quivered, a gasp escaping as I teased closer to her opening.

She unbuttoned my pants, and my erection sprang free. Gently, she gripped her hand around my length, rubbing up and down, slow at first, but quickening with every few strokes. She groaned behind closed lips as she felt me, tilting softly into a moan I wanted to bottle and own.

I slid three fingers inside her, pushing her to the edge, feeling her drip for me. An ache grew in my groin, waving through me as I craved every part of her.

Pushing my fingers in harder, until her wetness slicked down over my hand, I pressed my lips tight. She moaned a little louder this time, and I clamped my free hand back over her mouth, shaking my head. "Careful, baby girl. Moan into me." I pressed her head against my chest, and she bit down against me, her groans devoured by muscle.

"Gwen?" Astor called from right outside the door. "Are you okay?"

She stopped grinding against my fingers. Fucking asshole. I'd go out there and rip his head off if I could. If it wouldn't kill Gwen for me to do it.

I leaned down, carefully lowering my hand from her mouth. "Answer."

She obeyed. "I'm fine," she stuttered, but quickly cleared her throat. "Almost done."

"Yes, you are," I whispered breathily.

"Do you need me to come in?" he asked.

"No." She gulped, her voice strained. "Don't come."

"Or do," I teased, feeling her throb on my fingers.

I heard his footsteps leave, my heart pounding. I pushed my cock against her lower stomach, forcing her panties down to her knees. Grabbing her round ass, I tightened my grip, lifting her against the wall. Starting with the tip, I eased my way in, and she wrapped her legs around my waist, thrusting me deeper. Every moral dissolved into nothing as her pussy gripped my cock, holding me inside. My toes curled in my shoes as want rippled through my torso, a heavy ache building, one only satisfied by her.

Her teeth sank into my shoulder, her hot breaths on me as her fangs elongated, snapping any restraint I had left. Then, sliding my hand under her nightgown, I found her full tits, her nipples rock hard as I flicked one, coaxing a louder moan from her.

Shit. He'd had to have heard that. Even with the shower on.

Fuck it.

Locking the door with my other hand, I grabbed her hair, forcing her head back.

Liquid fire seared in my veins as I thrusted harder, her legs pulling me in deeper as if we somehow had any space left between us.

She ran her hands up my chest, unbuttoning my shirt. Steadying her on my dick, I pounded her to the sound of her boyfriend's knocks. The handle pulled down, the sound electrifying our desire as I fucked his girlfriend.

She clung to me as her boyfriend's shouting from outside the door lost to her groans. "Come for me, baby girl," I ordered.

She tensed, her vocal cords lost as her orgasm tightened her pussy around my dick, and I became undone.

I grabbed her ass as a hot pressure built in the base of my length and contractions rippled in my lower belly. My mind went numb as she screamed my name. The muscles in my thighs tensed, spasms shooting up my shaft, intensifying until I exploded inside her, my eyes rolling back in my head as if I felt like I left my soul.

I pumped faster, breathless, my nails biting into her ass as I spilled hot cum. Her groans synced with mine until they slowed, and I softly rocked the last of our orgasm, my legs twitching.

She slumped against me, her head resting on my shoulder. Astor banged on the door again, but we didn't give a fuck. I hoped he heard her scream—for me, only me.

THIRTY-FIVE

Sebastian

Olivia splayed her fingers over my chest as morning stole the night away from us far too soon. "Morning, love." I brushed a finger down the side of her face, admiring the flecks of pale brown in her green eyes. When the light hit them right, they appeared golden. Yet, behind them, I sensed her worry. "What's wrong?" She cast her eyes downward. "My eyes are up here," I teased, but she didn't smile. "Talk to me."

"How do you define evil?"

I sat upright, and she pushed back against the pillows, the sheets hugging the contours of her body. It was a question I'd often pondered since I'd been turned. I thought back to Velda, and when she'd slaughtered my family. Before then, I often believed evil was just someone who wanted to do bad things. Still, when I saw her, and the lack of anything behind her eyes, I felt the true darkness of what evil was. Sometimes it hid behind the prettiest of smiles. "It's an absence of light."

She fingered her bracelet, not meeting my eyes. "What if you do something bad and enjoy it?"

I sucked in a deep breath, thinking back to Hamza. I'd enjoyed torturing him, so much there was no room for remorse. But when I'd killed the guards, I'd spent nights trying to justify it, to come up with every reason under the sun so the guilt couldn't chip away enough. But I hurt from it, and even now, they trickled into my mind. "It depends on the context. Why do you ask?"

She swallowed thickly. "I-I tortured that server guy, Henry."

I sighed, lifting her chin, bringing her glossy gaze to mine. "Oh, baby girl, if you're worried you're evil, I can assure you, you're not. There is not an evil bone in your body." She opened her mouth to argue, but I interrupted. I couldn't bear the thought of her thinking she was a bad person. "If you were evil, you wouldn't be questioning it. That man cooked your friend and tried to feed him to you. He deserved whatever you did to him, and just because you liked it only makes you human, not bad. We are not ethereal beings. We're complicated, messy things, and often, the lines of morality get blurred."

"It felt too good," she admitted, her lips pursing. "I hate that I liked it so much."

I tucked a lock of hair behind her ear, gently touching her cheek as I moved my hand away. "That only means you have a heart. I've met evil—lived with it, even—and it looks nothing like you."

"I keep thinking about Draven's body." She choked out a cry. "His body was defiled, all to hurt me."

"His soul was not in there," I assured, knowing she needed to hear it. "That doesn't take away from it, but he's not in pain anymore." I struggled to find the right words, not wanting to burrow that agony deeper. Instead, I pulled her close as a sob quaked through her. "The ones responsible will pay for what they did. Erianna is trying to find out who else was there."

I selfishly wished Zach was still here. He was the best at finding out things, but I was also glad he was away from all of this. Things were getting worse by the day. People were growing bolder, and the whispers of Olivia not deserving the crown turned into discussions. Not even Sargon could control the opinions of others, as much as he'd like to.

She dug her nails into my biceps and slowly brought her lips up. Greif rocked her in waves. Sometimes, I felt it trickle through our bond. I didn't fully understand it yet, but I didn't care. I just knew when she needed me.

"I miss him," she whispered. "Sometimes I feel like I can't breathe when I think about him. It's killing me."

"This will get easier. I know that's hard to hear, but just know that it'll get a little easier with time. There will come a day when his memory will make you smile. Wounds from grief never really heal, but we learn to live with them." I squeezed her tighter, never wanting to let her go. "I will be with you through it all, always."

She rested her head against me. I know she was trying to be strong, to learn everything she could from Azia and manipulate her dad against Kalon. But when she came into the room at night, I saw the exhaustion behind her smile. That's when I held her closer, losing ourselves to each other instead of having to think about anything else. I brought my lips to her ear. "You can let yourself go around me. You know that, right?"

She nodded and ran her hands through my hair. "Tell me we'll get through this. That all this scheming is worth something."

I nudged the tip of my nose against hers. "We will get through this. I promise."

"Sebastian," she said tentatively, examining my expression. "When you talk about grief, I lose you for a moment. I know you lost your family…and all you wanted was to be mortal."

"Don't concern yourself with that," I told her, entwining my fingers with hers. "I'm happy right where I am."

She wetted her lips. "When I met the gods, they gave me the elixir I need to become mortal again someday. When I'm ready to resign from the throne. My father has one, too, and well, I plan on taking it from him. I know this is a lot for you, but I wanted you to know that I will make sure we both become mortal again. As for the underworld, Azia said there's always a way to get rid of things. I don't know how, but I want to destroy it. So Erianna and Zach won't end up there."

I closed my eyes, and snuggled into her, stroking her hair. "You are the kindest, most wonderful woman I've ever met." The thought of living a mortal life with Olivia, maybe even starting a family, set my heart on fire. It had always seemed like a dream, a fantasy that would never be fulfilled. "You are my salvation, sweetheart. But please know that I will never leave your side. Living my life with you, as your husband, is enough for me. Vampire or not."

She kissed me, stealing my next breath. Softly at first, parting my lips with her tongue, then all-consuming. Slowly, she pulled back. "I wish I could stay here all day."

"Then stay," I said. "Your duties can wait a day."

She shook her head. "I can't."

She didn't need to explain. We both knew the only thing stopping her from breaking completely was her vengeance against Kalon. I felt it, too—the desire to murder him was so far embedded in my core.

THIRTY-SIX

Olivia

Kalon smoothed the sides of his red, slicked-back hair, then adjusted his crown. "Good morning, niece. You look a little unwell. Have you not been eating?"

Of course, he was behind what happened. My father stood too close for me to say anything spiteful. I breathed in deeply, reminding myself that he would get what was coming to him. I just needed to be patient. "I'm immortal, so I can't be sick," I snapped back. "Perhaps it's the makeup." I shrugged him off. "Anyway, I need to go see your son."

"Are you bored with your husband already?" he asked, feigning concern.

"Oh no, this is about other matters." I sighed softly, pressing my lips tight. "You know, I just feel so bad."

He arched a brow. "Why?"

"Your own son is marrying the woman you were sleeping with. I mean, everyone seems to get what they want around here—except you." As my father moved his eyes to us, I touched his arm, feigning sympathy. "I hope you're doing okay, truly. And thank you for the concern, too. I'm glad we're getting along now. We have so much in common."

He covered his snort by clearing his throat. "How so, niece?"

"No one likes me either. At least everyone pretends to your face." My status was rock bottom. I was certain Kalon had added to the hatred building for me in court. "At least we can be there for each other." The muscle in his jaw twitched, and I hid my smirk. "I should go."

"Yes," he called before I could leave. "I am so sorry to hear about what happened the other day. Did you know they found that server dead in his cell?"

I turned on my heel. "Did they?" I raised my brows, blinking three times. "How disturbing."

"There were people who saw you going down there just before," he said loud enough for several vampires to hear. "Don't worry, I absolutely assured them they must be mistaken. I locked them away for spilling such treasonist claims. You would never do such a thing. As a princess, you take your role seriously, and anyone who speaks against you will end up in those same cells."

Sargon smiled, listening in from his throne. He didn't understand what Kalon was doing, the fucking prick. Every vampire in the vicinity was also listening, and their glares were darkening by the second.

"Goodbye, Uncle," I said, trying and failing to keep my seething tone pleasant. I raced away, toward Niall's ridiculous club. My father had sent me to deal with it, and from the rumors I heard, I was concerned about what I'd find behind those closed doors.

***

My lips parted as I took in the scene unfolding before my eyes. The large room in the west wing was thick with debauchery. Niall grinned at me as he moved his lips down to the women's neck, then released her into an unsuspecting vampire's arms, catching her in time. "Princess." He bowed at his waist, climbing his gaze to meet mine.

There was something cold in them, and unlike Sebastian, it was a darkness I didn't want to play with. It felt dangerous. I attempted to reach out, to feel his emotions, but the same as the last time, his walls were built high. "You look beautiful."

"Flattery doesn't work on me."

He grinned. "Noted. So, what *does* work on you?"

My breath caught in my throat as I sought the truth. "Kindness," I decided. "Something you lack."

He straightened his posture. "I've made a poor first impression. I'll have to remedy that."

"There's no need. Really."

"Yes, there is."

"Honestly, you barely made an impression."

His shoulders tensed, and the loudness of the room pierced into my ears. I focused on Niall's slow, steady breaths to numb the chatter and moans echoing around us.

"This club of yours. It's…"

A loud gagging sound cut through my thoughts, followed by a woman's voice. My words trailed into oblivion, and suddenly I forgot everything I had planned to say.

A naked vampire, with hair flowing out around him, lay upon the futon across the room as a woman forced another man's mouth onto his erection. The man's lips closed around his length, his gags growing less frequent.

The lady whispered in his ear as she twisted her auburn locks over one shoulder. "Go deeper. I want to watch when he comes in your mouth."

The vampire on the sofa thrusted his hips up, and the woman forced the other guy's head farther down until his lips were around the base of what was easily ten inches.

Fingers lightly touched the small of my back, lacing around my waist. Niall stepped up next to me, and I shuddered away from his grasp.

He smirked. "It's okay if you enjoy watching."

"I do not," I said through clenched teeth. "Is he…"

"He's doing it over his own free will. The couple frequent here often. The husband is our top member."

I turned away from them when the woman started touching herself and glared at Niall. "This is weird."

"Don't kink shame, Princess."

"That's not what I'm..." I let out a heavy breath. "It just encourages certain behaviors."

"Like?"

I placed a hand on my hip, adrenaline seeping into my veins. "Entitlement. These people think they can do whatever they want without consequences—like killing mortals."

His expression hardened, the power behind his stare unleashed as he stepped closer, leaving mere inches between us. "You're in our world now. Those people are your subjects, and when you deny them their pleasures and fetishes, all it does is push them to do them in secret. Shame leads further into darkness, so don't come in here and act superior to any of us." He flexed his fingers, then ran a hand through his hair, inhaling sharply. His gaze softened as she whistled out his next breath. "Respectfully, this is my club, and while you may not like it, no one here is harming anyone. Everything is consensual, and that is all that should matter. If you have an issue with us killing mortals, take it up with the king. I do not make the laws."

I put a finger up to argue, but there was a minor flaw in his words. I chewed the inside of my lip, digging my nails into my palms until they left half-crescent marks on my skin. My father didn't like secret clubs either, but he didn't want to publicly get involved. Not with Kalon advising against it.

"Fine, but this club still creates division with the invite-only to only the most influential, as I've been told."

He lightly booped the end of my nose, the corner of his thick lips curling. "Don't be upset, Princess. If you want an invitation, you only need to ask. Normally, we only have men, but you're different."

The audacity of this prick. "I have no desire to be a part of this. Besides, like you keep saying, I'm a princess. I wouldn't need an invite if I wanted to be in any club."

He shrugged, shoving his hands in his pockets. "It's a shame. I'd love for us to get to know each other better."

I scoffed out a laugh. "That makes one of us."

"I like a woman who's feisty," he admitted, grinning. "Don't worry, I won't give up. I'm not like your husband. I don't shy away from what I want or feel."

"You," I spat, "know nothing about Sebastian."

"I've known him longer than you."

My fists balled. "Don't pretend this—" I gestured around us. "—is all consensual. I've heard rumors of what happens here, and it's brutal."

He rolled his eyes up, then nodded along. "That's the awful thing with rumors. They lack evidence. It's such a shame. I really wish I could help you, but the Blood Brothers club is mine, and I protect what's mine. I hope you understand."

I stepped away. "You're going to regret this."

"No, I won't." I turned on my heel, heading to the door, when he called after me.

"Princess, did I make an impression this time?"

I didn't dignify his question with a response, and instead raced out the double doors, leaving behind the stench of blood and cum.

***

The day felt like it went on forever when I finally reached the grounds. Another party was happening inside, and now the Aslandians were gone, we were wall to wall with mortals for them to feed on.

I grasped the note Sebastian had left on my bed. Meet me in the gardens. With a slight smile, I walked outside, the trail of my navy-blue dress dragging along behind me. I gazed up at the moonlit black canvas pin-pricked with silver stars. At that moment, all I could think about was how my life had gotten so crazy. Less than a year ago, I was staring out my window at the same night sky, grieving Astor. It felt like a lifetime ago.

I made my way through the grounds, past Azia's cottage, until I reached the blooming lavender. Breathing in the evocative scent, I relaxed. The trees waved in the distance, and I listened to the wind whistling through the branches, frogs from the nearby pond ribbet, and crickets chirping. Every sound since becoming immortal was no longer just noise, but music.

A twig snapped, and I turned, expecting to see Sebastian. Instead, beady, soulless eyes watched me as the aniccipere licked its lipless mouth. Footsteps sounded from behind me, and I prepared my magic. Danger pricked my adrenaline, and I poised to fight.

"Wha—"

A bag was placed over my head before I could finish my question. I screamed, grasping at the fabric, willing my magic into my hands. A pungent, herbal smell coated the material. Before I could fight back, my knees buckled, and I fell into blackness.

THIRTY-SEVEN

Olivia

By the time I awoke, the world had changed.

It took five aniccipere to pin me down, gag me, then strip me bare before I was dragged into a derelict mansion. The walls creaked and groaned as the heavy winds swept through rotting wood. Eyes glared at me through the ominous, dark windows, penetrating the permeating darkness as a tower clock chimed in the distance.

I drove my nails into one of the aniccipere's arms, digging deep until I felt the bone under my fingertips. The creature flinched, shoving my hand off the now gaping wound, which healed far too fast for me to gain any satisfaction.

In an attempt to touch my magic, I closed my eyes, burying deep into my subconscious, but the thrum of power was reduced to a whisper of a melody, just beyond reach.

The past echoed within its walls as the old door creaked open, and I was pulled inside. Splatters of dried blood browned the peeling wallpaper and unvarnished floorboards. The surrounding energy flooded my barriers—terror. Terrible things had happened here. On the wall in the poorly lit corridor, symbols of demons were etched into the walls, smeared with blood.

One of the soul vampires hissed in my ear as they took me into what I presumed was once a grand living area, now an echo of what it was. I counted eight aniccipere, but I felt the energy from hundreds more, all waiting from the shadows. I had to be in the south. There was no way there were this many close to the castle.

A shiver puckered my skin into goosebumps as I was shoved, naked, into a hard chair, and tied with rope. Finally, they removed the gag, and I sucked in a deep breath. My magic was too far out of reach. The taste of poison was thick on my tongue, and the pungent herbal smell lingered on my hair from the bag. How long had I been out? Hours? Days?

My stomach grumbled with defiance, my body weakening from the lack of substance. While I was immortal, I still needed food, and the slow process of starvation knotted my stomach. I had been out for days. I had to have been.

I swallowed hard. My voice was raspy as I tried to speak. "Water."

"No," the creature who'd bound my hands hissed. "Not until he comes."

"Who's he?" I asked, squinting at the door. I bet it was Kalon.

My heart hammered when I saw him. I parted my parched lips, my tongue feeling like sandpaper in my mouth.

Astor tilted his head, sliding his icy eyes to mine. Out of everyone I expected to walk through that door—Kalon, Velda, hell, even Gwen, I didn't expect Astor. He should have been at the top of the suspect list. He'd lost everything, and I'd been horrible to him, for a good reason, but still. I was sure he didn't see it that way. Astor had faked his suicide before, and allowed the mass slaughter of his friends. This shouldn't be that surprising, yet, my stomach was in knots.

He looked me up and down. "I offered you the opportunity to marry me, but you had to choose Sebastian." His nostrils flared, the muscle above his lip feathering.

"So you—" I coughed, choking on my lack of saliva. "You sided with *them*? Because I wouldn't marry you?"

"That's not the only reason." He paced in a circle, and I stared at the man I'd spent years with, someone I once loved. That was when I saw what Sebastian had said—a lack of light. The boy I knew was gone, replaced by something monstrous. "Gwen," he continued, seeming uneasy around the aniccipere, too, with a slight tremble whenever he got too close to one, "chose Kalon's bastard son over me. The only reason I didn't leave the bitch is because she provided me with protection. It was fun for a while, though. She was such a tease, and gods, that mouth." He glanced down at my bare breasts. "Unlike you. You were always so—" He paused "—prudish. And now I'm left with nothing. Your mom has made several attempts to get me out of the castle and cast me into exile. Once Gwen and Velda's loyalties started waning, I realized I needed to take control of my own fate."

"So you joined Hamza's band of idiots?"

Pain stung through my cheek and nose, sending a ringing into my ears. It took me a moment to register I'd been slapped by an aniccipere. Blood spattered from my lip onto the ground, and I glared at the creature with deep loathing.

Astor didn't even wince, and I ran cold as I watched a sadistic smile curl on his lips. Lips I'd once kissed. "Like me, they have been cast aside. Forgotten by the precious monarchy and that fool, Sargon. Hamza felt the same way, until your actions killed him."

My heart raced. "He tried to rape me. He was a psychopath."

Astor shrugged. "Hamza sought me out when I arrived. He saw in me something none of you did."

I shuddered against the cold. "Evil?"

"Power," he snapped. "Then he was dead, and you were giving orders, talking of right and wrong as if you were so righteous. Then the gods gave you immortality—without vampirism—as if you're so fucking special. I know you, Olivia. You were always such a naive little bitch who cried over everything, and I still tried to protect you when they came for your mom at the guild. But you were so ungrateful, so hurtful, and now..." He trailed off, looking at one of the soul vampires. "I've chosen the right side."

I shook my head. "This is not the right side."

He closed the distance between us, grabbing my chin, and lifting my face to examine me. "You don't get to have everything! You did nothing to deserve this. I'm the one who sought the vampires out. I did my research and persuaded them to turn me, something most mortals never succeed in doing."

My jaw clenched as I wrestled against the ropes. "Congratulations."

He released me. "Well, now you know the true cost of such power. They want Sargon removed from the throne and Kalon dead. You're the key to tearing it all down. Gods know your father, mom, and Sebastian won't let anything happen to you. That's why I waited. I was so pleased when I learned you'd gotten close to your dad. You are his weakness."

My throat burned as fatigue and dizziness waved through me. "I need water."

His nose wrinkled as he turned to an aniccipere. "Bring it."

The creature nodded, then returned with a glass. "False princess." The creature angled its head. "Here's your drink."

I could smell the poison-laced in the liquid, one keeping me from my magic, but my body ached for the drink. "No."

The aniccipere dragged its long talon across my neck. Its lipless mouth curled into a sadistic smile, showing off its needle-like teeth.

I recalled the gutted mortal I'd once seen on the streets of the City of Nightmares.

The creature pinched my nose, forcing my mouth open for a gasp of air. He tipped the poison mixed into water into my mouth, then shut my jaw with such force my teeth trembled in my gums. "Swallow, or I'll cut out your eyes," he spat.

I swallowed hard, pinching my eyes shut. The poison burned the back of my throat, trickling into my stomach. Within seconds, it entered my bloodstream, weakening me from the inside. The memory of Sebastian having to drink the same poison when we were in the dungeons, floated back. Except they'd laced blood with it and gave him the choice of drinking that or dying from starvation.

I could barely make out what Astor was saying as a ringing sounded in my ears. My eyelids closed, and I heard Astor whisper, "When your husband comes for you, he'll be the first I kill," before the blackness stole me, and I fell to the mercy of my enemies.

The End…For now

The final two books in the series release soon

Preorder Darkest Heart now: https://mybook.to/DarkestHeart

Preorder Ruthless Royals now: https://mybook.to/RuthlessRoyals

BONUS CHAPTER

Download your free bonus chapter from Sebastian's point of view, carrying over from this last chapter of Shadow Kissed, set just before Midnight Crown begins, when you sign up for my monthly newsletter.

Get updates on the rest of the series, enter giveaways and see cover and title reveals before anyone else

Sign up here:
https://bit.ly/NewsletterBonusChapter

GLOSSARY

Sangaree: Species of vampire who drink blood. Made from the original vampire, Vener, and cursed by the goddess, Salenia. Sangaree are made when a mortal drinks the blood of a vampire and also has their venom in their system. Also called 'blood vampires.' They appear mortal, but they have wings and fangs.

Aniccipere. Species of vampire who eat souls. They are born from mortals who have mated with a demon from the underworld. Also called 'soul vampires.' They have small, beady eyes, needlelike teeth, and are willowy, gaunt creatures, with no lips. Most live in the south of Sanmorte, with a small number also living in the City of Nightmares.

Sorcerers: Sorcerers are descended from the offspring of gods and mortals. They have magical powers where they can influence the energy around them, and use the five elements: Air, Water, Fire, Earth, and spirit. Some can enhance their own gifts, such as empaths are able to take away others pain using their magic.

Gods: There are four gods who created the world: Vaneria, Laveniuess, Jaiunere and Salenia.
Vaneria: Goddess of love
Laveniuess: God of shadows
Jaiunere: God of light
Salenia: Goddess of the underworld

Underworld: A prison created by Salenia's magic. She is trapped inside by her own spell. However, there are some cracks which some souls have escaped through, but unlike them, she cannot pass through it. Salenia created the underworld as a prison for her lover, Vener and the woman he left her for. All immortal souls go to the underworld. There are emperor demons, and lesser demons, in charge of keeping the souls in the underworld. Most enjoy torturing the souls.

Sanmorte: The Vampire Kingdom ruled by Sargon. Sanmorte once belonged to mortals but was overrun by vampires centuries ago

Baldoria: The mortal kingdom closest to Sanmorte that Olivia and Ravena lived for most of Olivia's life

Laveniuess's Lake: The birthplace of the God, Laveniuess

Ismore: City in Baldoria where Olivia and Ravena lived

Asland: The biggest kingdom in the world. It has a hot climate, and shares a religion with Kibet of reincarnation and ancient gods

City of Nightmares: A walled city in the center of Sanmorte. Mostly Sangaree (referred to as vampires), and small groups of aniccipere live. There are many blood dens, sex shows, and other debauchery. This is the capital.

Black Mountain Retreat: Exclusive hotel for the elite, south of the castle

Polgoria: A small island off the coast of Istinia, where ships refuse to pass through. It is rumored there are deadly creatures that drown crews and drag ships into the depths

Istinia and Salvius: A large land split into two by mountains. One side is the kingdom, Salvius, and the other, a country, Istinia.

Istinia is filled with witches and warlocks (known in Sanmorte as sorcerers). Salvius is a mortal kingdom

Kibet: A large, hot country next to Asland. They share in the same religion which is based on ancient gods and reincarnation

Nightshade: An order that serves Kalon

Midnight Lotus: A select group of trusted guards close to Sargon that serve him

Blood Brothers Club: A society created by Niall and Adrian for elite members of the castle who all help achieve each other's goals. Members are normally men.

Guild for the Protection of Mortal Beings: Protectors of the mortal world, based in Baldoria

Cane of Cineris: A cane gifted to the kings from the gods that will turn any vampire it touches into ash

Trailic: A thin, see-through dress worn before a wedding by the woman so they can see if there are any visible signs of abuse from the man. It's an outdated tradition.

Shadow Kissed Ceremony: A ceremony where a mortal is made into a vampire. With normal mortals, they are killed by either being fed on and drained of blood. Royals are killed using a dagger

Vitarem: A holiday to honor the dead who have passed on from that year

Adormai: A holiday celebrating passion and love. It's the most erotic of all the holidays and celebrates the goddess Vaneria.

People often get married, propose, or engage in sexual activities during this time

ACKNOWLEDGMENTS

A huge thank-you, as always, to my incredible beta readers for your input: Kelly Kortright, Sherri Stovall, Christine Hutton, Lauren Churchwell, Jennifer Rose, Val Forness, Sarah Elyse, Carla Sosa, Rebecca Waggner, Linda Hamonou and Heather Taylor.

A big thanks to my Angel & Fairy patrons for continuing to support my art every month:, Tara Stallard, Laura Lea Davidson, Renee Balestra, Shemri Harris, Jennifer Rose, Mary Duke, Amelia Pluck, Keshia Mahi Penny Riley, Tamiya, and Megara.

Thank you to my editor, Belle, for staying up late with me, talking about this world, and helping polish the Shadow Kissed Series.

A big shout-out to She-Wolf Pack! Sarah Cradit & K. L. Kolarich, for being incredible friends both in my professional and personal life, and for always being there to bounce ideas off.

Thank you to you for reading this series, and for your incredible comments and love.

ALSO BY REBECCA L. GARCIA

THE FATE OF CROWNS SERIES

The Fate of Crowns

The Princess of Nothing

The Court of Secrets

Ruin

EMBRACING DARKNESS COLLECTION

Spellbound

Heart of a Witch

SHADOW KISSED SERIES

Shadow Kissed

Midnight Crown

Darkest Heart

Ruthless Royals

ABOUT THE AUTHOR

Rebecca lives in San Antonio, Texas, with her husband and son. Originally from England, you can find her drinking tea and writing new fantasy worlds filled with romance. She devoured every book she was given, and when she got older, her imagination grew with her.

When she's not writing or spending time with her family, you can find her traveling and hosting book signings with Spellbinding Events.

Find out more on my website: www.rebeccagarciabooks.com

Check out her Patreon account to read chapters of her upcoming releases, get goodies, and so much more: www.patreon.com/rebeccagarciabooks

Follow Rebecca on Instagram: www.instagram.com/rebeccalgarciabooks/

Join her Facebook Group here and become a member of her Royal Court: www.facebook.com/groups/rebeccasroyalcourt

www.ingramcontent.com/pod-product-compliance
Lightning Source LLC
Chambersburg PA
CBHW020458310726
48979CB00016B/2710/J

* 9 7 8 1 9 1 2 4 0 5 9 6 1 *